Sweet Home
Stories of Alabama

William Cobb

SixFinger

First Published in 2013
by SixFinger Publishing
an imprint of Great War Literature Publishing LLP

Produced in United Kingdom

ISBN 978-1905378319 (1905378319) Paperback Edition

SixFinger Publishing
Forum House
Sterling Road
Chichester PO19 7DN
www.gwlpublishing.co.uk
www.sixfingerpublishing.com

Born in Demopolis, Alabama, William Cobb was educated at Livingston State College before attending Vanderbilt University. He taught at the University of Montevallo, serving as writer in residence of twelve years. His novels and short stories have reached a wide audience and he has won many awards, including Story Magazine's Story of the Year in 1965, the Alabama Library Association's Fiction Book of the Year (2000) and the Harper Lee Award (2007). He has also written an autobiography (Captain Billy's Troopers), and non-fiction. William is married to the short story writer, Loretta Cobb. They have one daughter and two grandchildren and continue to live in Montevallo.

Raised in New York State, Dr Don Noble is Professor of English, Emeritus at the University of Alabama. His particular fields of expertise include Southern literature, especially fiction. He is the editor of ten books and 550 short pieces, most of which focus on the literature of the South. Now resident in Cottondale, Alabama, Dr Noble is the host of a weekly author interview show, Bookmark, on APTV.

iv

PUBLISHER'S DISCLAIMER

Due to the historical nature and setting of these stories, some of the language employed could, by modern standards, be deemed offensive. Whilst the publisher recognizes the sensitive nature of the language, it is deemed that this is acceptable within the context of the period in which the stories are set.

Alabama

CONTENTS

(dates in which the stories are set are shown in italics)

FOREWORD

A reader could hardly find a stronger and more representative southern fiction writer of stories in his generation than William Cobb. It is all here.

While he is certainly in the tradition of William Faulkner, Eudora Welty, Flannery O'Connor, Erskine Caldwell and the other writers of the Southern Literary Renascence, Cobb's vision was formed in the second half of the twentieth century. William Cobb , born in 1937, grew up in Demopolis, Alabama, attended college at West Alabama in Livingston, and has made his career in Montevallo, Alabama; he is of the next generation, that of Harry Crews, Barry Hannah and Larry Brown.

His is a South with slightly more contact with the rest of the country, a South in the process of modernizing into the Sun Belt, with a certain number of Northern transplants, and even more Southerners who have sought their fortunes in the North. It is a South of television, air conditioning, and, most importantly, a culture having to cope with the increasingly powerful Civil Rights Movement.

Cobb's own literary consciousness was formed in post–World War II Alabama, but his stories, here arranged, to good effect, in chronological order by setting, reflect the ways in which the South, especially Alabama, has changed over a period of 130 years, with some cultural values holding steady and others undergoing abrupt and difficult shifts.

Of all the tropes or recurring motifs in Southern fiction, a powerful sense of place and of individuals rooted in that may be the most prevalent.

Southerners, more than any other Americans, are attached to their piece of native ground and stay put. William Cobb, with some excursions to Nashville, Tennessee; Vermont; New York City to guide his plays through production; and some trips to Europe, especially France and Bulgaria, lives in his native Alabama. He has made his life and career within a forty-mile radius of his present home.

As Faulkner's fictional "postage stamp of soil" Yoknapatawpha County and its county seat, Jefferson, supplied him with more than enough material, so does Cobb's creation of Hammond, Alabama, based mainly on Demopolis, give Cobb more than enough to work with.

The town is small, with only a few thousand residents, a few merchants, a miniscule professional class of physicians and lawyers, and a black section for the African-American community.

The surrounding countryside is relatively impoverished with mainly yeoman farmers, some poor whites and a number of sharecroppers.

As poor as almost everyone is, a rigid racial and caste system is in place and love and marriage are often constrained by these divisions. In *"A Very Proper Resting Place"*, the reader is saddened to the core by the failure of the love between well-to-do Mr. Cincy and Clara, a girl from across the river. He would marry her, but she refuses to let him destroy himself by that marriage and so breaks his heart.

Hammond, Alabama, is all Cobb needs. Every form of human pleasure and pain, all the experiences of family, church, community, love and loneliness can be explored with those few thousand people.

This area of the South, like Faulkner's section of Mississippi, was not the scene of major battles such as took place in Virginia and Tennessee. Alabama volunteers went off to fight. Many came back grievously injured and some never returned. The effects of The War were profound and lasting, and Cobb appropriately shows these effects, indirectly, in story after story. In *"The Stone Soldier"*, the war is only five years in the past, and Major Hammond cannot speak of it, even think of it, without tears. His brother was lost, as was the hero of the South, General J.E.B. Stuart, at the Battle of Chancellorsville.

The "monument" the salesman Sparks wishes to see erected is a travesty; it will bring no solace at all, indeed it will serve as a perpetual reminder of loss.

A source of both solace and the object of considerable satire in Southern fiction is religion, black and white, from evangelical tent revivals to ritual, orderly Episcopalian ceremonies.

Cobb generally eschews the brush arbors and the snake handlers, although there are some ecstatic moments in *"Suffer Little Children..."* in which Martin, an eight-year-white old boy, with the help of a black washerwoman, Hess, sees Jesus at a church revival, to the embarrassment of his family.

Most of the stories in this collection that deal with religion concern the difficulties of change within a formal tradition. The old rich lady, Mrs. Bridges, in *"Old Wars and New Sorrow"* is contemptuous of change in the Episcopal church but, nevertheless, serves as a catalyst for the young rector, Father Simmons White, putting him back in touch with his faith and with his social conscience.

Although Cobb's stories do not focus on faith, many of them contain visions, fantasies, hallucinations, dream-like experiences. In Cobb's fiction it seems there may be a world parallel to this one. This is not to say Cobb is a "magical realist" in the sense of the Latin American fictions such as *One Hundred Years of Solitude*. He is more in the tradition of Flannery O'Connor, whose stories are peopled with physically maimed characters and religious fanatics, or Carson McCullers with her deaf-mute Mr. Singer in *The Heart is a Lonely Hunter*. Most directly, Cobb has a number of characters who may claim Benjy Compson, literature's most famous idiot, as their fictional ancestor.

William Cobb can be scrupulously realistic when he chooses but he is also one of the last practitioners of the Southern Gothic. He is possessed of a powerful and unusual imagination. The supernatural is presented, not in a calm and realistic manner accepted by all observers but as a deeply personal experience, either not shared with others or ridiculed by those who learn of it.

In *"The Hunted"* Buck has a chance, powerful, sexual experience in the deep woods with a mysterious black woman. Is she a witch?

He is ensorcelled. She seems to have been seeking his sperm; we don't learn why. He will, in all likelihood, tell no one.

Doyle Sprayberry first dreams of yellow butterflies and then more and more of them begin appearing in his life: on a dog's head, on other people's shoulders. Near the end of the story an entire baseball outfield is " ...aswarm with yellow butterflies, but nobody else seemed to notice".

In one of Cobb's best stories, *"Brother Bobby's Eye"*, Bobby has his eye knocked out in an accident. The eye is buried in a clear glass jar, but Bobby continues to see through it. He not only watches the world around him but also believes he can see into the secret, sinful, depraved lives of others, including his wife. But are his visions accurate, or are they paranoid delusions, a phantasmagoria, the product of a genuinely disturbed mind? At the end of the story, what seems to be a miracle occurs, but the visions may be mania and the miracle a stroke of really good luck.

Although Southern states have their asylums for the mentally ill and deficient — Bryce Hospital in Tuscaloosa, Alabama for example — there is a tradition of keeping afflicted members of the family at home if at all possible. Benjy Compson in *The Sound and the Fury* is one example. In Cobb, especially in his newest stories, examples abound.

In *"The Best of It"* Gideon is unforgiving of how his father treated his afflicted sister Celeste. In *"Birmingham: Mother's Day, 1961"* Doc will be burdened by the care of his boy Martin all the rest of his life. Jimmy, the retarded twelve-year-old in *"Walk the Fertile Fields"*, is six feet tall at twelve and half years old in his elementary school special education class.

The afflicted are legion in Cobb's fiction; the challenge to the reader is to come to understand why they are there. Amy, the special ed. teacher is driven to distraction by Jimmy, but finally has her epiphany: Jimmy can't learn much but he can receive love — her love. In each case in Cobb's stories, the deluded or retarded character is there to illustrate some lesson of the human heart that the "normal" could not effect.

On a lighter note, sport has been a major element in Southern life and fiction from the start but the activity has changed enormously. In early Southern literature the sports were riding, cockfighting, and hunting. In William Cobb's South baseball is the sport of choice. Baseball and its slightly gentler equivalent, softball, is watched and played all over Dixie.

It is on the softball field that D.O. Prants has a possible heart attack and a revelation in *"Glad My Eyes"*, as he collapses heading for home which is, in this story, both the home plate of the softball field and his marriage to Mayfrances.

The talented baseball manager Doyle Sprayberry is having an extraordinarily successful season with the Hammond Rebels, but we fear he will throw it all away as he moves from only two beers a day to a six-pack and finally back to bourbon, starting at breakfast.

A major subject in Southern fiction is and always has been the subject of race: slavery, Jim Crow, injustice, civil rights. The state of Alabama, especially the lower half, was a land of cotton plantations. Consequently, statewide the population is about 24 percent African-American and in Cobb's home territory, the Black Belt, so-called because of the deep rich soil, African-Americans are in the majority. As a reader might expect, Cobb's stories deal with race but in a far from sensational way.

Cobb has not chosen to write of the more sensational aspects of the racial issue, plantation cruelties, lynchings, and so on. In most of his stories, beginning with the first, black characters are just that: characters.

In the first, *"The Stone Soldier"*, the black John Thomas, known as "Lip," rejects Sparks' ploy to engage him selling Bibles to the black community, in fact rejects the Bible Sparks gives him, gratis.

John Thomas' loyalties are with Major Hammond. "Lip" and Carla, the Hammonds' serving girl, understand the loss and pain of Major Hammond and the emotionally ignorant and self-serving motives of the drummer.

A lifelong Alabamian, Cobb was of course informed and involved with the Civil Rights Movement and uses it as the theme of perhaps his best novel, *A Walk Through Fire* (1992). In that novel The Movement comes to Hammond and we see depicted the confusion and violence of the struggle for equal rights.

Among the stories, the only one to treat the Civil Rights Movement is *"Birmingham: Mother's Day, 1961"* and here, as usual, indirectly. Doc, an optometrist, and his retarded son Martin, find themselves by chance at the Greyhound station in Birmingham, Alabama, on the day of the attack on the Freedom Riders by the Ku Klux Klan and other violent racists.

Already in a state of emotional chaos and frustration over the difficulties with Martin, Doc, seemingly not a bigoted man, gets caught up in the vicious actions, the nightmare around him. His own racism is, we see, not far beneath the surface.

As with many other Southern tropes or motifs, several of Cobb's stories deal with the issue of alcohol and alcoholism, but from an oblique angle.

Readers might expect to find stories about moonshiners, stills, outwitting or even engaging in gun battles with agents of the Internal Revenue Service, sometimes outrunning the agents in souped-up cars around twisting mountain roads. (These conventional-looking cars with special engines are thought by many to be the origins of the popular Southern racing sport NASCAR.)

These activities happened often enough, but in the Appalachian South, not the Black Belt, plantation South of Bill Cobb.

In these stories, alcohol is rarely presented as a casual, everyday pleasure or a matter of cultural sophistication, as in a fine wine with dinner. It is, in fact, usually destructive and indicative of poor character or emotional distress. In the very first story the monument salesman Lyman Sparks, leaving town, is described as "squinting in the sun, his eyes red-rimmed from the bottle of corn whiskey that he'd drunk in his room in the hotel last night. He'd been plagued by a sense of guilt that he could not understand, and he'd drunk the whiskey and had passed out, fully clothed, across the bed...."

The narrator of the last story, *"The Best of It"*, is a recovering alcoholic whose anger at his father had fueled his thirst to the point where he "had wound up in the psycho ward in Bellevue, with bars on the windows. That was where they put drunks in those days."

This collection of eighteen stories, set from 1870 to 2000, offers the reader a deep and varied reading experience, and one which illuminates the major concerns of the American South, dealt with masterfully, by one of our finest and most honored living short story writers.

Don Noble
2013

The Stone Soldier

(First Published in "Story Magazine", 1965)

I

It was nine thirty in the morning when he stepped off the train, and the first thing he did was to pull the wrinkled, big, red bandana out of his hip pocket and slowly wipe his face. He grunted under the heat and stood looking around — at the deserted platform with only one old Negro standing in the two-foot strip of shade next to the yellow wall, under the sign that said, in peeling whitish letters, HAMMOND; at the dusty street that ran away from the station toward the east and toward the new sun; at the small frame buildings lining the street and the few brick ones; and halfway up the street at the sign that said MADISON HOTEL, and under that *Dining Room* in smaller letters. He grunted again and looked at the Negro.

"Mornin', Uncle," he said. His white suit was stained under his armpits and wrinkled up the back; it was tight across his bulging belly, and the pants hugged his legs and made his thighs look like fat sausages under his belly. There was an early-morning stubble on his fleshy jowls, and he exuded an odor that was part sweat, part cheap bourbon, and part that universal smell of the fat person emerging from close quarters. His hat was pushed back to reveal a matted, yellow widow's peak over his squinting eyes as he looked at the small straw suitcase beside him and then at the Negro, who hadn't answered him.

"I said mornin', Uncle" he said.

"I said morning," the Negro answered. His face was in a shadow, and the fat man couldn't tell by his tone of voice if he were trying to be smart with him. He paused a moment, looking around.

"The Lord doth send heat and make white and nigger alike sweat under it, don't he?" the fat man said. "Lord if he don't."

"Yes sir," the Negro said.

"But Goddam if a man got to stay out in it, has he? I'll just be getting on up to the Madison Hotel for a bath and a shave, and then I'll be tendin' to my business and be gettin' on my way. But Lord if it ain't hot as the fires of almighty hell." The Negro said nothing, and the fat man widened his eyes and peered into the shadows at his face. The fat man's eyes bulged in their sockets; they looked as though they were loosed inside his head. They kept moving back and forth, just slightly, a slight wiggle as if they might have been too well greased and he couldn't quite control them; it made him tilt his face slightly to the side and peer like an old woman trying to thread a needle. He stood there looking at the Negro for a minute, and he couldn't say anything. Because the Negro's lower lip was stretched. It hung down over his chin, glistening wetly, startlingly red against the dull, brown skin like the meat of a dog torn open by buzzards looks red against the bloated brown belly. The Negro moved his head, and the lip flapped, and his eyes bored into the fat man's with an incomprehensible message. The fat man felt the heat of the sun against the side of his sweating neck.

"It's open for business," the Negro said.

"What?"

"Madison Hotel," he said, and the lip flapped.

"My name is Lyman Sparks," the fat man said. He pulled out the bandana and swiped it around his neck; he reached into the folds of fat over his belly, into a pocket of his vest, and pulled out a small card and handed it to the Negro. The Negro didn't look at it; he just held it in his hand, at his side. "I do quite a bit of business with colored folks," the man said. "Not that that's what I'm here for, but you just well kill two birds with one stone, I always say."

He looked slyly at the Negro, and a grin revealed blackened, twisted teeth. "And that's what the boss says too. Got to please the boss, ain't that right?"

The Negro moved out of the shadow. He was much taller than Sparks, with a high, slanting forehead and tight black hair sticking closely to his head; his arms hung loosely at his sides, and his legs were thin under the coarse cloth of his breeches. Sparks found himself looking at the soft, moist underlip, which was even more red when the sun hit it.

"Now," Sparks said, "what is your name?"

"Lip," the Negro said. His eyes bored into Sparks.

"Well now," Sparks said. "Well now. I reckon you're a freed man?"

"That's right," Lip said.

"Well then, I reckon I can talk to you man to man, or salesman with somethin' you need and want to buyer who's goin'ta be eternally grateful that I happened along. Ain't that right? Like, now that you your own boss, ain't no reason why you can't decide what you want to buy and what you don't, now is it?"

"It ain't much I want to buy," Lip said. Sparks grinned slyly at him again.

"Well now, suppose I was to take you in with me on the selling side? Suppose I didn't want you to buy anything. Suppose I wanted you to sell with me?"

Lip didn't answer him. He just stood there, his dark eyes level on Sparks.

"Course when I show you what I got, ain't no doubt in my mind that you goin'ta want one, too. And ain't no reason why I can't just give *you* one, long as we gone be partners, now is it?" He tilted his head to the side, as though he couldn't quite get Lip into focus. "Well now," he said, and he grunted as he knelt to open up the straw suitcase and began to rummage around among papers and pieces of clothing until he found what he was looking for, a small black book that was unmistakably a Bible.

"Now, I know you go to church, am I right? Sho you do. I know that by just lookin' at you. And I can see you know what this here is I'm holdin' in my hand. But you reckon you do? Now just reckon you do?" He opened it and shoved it under Lip's nose, and the Negro took it and looked at the picture in front of him.

It was a well-known picture; Lip had seen it in the Episcopal church, made out of glass in a window; he had seen it when he helped Johnny Pope clean up down there. It was the one of Jesus, holding a little sheep in his arms and with other lambs around his feet rubbing up against his legs like cats will do. Only one thing was different. Jesus' face was dark, and his lips were thick, and his hair was darker, only still long and soft looking, and his hands holding the little sheep were dark, too.

Lip stood there looking down at it; he could hear Sparks breathing heavily beside him as he let the pages flip through his fingers, and it opened to the picture of the boy Jesus in the temple, when he was twelve years old. Here, too, he was a young colored boy, with some sand stuck to the paper that reflected the sunlight and made it look like a bright halo over the boy's head. The book seemed light and flimsy in Lip's hand; the pages were not slick like the ones in the Bible he had at home, but rough and coarse, and the printing was in places light and faded looking.

"Well?" Sparks said. And when the Negro didn't answer, he said, "Well, what do you think of it?"

"I reckon I already got a Bible," Lip said.

"But not like this one I bet," Sparks said. He laughed then. "Go on. Take it. I'm givin' it to you, ain't gone charge you a cent for it. I do like that sometimes, good business, I always say. So you can just take it, and it don't obligate you in no way whatsoever. No sir." He looked slyly at Lip again and grinned. "Only thing is, I sho do think you ought to show it around. You know, show it to all your good friends, cause they gone sho want one, too, don't you reckon? After all, they freed men now too; ain't nobody to tell em what they can't have and what they can, and that's just what my company felt like after the war. Figured you colored folks ought to have products of your own, that's all."

"I don't know," Lip said.

"Hell, ahhh, Lip, I ain't askin' you to sell for me. Nothing like that. Just let folks know that I got 'em, and where they can get 'em. That's all. You gone be doin' them a favor."

Lip didn't answer. He just stood there, looking at the fat man with those deep eyes, large and red-rimmed, but steady.

"You understand that that ain't my business. Hell no. That's just a little sideline. A little service, you might say. A public service. I don't charge but a quarter for 'em, and that's some fine workmanship goes into that artwork, you can see that. And hell, the quarter don't hardly pay for toting em around. No, I got other business round here, big business — but I figured I just might kill two birds with one stone."

He grinned again and tilted his head.

"Well, you just take that one, anyhow hear? I want you to have it, free of charge. Let's just say, as a gift from a stranger who ain't never been in Hammond before. Maybe that'll bring me some luck on my other deal, my big deal." He winked at Lip and wiped his neck with the balled-up bandana. "I didn't come here just to sell no Bibles. No sir. But you just keep it, and you know where I'll be. The Madison Hotel. Ask for Mr. Sparks." He closed the straw suitcase and glanced up the sun-bright street to the hotel. A cotton wagon was coming very slowly down the street, and the mule's hooves made little clouds of dust rise out of the motionless air. "Good to seen you, Lip. And that's Sparks, Lyman Sparks from Mobile." He pulled at his crotch, set his hat low over his eyes, and headed up the street on his sausage legs.

FROM WHERE Dale Spivey was sitting, on the porch of the hotel, he could see Sparks leave the platform and start up the street. He had been watching while Sparks and the Negro were talking, his cane-bottom chair leaning back against a post at the edge of the porch. He was holding a pipe on his lap, and his eyes were half-closed like the eyes of an old cow standing in the shade. He watched Sparks, lugging the straw suitcase, pass the wagon and tip his hat to the old Negro on the seat and wipe at his neck with the red bandana.

"Walks straddle-legged like he scared some of that fat on his legs gonna rub off his privates," Dale Spivey said.

He was speaking to Mr.Downey, who had been sitting in exactly the same position as Dale Spivey, only with his chair leaning back against the wall of the hotel.

"Who?" Mr. Downey said.

"That drummer."

Mr. Downey let his chair fall with a dull thump, and he leaned forward to look up the street at Sparks. Sparks came on slowly, already out of breath, bent at the waist and craning his short neck toward the two men on the porch. They watched him come up and stand in the street until he got his breath, wiping at his sweating face; then he came up the steps onto the porch.

"Mornin'." His breath wheezed out around the word. "Lord if it ain't hot."

"Mornin'," the two men said at the same time.

"My name is Sparks, Lyman Sparks," he said. "And I would assume you to be Mr. J. P. Downey, owner and proprietor of the Madison Hotel."

"That's right," Downey said.

"Well, I'm pleased to meet you," Sparks said. Then he looked at Dale, still leaning back in the cane-bottom chair, his eyes half closed and the cold pipe clenched between his teeth.

"That's Dale Spivey," Mr. Downey said.

"I'm happy to make your acquaintance, Mr. Spivey," Sparks said. Dale just nodded, and Mr. Sparks tilted his head to the side, and his eyes shifted; then he looked off up the street and at the buildings giving way to a few houses as the road ran down a hill. In the distance he could see the river, pale and shimmering under the sun, and the white-limerock ditches at the side of the street reflected the sun back at him. "Lord, it's goin'ta be another one, ain't it?" he said.

"It's September," Dale said.

"And rightly so. Rightly so," Sparks said. "But it sho nuff makes it uncomfortable for heavy folks." He sat in an empty chair and placed the straw suitcase carefully against the wall. The chair creaked under him as he pulled at and straightened his crotch. "Well now, Mr. Downey, I'll be wantin' to put up with you for a while, but it's sho no hurry about it. I trust you do have room for me." Downey nodded. "I'll be transactin' some business from here, but it's a mite early in the day to be talkin' business deals, so I'll just set here for awhile with you all if you don't mind."

"Fine," Mr. Downey said.

They sat quietly for a while and Sparks watched the heat waves rising off the road. An occasional wagon would go by, loaded with cotton, and the driver would raise his hand in greeting, and the men on the porch would do the same. Mr. Downey was a small man, with a thick, rough-looking shirt and a string tie and a graying moustache; his face was sun-spotted and deeply tanned, and his eyes were small and bright and quick. Dale hardly moved at all; his heavy boots rested on the heels and his breeches were drawn up his legs for the occasional slight breeze. His chin rested on his chest and his drooping eyes kept closing and opening and he kept taking the pipe from his mouth and putting it back. When he spoke suddenly, Sparks thought that someone else had come onto the porch.

"You had some business with John Thomas?" Dale said, and Sparks' eyes shifted to Dale.

"Who's that?" he said.

"John Thomas, the nigger down there at the station."

"Oh yes. Well, not business, I don't guess you'd say." He paused a minute. "That nigger told me his name was Lip."

"It is," Mr. Downey said. "John Thomas Lip."

"Oh," Sparks said. Then, after a minute, "Wonder what make his lip hang down like that?"

"He come right from Africa like that," Dale said. "One of them tribes in Africa, that he come from. They lips growed like that."

"Well, I declare," Sparks said. "Now don't that beat it all? I never seen one of them before. I reckon you learn somethin' every day, don't you?"

"His mammy was like that too," Dale said. "Both of em belonged to Major Hammond. The old woman died before the war." Then his eyes closed.

"Well, I declare," Sparks said. "Beats all, don't it?"

Sparks watched Mr. Downey take a plug of tobacco from his pocket, pick a few pieces of lint off of it, cut a neat plug, and put it into his mouth. He waited until the hotel proprietor had chewed it a while, and he could see that Mr. Downey could talk.

"How is Major Hammond?" he asked, looking at Mr. Downey.

"Not good, I don't think," Mr. Downey said.

"Sick?"

"Well, he don't ever leave the house anymore. Miss Iva, she takes care of him, but he just sets there in the house and rocks."

"Well now, that's a pity," Sparks said. "That's sho bad. Man like that."

"You know the Major?" Dale asked, and his eyes opened a little. His chin came up off his chest a fraction.

"Well, no, not really. But Lord if I don't feel like I do. I heard enough about him." He wiped at his face. "Sho bad. Hear he lost ever thing he had. Sho bad."

Dale laughed. It was a low, muffled rumbling from out of his chest. "He could still write you a check for ten thousand dollars."

"Well now, I could too. I could write you a check for a million dollars, but that don't mean it'd be any good."

Sparks knew right then that he had moved too fast, and his eyes wiggled as he looked at Dale and then at Mr. Downey. They looked straight ahead, and he couldn't read their eyes. "But Lord, what does it matter?" he said. Mr. Downey let his chair fall again with a thump, and he leaned forward and spat a yellow stream over the edge of the porch. "Yes sir, I always say what does it matter?" Sparks repeated.

But they didn't answer him. Sparks wiped at his face and neck and stood up. "Well, I just might get inta that room and get me a clean shirt on befo dinner, yes sir," he said. He picked up the suitcase and looked at Mr. Downey.

"Just tell the nigger," Mr. Downey said, hooking his thumb over his shoulder at the door. "He'll show you."

"Fine," said Sparks. He moved toward the door. "I hope you gentleman will take dinner with me," he said. "In any case, I'll be down after a while. And it was certainly nice to've met cha." After he heaved through the door and into the gloom of the hotel, the two men sat without speaking for a while.

Then Dale said, "That son-of-a-bitch has got shifty eyes." And Mr. Downey just nodded and reached for his plug.

II

SPARKS COULD feel the sweat running down the insides of his legs and down his collar as he walked through the town and he took out the fresh bandana, his third for the day, to mop his face. And then, at last, he was standing at the gate, looking up the sandy walk to the house, lined with dusty verbena, and at the hint of lace curtains at the darkened windows and the smilax shading the veranda. The iron plowshare rattled on its chain as he pushed through the gate and puffed up the path to the porch. He knocked and then looked through the colored glass at the side of the door, cocking his head like a man trying to look at another man's woman without his knowing it, but when he saw the Negro woman coming up the hall he snatched his hat from his head and stood holding it over his belly and waiting for the door to open.

"Good afternoon," he said before the Negress could speak. "I was wonderin' if I might have a audience with the Major. With Major Hammond."

The Negro woman was as big as he was; she stood blocking the door, looking levelly at him. Her broad face was bright yellow, and her skin was as moist and looked as soft as baked bread; it shone dully over her broad nose, and her biceps bulged under the sleeves of a white house dress. She looked him up and down, at his dusty shoes and wrinkled suit, at his sweating face and matted hair.

"What?" she said.

"See him," he said. "See Major Hammond."

"The Major don't see nobody," she said and made a step back as though to close the door in his face.

"Well then," he said, "I'd like to see Miss Iva Ward Hammond, then, if you don't mind."

"Miss Ida restin'," she said.

"Well now, this is a matter of great importance, Auntie, and I'd be glad to wait," he said and moved toward the door.

"You wait here," she said and pushed the door gently to. After a minute she reappeared and opened the door widely for him to enter.

"Miss Ida say for you to wait in the parlor," she said; "she be downstairs in a minute." She disappeared into the damp gloom of the hall toward the back of the house. Sparks realized with a sudden sense of pleasure that the house was much larger than it had looked from the outside; he went into the parlor and put his hat carefully on a deep-crimson sofa, slightly worn at the corners, and walked over to the window. He would see all the way down to the river from the window, to where the dusty road wound down to the landing and the big, stone storage barn that the young Negro at the hotel had told him was haunted because the walls ran water. But Dale Spivey had told him that the walls sweated because they had stored salt in it during the war. Then he looked around the room, at the two oil portraits over the mantel, in peeling gilt frames, the man looking stiff and staring, with steel-gray eyes and hair, and the woman looking stiff and rosy-cheeked, with a mountain of black curls piled over her head. He noticed the framed Stars and Bars on one wall, with black-edged holes in it, and brownish stains in one corner, and the bookcase crammed with leather-bound volumes between the windows. He took one of the books out and looked at the flyleaf. It was spotted and brown, and in faded ink was scrawled across the page: "Winslow Hammond, Rose Hill, 1834."

"My brother, Winslow, the oldest," he heard a voice say, and it startled him. He turned to see her standing just inside the parlor. "He was the only one of us that liked books and literature," she said. "Really liked them."

She came into the room and stood across from him, and his eyes flicked over her, from the dark dress, black or navy blue, down to the floor where he could hardly see the tiny shoes beneath, back to where her blouse gathered around her neck with white lace, to the face with the high white forehead that might have been chiseled from the limerock river bluff at the edge of town. Her gray-black hair was pulled back sharply to a knot at the back of her head. Her eyes were wide, but not staring, and were a clear, deep brown, steady on him as she came across the parlor. The thought that he had seen them before flickered into his consciousness and out again as she stopped and looked at him.

"I'm Iva Hammond," she said, and her lips were just a thin line over the strong, jutting chin. "Carla says you'd like to see me, Mr. —"

"Sparks. Lyman Sparks," he said. He looked at her eyes again, and there was the same question, the same look. He cleared his throat.

"I was hoping to see the Major, Miss Hammond," he said. "but I think you can help me."

"Won't you sit down, Mr. Sparks?" she said and sat herself on the slightly worn red sofa. He took the rocker across from her, put his bulging legs out before him, and smiled his twisted smile at her. She looked steadily back at him, and he could read nothing in her face.

"Would you like a cool glass of water, Mr. Sparks?" she said. Before he could answer she called Carla, who came with a tray and a pitcher and two tall glasses and poured him a glass. He tasted it and smacked his lips.

"Ahhhh, that's good," he said. "I don't know when it's been so hot."

"It's the lime," she said.

"I beg your pardon mam?" he said.

"The lime, in the water. Makes it so good. My father always used to say that that was one of the best advantages of this river bend, the lime water."

"It is good," Sparks said. He tilted the glass and had another swallow, and smiled at her, and said "Ahhhh" again. They sat quietly, and he could hear a clock ticking somewhere, and he heard Carla moving around in the back of the house.

"Well, Mr. Sparks, what was it you wanted to talk with me about?" she said.

"Well now," he said. He reached into his vest, pulled out a card, and leaning forward with effort, passed it to her. "Miss Iva — " He paused and grinned. "Miss Hammond, is your name Iva or Ida?"

A slight smile flickered at her thin lips, and she said, "It's Iva, Mr. Sparks. Though most of the Negroes call me Miss Ida. They have as long as I can remember."

"Well, Miss Iva," he said grinning, "as you can see by my card, I represent the Dixie Monument Company, Mobile branch."

"Yes," she said.

"And I'm in this area, what you might call, solicitin' for future buildin' of monuments and callin' on the most prominent citizens in each town to discuss it. Naturally, the first folks I'd call on in Hammond would be the Hammonds theirselves," he said, and he grinned and nodded to her.

"What sort of monuments would these be, sir?" she said.

"Why, Confederate monuments, Miss Iva, of course." Her expression didn't change, and the brown, deep eyes seemed even deeper. "Now we've sold one over at Livingston; it's possible that you've seen that one, and well, most of the towns goin'ta be puttin' em up sooner or later, and well, Miss Iva, we just feel like we got the best product for the people. Yes mam, ours is guaranteed to be standin' long after a hundred years is up."

Miss Iva got up from the sofa and went to the window. His eyes followed her and then turned inward as if he were examining what he would say next, or making it up, or trying to figure whether he had been too quick, as he had been with Spivey and Mr. Downey. Then he fished into his coat and pulled out several pieces of paper, with drawings. They were slightly damp, and he brushed at the lint and bits of tobacco stuck on them and heaved himself up from the rocker.

"You might like to look these over, Miss Ida. Of course, you'd want to see the real thing. But I can tell you, it's some fine art work goes into these statues, yes mam. And, too, right now we got cannons from about every major battle in the war. Any one you want, you just name it and we'll supply. And it'll be the real thing, yes mam, the real thing. We don't believe in pushing off cannons made up there in some factory after the war like some of the companies are doin'. Why, they's a company in Georgia claimed they had all the cannons from Chancellorsville for sale with their statues, and by God, they wasn't a one of 'em the real thing." He couldn't tell what she was thinking, or even if she was listening to him.

Then she turned from the window, and the dark eyes bored into him as she came back to the sofa and sat down.

"Mr. Sparks," she said, "I don't think you understand how scarce money is in Hammond right now. I don't think you know about our situation here."

He quickly arranged a sorrowful expression on his face. "Of course I do, Miss Ida. My company does, I mean. Why, we've taken that into consideration. Let me tell you, mam, that we've got a plan, yes mam, a plan for your whole town. Why, you can take up to fifty years to pay for it. We can arrange just about anything you want."

"Why?"

"I beg your pardon mam?"

"I only asked why, Mr. Sparks," she said.

His eyes seemed to be jumping from one side of her face to the other.

"Never mind," she said. And then, "But why do you come to me?"

He grinned. "Why, well now, Miss Ida, you ought to know that. A man like me wants to do business with the right kind of people. And you know that if you, or the Major, said to the people of this town that they ought to buy one a these statues, which they sho ought, ain't no doubt about that, then they'd buy one. Now that's my business. I know what the people need, but I can't always get it over to 'em what they need. But the right kind of folks, you ain't got to sell, now ain't that right?"

"Well, I don't think that this is the time."

"Well now, Miss Ida, you just ought to think about that. Now is the time to," and here he paused, "honor your dead. Our dead. Folks need to be reminded of those young boys that gave they lives for they country. Now, you sho believe that, now don't you?"

She glanced quickly at him, and he could detect that question in her eyes, that question that he'd seen before, and she said, "Mr. Sparks, I don't need to be reminded of the tragedy of the war."

"You don't, Miss Ida, now don't you think I know that? But what about all them folks that're goin'ta come after you? What about them? What about —"

He stopped, and his eyes were on the door to the parlor, and she knew even before she turned that her brother was standing there, and she knew what he looked like. Sparks's mouth was standing open and his eyes were active, and the beads of sweat were standing out on his face.

And she thought about the Bible that Carla had told her about, the one the man had given Lip, and that Lip had brought to the kitchen door when he came to eat and had shown Carla, and that Carla had laughed at with the still strong laugh that echoed all over the house. And she disliked Mr. Sparks even more than she had before, because her brother was in the room now. She turned and looked at him.

He was leaning on the carved walking stick, in the old robe, his bad foot trailing behind him. He was small and frail, and his pale-blue eyes were so light as to look all white, except for the red rims and the tiny red veins. He had a high forehead, but his hair was thin and short and stuck out from his head in a mad tangle; his mouth hung open, and his head nodded forward and jerked. His hands on the cane were thick and wrinkled and the veins stood up on the backs. He hobbled slowly into the room and squinted at Sparks.

"This is my brother, Clayton Hammond, Mr. Sparks," she said. "He's not well," she added.

Sparks went forward toward her brother. "Why, Major, I'm indeed happy to make your acquaintance. Why, I've heard so much about you, and well, it's a honor to meet a great officer like you."

The Major stood there like a weak sapling, his head moving slowly back and forth as he looked at Sparks. "What's your business, sir?" he said, and his voice grated like the bottom of a skiff when it's pulled out of the river onto sand.

"Mr. Sparks was just —" and she was going to say leaving.

But Sparks, moving with surprising quickness, was across the room in front of her brother, saying, "Sparks, Lyman Sparks, Major Hammond, and I'm happy to make your acquaintance. Yes, indeed, I really come to Hammond just to see you, and it woulda been a disappointment sho nuff if I hadn't got to talk with you."

The Major looked at him with his pale-blue eyes, and Sparks grinned. The Major's lips were thin and quivering, and sparse gray whiskers clung to his wrinkled chin.

"Well now," Sparks said, rocking back on his heels to pat his bulging belly with both palms. "Well now, I reckon we can talk business now." And he glanced over at Miss Iva.

"No, I don't think we will, Mr. Sparks," she said.

"But, Miss Ida —"

"I've already told you, Mr. Sparks," she said. "We can't help you. It's not us that you ought to be talking to."

"Well now, Miss Ida," Sparks said, "I reckon the Major just ought to hear what I've got to say."

Miss Iva stood looking at him, one hand on the back of the rocker in front of her, her lips in a straight line and so tightly drawn as to be almost invisible. Sparks turned away from her smoldering eyes to the Major, who stood hunched over his cane.

"State your business, sir," the Major said.

And so Sparks told him about it, his eyes shifting from one to the other while Miss Iva stood watching him, watching him show the drawings to the Major, or rather, holding them in front of his face. He had begun to sweat with the effort and had pulled out a wrinkled, red bandana to pass it over his face from time to time. When he finished the whole spiel, he stood waiting, tilting his head at the Major.

"Chancellorsville," the Major said. "Chancellorsville."

"Yes, those fellers claimed they had the cannons from that battle, and Lord if they weren't ever one a fake," Sparks chuckled.

Miss Iva crossed the room and stood beside her brother. "Mr. Sparks, I think my brother is tired now, so if you don't mind, I'll take him back."

But the old man stood rooted to the spot, looking at Sparks, a gleam came into the dull eyes, a glimmer of understanding, and his old lips moved slowly.

"A soldier," he said. "A stone soldier?"

"Why that's right, Major Hammond," Sparks boomed. "That's right. A stone soldier, standin' there guardin' the town." And his finger pounded the drawings in his other hand. "Never thought of it like that, no sir."

And then the old man was crying, dry rasping sobs coming from deep down inside his body, so that his head shook, and two tiny tears made a path across his leathery cheek. Sparks straightened up, and Miss Iva put her arm across the withered shoulders.

"What, Miss Ida," Sparks said. "Why, what did I say?"

"It was nothing you said, Mr. Sparks," she said. "He's just sick, you understand."

The old man's head was down, and he was mumbling something about Chancellorsville and a river, and Sparks backed up against the wall, suddenly afraid again, afraid for his deal, and he quickly wiped his face.

"Well now," he said, "I reckon I'm sorry."

Her eyes were on him for a moment before she spoke and he looked away. She spoke quietly, "It's not your fault." She paused, and then she said, "It's not your fault that you're the way you are, Mr. Sparks, anymore than it's his fault." She stopped speaking, and he hung his head, felt the clammy, wrinkled suit sticking to him. Carla had come to the door, and Miss Iva walked the old man over to her, and the servant disappeared down the hall with him; then Miss Iva crossed the room to the window, walking slowly as though she had suddenly grown very tired, and Sparks, as quietly as he could, walked over to the sofa and picked up his hat and twisted it in his hands. Then she turned from the window and came toward him.

"Mr. Sparks," she said, "what you've brought here is no concern to me. If this town wants a monument, then it's all right with me, but it's not up to me to make the arrangements with you, do you understand?"

"Some great art work goes into these statues, Miss Ida," he said, a hint of a whine in his voice.

She was still standing across from him, a hand on the rocker. "You go to see George Mayhew, at the *Hammond Express*," she said. "Talk to him. Tell him I sent you, if you want to."

He tilted his head to the side and saw her sharply and clearly, standing in the dim parlor as her eyes bore into him. And there was the question, the burning question; but he thought only of leaving, of fleeing, because he had what he had come for. There was nothing else for him in that house, the house that held the Major and his sister; he wanted only to get away, to complete his deal and get away. She had thrown open the door for him, but he couldn't understand why. He had only to walk out and put her behind him, to get on the train and walk into his boss's office and be patted on the back and start getting his commission checks; but he stood looking at her. Instead of elation, there was a hollow, cold lump in the pit of his stomach, and he felt ugly and fat and sweating; he twisted his hat in his hands.

"Miss Ida," he began and stopped. After a long, hollow minute, he said, "Well now, it was a pleasure meeting you, Miss Ida," and he walked quickly across the room and down the hall and out the door. Once in the street he could see the Madison Hotel sign in the distance, through the rising waves of late afternoon heat. He began the long haul up the hill, in the dust, the sky red with sunset behind him. There was a tightness in his chest that was not caused by breathlessness; and he felt it again, stronger, when he passed a small frame building where some Negroes were sitting, and heard the low, ringing laugh. He looked at the faces, at the large, white eyes with the dark pupils and the shining white teeth; and at the one face that was not smiling, but was twisted grotesquely by the bulging, bulbous, red lip that hung down over his chin. Sparks turned his face toward the hotel and moved on, the sweat on his neck moving unchecked down over his collar and down the wrinkled back of the grayish suit, orange-tinted now in the dying sun.

III

HE WAS standing on the platform, and he had just heard the 11:15 blowing before it crossed the trestle upriver, the trestle that Dale Spivey told him had been rebuilt by Bedford Forrest just a month before he was captured up at Gainesville. It would be a matter of minutes before Sparks would be away from Hammond, speeding toward Mobile. He stood squinting in the sun, his eyes red-rimmed from the bottle of corn whiskey that he'd drunk in his room in the hotel last night. He had been plagued by a sense of guilt that he could not understand, and he'd drunk the whiskey and passed out, fully clothed, across the bed about daylight. George Mayhew had his ad for the *Hammond Express*, the one drawn up by his company in Mobile; he had the sanction of the leading citizen of Hammond (a fact that he had wasted no time in spreading around)

25

and there was no doubt in his mind that he had made a sale. Once Hammond put up a statue, a stone soldier (that's what he thought of it as, now, because of the Major; and every time he thought about the stone soldier the image of Major Hammond leaning on the cane, sobbing quietly, would flash across his mind, but would manage to put it quickly away, out of sight), he knew that the other towns across the state would soon follow suit and they would be his. Of course, the deal wasn't closed, but it would be. He allowed himself to smile, and he glanced around the platform and up the street toward the hotel, where he could make out Dale Spivey, tilted back in the chair on the porch; then he heard footsteps beside him and he looked around, and up, into the dark eyes, and his own eyes flickered over the lip and the white shirt with the sleeves torn out and with the collar missing.

"Well now, mornin', John Thomas," he said, squinting up in the near-noon sunlight. The Negro nodded to him, and after a moment held out his hand; Sparks looked, and there was the Bible. He'd almost forgotten about it, and it was a moment before he realized that the Negro wanted him to take it back.

"Why, that's all right, boy, you can keep it," he said, grinning. "You understand, I didn't come here for that, and well, I'm too busy for it anyway, and it don't matter that I didn't sell any. That one is yours to keep. I give it to you, and it's yours."

The Negro lowered his arm for a moment, and then held out the book to him again. "I don't want it, Mr. Sparks," he said. "I got a Bible give to me by Major Hammond a long time ago."

"But not one like this'n," Sparks said.

He avoided looking into the Negro's eyes.

"I thank you," John Thomas said, "but I reckon I want you to take it back. I don't want it."

The train, with a roar, was approaching the platform now, and Sparks picked up the straw suitcase and wiped at his face.

"Well, Goddam, if a man don't take somethin' give to him free, he don't deserve it, I don't reckon," and he took the Bible. "Well I see you, Lip," he said, and he moved toward the train.

From his seat he could look out onto the platform and the yellow station and the dusty street leading up the middle of the town. The train moved away, and the scene got smaller, and Sparks could see the Negro standing on the platform, moving back into the shadow against the wall. He was leaving, and the image of the Major and of Miss Iva standing in the dim parlor welled up in him, and he swallowed them down. The train was cool after the sun of the dusty street and he looked down at the Bible in his hand. Then he opened the straw suitcase and put it back with the others, among the dirty shirts and wrinkled underwear and damp bandanas. He settled again in the seat, tugging at his crotch and pulling his breeches legs down so that they did not cut into his thighs. He placed the wrinkled hat in the other seat and relaxed, looking out at the rolling pastures and clumps of trees in the distance.

"I'll just never understand some folks," he said. And a sense of relief swept over him when he closed his eyes, for he realized, now that he was on his way back to Mobile, that he did not have to understand.

A Very Proper Resting Place

(First Published in "Comment", 1967)

I

Even though it looked like it was going to start to rain any second and all the other people were going back in little groups to their cars, I stood there for a long time looking down at Old Mr. Cincy's grave. It had been a short funeral; the kind where there's not much grief, or, I should say, not much outward show of it. Though he had lived there in Hammond for his eighty-four years, and though he had all sorts of kinfolks (he never married), he wasn't the type of man that you'd really cry over when he died. I guess I'm putting this badly, in a way; what I mean is, everybody, or most everybody, loved and respected Mr. Cincy, it was just that there was nobody to break down and cry over when he died. He had a sister and a brother, both still alive and at the funeral, with dry eyes, both of them having come over from where they lived in Montgomery the night before after tending to arrangements by phone. It was rare enough, really, when they ever visited in Hammond; they had moved away forty years ago, had changed homes, and the family never visited back and forth except when one of them had to come back to check on some property that Mr.

Cincy had mismanaged, which didn't happen too often, and which, when it happened, according to Mr. Richard Barbour, the president of our local bank, was mostly just the figment of the brother or the sister's imagination. I was standing there watching Mr. Cincy's brother's Cadillac drive off then, with Miss Emma sitting up on the front seat with a little black straw hat on, and Mr. Earl already with a big, lit cigar in his mouth, and I looked up at the late summer sky where it was heavy with rain; there were two Negro men standing near the grave, looking at me every now and then, not knowing whether to go on filling the grave in, disturbing the flowers and the little tarpaulin, or not, while I was standing there. Finally one of them started in to shovel, maybe because they could tell by looking at me that I wasn't mourning, not really, but was just sort of day dreaming.

What I said awhile ago might have made you think that nobody cared much about Mr. Cincy, and maybe a lot of people didn't. It wasn't that, so much, as the fact that most of his life Mr. Cincy didn't care much for other people. And that's not exactly right either.

He did live by himself in a big yellow house down near the river in the oldest section of town; and he had his law offices over Willingham's Drug Store across from the city square, and you could see him walking to his office in the morning and back home in the evenings, a tall, lean man with a hooked nose and one of those real old-fashioned looking suits on, with a vest and all, and a chain across his vest. Nobody much that I knew of used his services; I think he must have lived off his share of the rent from some downtown property that his daddy had owned; he never wanted. I think that I was one of the few people who ever went up those dark, crickety stairs to his offices, one big room lined with books and another, practically empty, which was supposed, I guess, to hold a secretary. He would be sitting there in his shirt sleeves, with armbands around his biceps and with his vest unbuttoned down the front, usually reading, or writing letters, or sometimes just sitting there looking out the dusty window at the square across the street, smoking an old, worn meerschaum with friction tape around the stem. That was when I was a lot younger, of course, much younger than him. But he considered me a friend, I believe, if only because of all I knew; in fact he's the one who loaned me five hundred dollars to repair my dairy barn the time of the big Baptist storm. (That's another story.) Anyway, even after I moved out to Gallion he'd sometimes invite me in to dinner, in that big old house, and he'd have on his suit coat and have the old Negro woman fix us a toddy, and then we'd eat something like chicken salad on toast or asparagus casserole, and follow it up with great big hunk of pound cake and coffee. And then afterwards, we'd talk, and he'd get down books and read to me out of them, and he let me carry some home with me, though most of them I never understood until he talked about them, folks like Keats and Shelley and WIlliam Wordsworth. And others, too. But I remember particularly listening to him read William Wordsworth's poetry. And he would smoke his pipe and sometimes go to sleep in his chair, and the old Negro woman would come in and rouse him.

"Mr. Cincy a growed baby," she'd say, clucking her tongue at me, while he coughed and snorted and look at me out the corners of his eyes. And all those times, when we'd sit, either in his office or his parlor, or sometimes when we'd walk along the river bank in the spring, during all those times he only mentioned Clara Youngblood twice, and those two times were not long after she died, but he never talked about it, all that happened and all I knew about it. Which was why I ever knew him at all in the first place.

Both the Negroes had started working at the grave then, and I could hear the shovelfuls of dirt thumping on the coffin, so I turned and walked down the little gravel walkway that led away from that part of the cemetery and over to what I guess you could say was the newer part, though there were some mighty old graves there. It had started to sprinkle rain a little bit, big drops that made dust rise in the road, but it stopped just as quick as it had begun, the way it will do in Hammond in the late summer, so I kept on walking until I came to the section of the cemetery where I knew Clara Youngblood was buried. I didn't have much trouble finding the grave, because she was buried right near my Aunt Hattie Michaels, and I walked right to it and stood there looking down at it, thinking about Clara, and what all happened, really thinking about it for the first time in what I suppose was just about thirty-five years.

CLARA YOUNGBLOOD
1881-1904
She seemed a thing that could not feel
The touch of earthly years.

I GUESS it would take a long enough time to tell about the Youngblood family. There are not any of them around here now that I know of; you see, I was there when Clara's brother, Ben Youngblood, was killed, and I remember when Clara died, and even then their parents (I knew them only as Mrs. and Old Man) were way up in years. But as I stood there by that little stone with its little empty plastic pots half full of reddish brown rain water and a couple of brown, barren stems, I could see them just as clearly as if they had been living over there along the river right today.

They lived in a great big old house that somebody had deserted, on land that wouldn't grow anything, I don't think, but maybe a little corn, which was really all that the Old Man and Ben needed to run their business, up along the river bank about seven or eight miles from town. How long they'd been up there I don't know, but I do know that I can remember seeing Old Man Youngblood, a humped over man with a great, shaggy beard, coming into town in a wagon, even when I was just a little kid, and I remembered Ben, then, too, a big boy with a round, red face, in wrinkled and tattered overalls sitting up in the wagon beside his pa glowering down at whoever might be standing along the street and hollering at their old hound when he left his trot under the wagon and struck out after some town dog up in somebody's yard. And it seems that I saw Clara a couple of times, too, along about then, but I never could put the Clara that I saw then together with the Clara I knew later; then she was a thin, sandy haired little girl who must have been about my age, sitting up in the back in a straight chair, in a faded, loose fitting cotton dress that just barely covered her scrawny legs, looking directly ahead, not even looking when the hound darted out from under the wagon and started Ben to yelling. It was a rickety old wagon with warped wheels held together with baling twine; I guess the reason I remember it so clearly is that everybody knew, all the folks I played with, anyway, that if you got too close the Old Man would spit tobacco juice on you.

I guess that was just about the time that Mr. Cincy was getting out of the University and coming back to Hammond to set up his law practice. I knew him, in the way that everybody in a small town knows everybody else; I knew his name was Cincinattis Harrison and that he lived with his sister, Miss Emma Harrison, and his younger brother Earl, who was just about the biggest bully in town, in a big house near the Methodist Church. I knew that he was different, but I really didn't know why; different, I mean, from the other men about his age around town. Maybe it was because he didn't wear fancy hats and strut up and down the streets, like some of them did; I don't know. He seemed sort of quiet, and dreamy, the kind of thing a boy my age would notice, I supposed. But then, all those years, he was just there, I never thought much about it, one way or the other.

Until all that happened when I was twenty and a part time deputy sheriff. I was building houses then for my Uncle Caswell Michaels, and being a deputy sheriff didn't amount to much. L.S. Tate, our sheriff, would call me sometimes to go with him down to Gritney to check out a cutting or a fight on Saturday night, and that's what I figured he wanted when he stopped his hack by the front gate of Uncle Caswell's house (I was living with them, then, too) and hollered at me to come down off the porch where I was sitting with the paper. I went down the walk to where he was sitting, all three hundred pounds of him, and he always looked like he was squatting down instead of sitting, which made him look forever uncomfortable.

"Good evening, Finney," he grunted, when I came up to the wagon. It was six o' clock, but still light and hot; it must've been around the middle of September, though I couldn't really say exactly, and the sheriff's light tan hat was sweat-stained around the band. "What you doin' tomorrow?" he said, before I could say anything, and I looked up at him, at the cold cigar in the corner of his mouth, and he shifted on the seat and the iron springs creaked under him.

"Why?" I said.

"Cause we got a job to do," he said. "We goin' over and get Ben Youngblood."

For a minute I didn't even know who he was talking about; and then I knew. I remembered him sitting up in the wagon with his pa.

"What for?" I said.

"He shot Asa Logan's boy this afternoon," Mr. Tate said. "Left him to bleed to death over near the ferry."

I just stood there looking at the sheriff. "Nigger woman, Justina Beasley, seen him do it; said Logan caught Ben tryn'a run one'a his hogs into the swamp."

"Goddam," was all I said. I remembered that I knew Ben Youngblood was doing that; at least I'd hear it, driving somebody's hog into the swamp and then tracking it down and shooting it for wild, but usually it was some nigger's hog and nothing ever came of it. "Mr. Tate," I said, then, and stopped. He was looking down at me, chewing on the cigar butt.

"I know what you goin'ta say. I got four others to go out there with us."

I sort of shuffled my foot around in the dust at the edge of the road. "From what I hear," I said. "that fellow can hit a Keeldee on the wing with a twenty-two."

Mr. Tate just sat there for a minute, then he took the butt out of his mouth and spit over the side of the hack. "That's what I hear too," he said. "Five o' clock. Git, sumbitch," he said to the horse; the hack creaked on into the road.

III

I WAS standing out beside the road when the hack came around the corner the next morning about daylight. I could see the other men up in the hack with Mr. Tate, and the gun-barrels pointing up at the still gray sky, and I don't mind admitting that I was feeling mighty low along about then. (I'm not going to give the names of the other men; all but one of them is still alive and if they want to tell the story, they can, as good as I can, I suppose.) They made room for me, and I crawled up there onto the rear seat, with my gun propped between my legs, a little pump twenty-two, which was all I had except my twelve gauge, and I wasn't figuring on getting close enough to Ben Youngblood to use any shotgun. I saw the sheriff give a quick glance at my rifle, and sort of frown, but he didn't say anything, and the old hack went creaking off toward the river and the ferry north of town. We rode along for a long time in silence that morning, the only sound being the creaking of the springs under Mr. Tate and the jingling of the harness, and I guess everybody was thinking the same thing as I was, that here we were going off hunting, but this time for game that not only could, but was likely to, shoot back.

It was good daylight when we came up the little rise in the gutted limerock road that was little more than a ditch and caught sight of the house, across a cornfield, or what passed, I guess, for a cornfield to the Youngbloods. There was a thin curl of smoke coming out of a chimney at the back of the house, which made Mr. Tate pull the horse up fast; we had got to talking along the way, and about everybody was hoping that nobody would be up, this being Sunday morning and all, but we didn't have any such luck. A cook-fire meant that everybody was up, or soon would be, and so we all got down out of the hack and gathered behind this scrawning clump of cedars that was growing out of the limerock at the edge of the roadbed. Mr. Tate stood shading his eyes from the new, red sun, with one hand on the pistol strapped to his bulging hip, peering out across the field at the house.

There was one big house, with a wide gallery across the front; from here we could see a row of chamber pots with crawling plants growing out of them, hanging from the rail of the porch on wires. And there was a set of horns tacked to the wall, and the wheelless body of a wagon set up on blocks in the front yard, (I remembered then this story I'd heard in the drugstore, from a surveyor for one of the lumber companies around town, who told how he'd come up on the house one day and seen Old Man Youngblood sitting on the front porch whittling and the surveyor swore there was a half-decayed dead cow in the front yard covered with flies and maggots. He said he'd been smelling the stink for over a mile, and the old man was just sitting there, whittling.) Out in the back of the house was a barn that was leaning to one side and propped up by logs, and next to it was an outhouse; and that was all. There was only one tree near the house, a crooked and gnarled looking fig tree just to the side of the barn.

"Boys," the sheriff said, and then stopped. He took a handkerchief from the hip pocket of his breeches and slowly wiped his face. "Well," he said, after a minute, holding the handkerchief over his face, "How you suppose we to go about this?"

"In that wagon," one of the men said, "turned around and gettin' back to town as fast as that fat-assed mule will go."

One of the other men chuckled, and I looked over at him, and he wasn't tickled. He looked back at me with heavy eyes, and spit out a wad of tobacco like it had just gone sour on him.

"What I figure," the sheriff said, "is we ought to surround the house."

"Suppose that son-of-a-bitch starts shootin'?" another of the men said.

"Shoot back," the sheriff said, and I was thinking about that skinny little girl that I had seen sitting up in the straight chair in the wagon.

"What about the other folks there?" I said. "His sister?"

"Yeah," the sheriff said. He just stood there, mopping his face with the handkerchief. We were already starting to sweat in the sun. "Yeah," the sheriff said again. "Now listen here. Phineas?"

He hardly ever called me anything but Finney. "Yessir," I said.

"I want you to circle around and come up on the house by the barn. You can use that for cover." He told all the others what they ought to do, then, but I was looking at that open field surrounding the barn; I was going to have to cross it. "Maybe we can flush him out," Mr. Tate said. "If we do, try to hit him in the leg or something, you hear me? Ain't no use to kill him. Holler 'fore you shoot, hear?"

That was the longest field I ever crossed; I remember there was some cotton growing after awhile, dusty and not even knee high, and then corn again, both crops sort of strung out in that field without any pattern at all that I could see. I'd sprint a little, and then I'd crouch down and look around at the other men, most of them already disappearing in the scrub cedars and high grass way around front of the house. I kept thinking about hearing my Uncle Caswell tell about how he as a young man had to run across a field during the Battle of Franklin up in Tennessee, how he'd run and then fall down and get up and run again; more than once I considered diving down into the dusty cotton, but nothing was stirring from the house except the little curl of smoke; not even any dogs had barked. So after what seemed like three or four hours, I went leaping up to the corner of the barn, and there I was, peeping around at the house, and I was just in time, too, because just about then I heard Mr. Tate hollering.

"Ben Youngblood!" I heard him yell. It set up a sudden yapping and barking from under the house. "We just want Ben!" There wasn't a sound or a movement from in the house but all of a sudden four or five hounds came boiling out from under the porch, howling and carrying on fit to kill. They ran around in the yard, barking and looking at one another and then to the house. "Come on out now, Ben!" Mr. Tate shouted.

About that time there were three quick shots, which I figured came from the house, because I saw Sheriff Tate waddling across an open space faster than I ever thought he could move and saw him dive behind a little stand of willows about fifty yards to the side of the house. Everything was quiet for a minute, even the dogs, who had wheeled with the gunshots and headed back under the porch. Then I heard Mr. Tate yell again.

"Awww, goddamit, now Ben!" he yelled.

And Ben, or whoever was doing the shooting, answered him with another shot; I could see the dust rise about twenty feet in front of the clump of willows where Mr. Tate was hiding. Nobody said anything then, for a minute or two, so I slid along the wall of the barn until I came to the door. I don't really remember why I decided to go in there, unless it was to crouch down and look out a window or the front door of the place, but I did. The door wasn't even fastened, so I pushed it open with my rifle barrel and slipped inside; it was dark, except where the light filtered in through the closed shutters on the windows, and I couldn't make out much of what was inside for a minute. There was a smell of corn mash in the air, I remember, and the floor was stone. I just stood there, waiting for my eyes to get accustomed to the dark, and I guess I was silhouetted against the light from the partly opened door because it was then that I heard this tiny sound, like a sigh, and I peered at where it came from and could make out what looked like a pile of sacks, but what wasn't, because just then this voice said:

"Phineas?" and I nearly jumped out of my breeches. I just stood there with my mouth open, not knowing whether to open fire or what, when the voice said again, "Phineas?" and I could see somebody moving toward me, and I didn't even think about it being Ben, which I guess it was lucky for me it wasn't, because he was right up next to me before I knew what was happening, and I could see that it was Mr. Cincy. I was gaping at him because he just had on his breeches and the tops of his underwear, and he was barefooted, and his hair was mussed. "What the hells goin' on, Phineas?" he said, in sort of a whisper.

"We come to get Ben," I said, and Mr. Cincy just shook his head up and down, and then I saw this movement over where he had come from, and gradually I could make out that it was a woman, or a girl, dressed in one of these long nightgowns; I could hear her bare feet padding on the floor as she came over to where we were. She walked into the light from the door, and shook some straw out of her long, blonde hair, and just looked at me with these solid black eyes, with sort of a pleading look in them, and I said:

"He killed a fellow," and she just kept looking at me, and then I knew who she was.

So I just stood there, looking from one to the other, at Mr. Cincy looking sleepy and mussed, and at Clara, looking fresh and clean: she was about the most beautiful woman I had ever seen, and that's no lie, even dressed in that old nightgown that I could tell had been made out of flour sacking; and to tell the truth, I didn't know what to think, much less what to say. Just about then we heard another shot, and Clara ran over to the front window and threw it open and looked out, and I could see, in the new light, that the room was made up like a bedroom, with a bed over against the wall, and a couple of chairs and a table.

"Cincinattis!" she said, and it sounded peculiar, not like you would expect it to sound coming from a scared girl, "What...?"

"They come to get Ben," I said, again, and she turned around and walked back over to where we were. I could see Mr. Cincy, the way he was looking at her, the way her hair looked in the morning sunlight, all golden and flecked with bits of silver, and her skin the color of delicate china, and the eyes that you wouldn't expect to be black, looking twice as black in her face. Then Mr. Cincy looked at me.

"Phineas," he said, and then he stopped.

"They ain't got to know," I said, and his eyes jerked to mine, and he mouthed some words and coughed and said, "You don't understand, Phineas," and I didn't. She was looking steadily at me, too, and then she looked at Mr. Cincy.

"Cincinattis," she said, gently.

About then we heard some real shooting going on, and we all three ran to the front window just in time to see Ben come tumbling out a side window and go running out across a field, and I heard Mr. Tate hollering:

"Wing 'im, wing 'im!" and there were a couple of shots, and then a couple more, and Ben went flopping to the ground and rolled over one time and then was still, and you couldn't hear anything but the dogs barking under the house, and the three of us were just standing there, me with my cold rifle in my hands, looking at the motionless Ben lying in the field, with one leg twisted around him like he had broken it. And then I heard this high moaning wail, and the back door opened and I saw Mrs. Youngblood coming down the back steps, moaning, and she started across the field toward Ben, and I saw Mr. Tate, then, running out there, too.

"They just figured to wing 'im," I said then; neither one of them said anything, until Clara said:

"I got to go to her," and Mr. Cincy said:

"We," and it was then I understood; it seemed to all come to me at once, how I had sense it when I first saw them together, that it wasn't at all what you would expect; and I could see Mr. Cincy's hand on her arm, just gently resting there, and her not moving, until she turned her head and looked at him, and said:

"No. Not now, not ever," and I could suddenly see, in my mind, Miss Emma in the big house, and Mr. Earl tearing down the middle of the street on his big black horse, and then the two of them in the old barn. Then she looked at me, and said:

"Tell him," and I just stood there.

"I guess it's about time," Mr. Cincy said, taking her arm, and she pulled it away.

"No," she said again. Then she looked at me again, and then off out the window to where the little group was gathering in the field. "My place is out there with her," she said. Then Mr. Cincy took her arm again, and she looked long at him, and they started to move toward the door, walking silently and easily, as though they went together; I watched them go through the door, and I stood there with my rifle and looked around the little room, at Mr. Cincy's shirt and vest hung over the back of a chair, and his coat hanging on a nail that had been driven in one of the wall beams, with the look of having been carefully hung there.

So I followed them out, and the three of us went across the field to where the others were gathered; I knew that he was dead long before we got there because the old woman was walking slowly, and I caught up to them, and I could see that Clara was crying too, the tears running silently down her cheeks; all the men who were there were looking at them, one or two with their mouths hanging open, and nobody said a word when the three of us walked up there. Clara was holding her head high, and she would look from Ben to her mother to Mr. Cincy to the men, standing with their rifle butts down in the dust between their feet, and Mr. Cincy had his arm around her shoulders.

We got Ben's body into the hack after awhile, and Mr. Cincy got his buggy out of the shed at the side of the old barn, so some of the men could ride back with him; the old man wouldn't ride with us, he just went over and without a word started saddling this old mule. So we started in; I was in the hack, in the lead, and I looked back and saw Mr. Cincy sitting up on the seat, with Clara up next to him, wearing a heavy coat over her night dress now, holding onto his arm; and behind them, getting smaller and smaller, the old woman, still standing out in the field, looking off at the river.

IV

I GUESS Mr. Cincy had his mind made up when he got into town that morning, because he drove the buggy right up the street to the big house where he lived with Miss Emma and his brother; Clara was sitting up on the seat beside him with a blank look in her eyes, looking directly ahead, and I couldn't help but think about the times when I'd seen her, a long time before, sitting up behind the old man and Ben in a straight chair in the back of their wagon, staring ahead and not looking at anything they were passing, a skinny little girl who had grown into the woman who was in the buggy with Mr. Cincy now; somehow she had the same look in her eyes, like a buck you've brought down, the way he looks at you when you walk up and grab his horns to slit his throat.

Nobody really knows, except Miss Emma, and one just dead, and one long dead, just what happened in that house that morning. I know that Mr. Cincy took her in the front door, and the door closed just as the Negro servant came from around to take in the buggy. (I got all this from a yard boy who sat in the yard sharpening a swing blade for four hours that morning.) About an hour later, Mr. Earl came back from his morning ride and came pounding up the drive and dismounted and went in; two hours later the Negro brought the buggy around front, and went inside, and came back out with two suitcases, followed by the cook with a hatbox, and then Miss Emma came out and got into the buggy, and she and the Negro drove off. (I found out later that she had gone over to her first cousin's house). A little while later Mr. Earl and Mr. Cincy came out onto the gallery and talked for about half an hour, and several times Mr. Earl flung his arms over his head and stomped around. Then they went back inside.

By noon it was all over town that Mr. Cincy had brought home Clara Youngblood to marry and live in the house with Miss Emma, and that Miss Emma had left in a huff and had told anyone who would listen that she would not, and had no intention of ever, staying under the same roof with a "river whore, and no-good Youngblood white trash to boot!" And that afternoon Mr. Earl rode his horse as fast it would run right down Washington Street, with his coat flying out behind him and a cigar in his mouth and those who were closest to him said he had a pistol strapped to his hip, though it wasn't clear just who he might be planning on shooting. By late afternoon, I heard in the drugstore that Miss Emma had to have the doctor called to her and was all hysterical about how Mr. Cincy had disgraced the family name forever.

THEY BURIED Ben the next afternoon. I went, and I saw all the other fellows who'd gone out there to get him there, too, standing in a little group off by themselves, looking sick and uncomfortable in their suits and stiff collars. It was just a grave-side service and was very short. The old man and Mrs. Youngblood were standing nearest the grave, near the preacher, both standing with their hands hanging down beside them, straight and unmoving, the old man in overalls and Mrs. Youngblood in the same dress from yesterday; near them was Clara and Mr. Cincy. She was looking at the ground, and her hair was combed straight down her back, and she was standing very still in a loose black dress; Mr. Cincy had on his suit, and was standing beside her, one hand on her arm; his face looked drawn and his eyes were sunk back in his head, with dark rings under them; he was staring straight ahead. The only other person there was an old man named Asa Logan, whose son Ben had shot and killed; he had his head down and seemed to be praying.

When I got back to the house that afternoon, there was a Negro boy sitting on the front steps and he handed me a message; it was from Mr. Cincy. "Can you bring a buggy and come over here? C.H." was all it said. So I told the Negro to wait and got Uncle Caswell's buggy out and hitched up the mule and we rode over to Mr. Cincy's house. It was getting real late in the afternoon, and even though it was still very hot, there was a sign of fall in the air, a smell, or maybe

42

just the way the late afternoon sun played over the dry and getting ready to die leaves. We rode up the driveway to the galley, and Mr. Cincy must have been watching out a window because just as we pulled up he came out the front door.

"Evening, Phineas," he said, and then he just stopped dead in his tracks, and looked around like he'd forgotten something, and then looked at me again.

"Mr. Cincy," I said, nodding my head to him, and he peered at me out of these red-rimmed eyes that seemed to be sinking deeper into his head. I was still sitting in the wagon and he was looking at me like he didn't know who I was. "I got your note," I said, then, and he slowly shook his head up and down. Then he looked at the wagon and back up at me.

"Get down, get down," he said, and though he suddenly realized that he wasn't being polite or something, so I crawled down off the seat and walked up on the porch, and he walked over to the front door and opened it and stepped back for me to go in.

It was the first and the last time I ever was in that house; I remember that there was a big hallway, with one of these curved staircases with a dark rail that reflected the light. The door to the parlor, just to the right of the front door, was open, and Mr. Cincy guided me in there and motioned for me to sit on the sofa. It was a long room, running the length of the house, and there were bookcases and a big fireplace, and the room was crammed full of furniture, sofas and comfortable looking chairs.

I sat there on the sofa and Mr. Cincy paced the length of the room and then back to stand in front of where I was sitting. He paused a minute.

"Phineas," he said. Then he stopped.

"Yessir," I said.

"Phineas," he said again, "she's bound to go back over on the river."

I just sat there. He scratched his head and swallered. He had a prickly looking beard, as though he might not have shaved too well that morning. "She won't listen," he said. "She's got her mind made up.

"Why?" I said, and he tilted his head to the side and looked at me; I had the idea that my voice startled him.

"Why?" he repeated, and he kept looking at me. "Phineas," he said, shaking his head, "she wants to go back," just as though he'd never said it before, or I hadn't asked the question. The big house was very quiet, with Mr. Cincy just standing there rubbing his hand across his unshaven chin. His hands were shaking, and he seemed almost ready to fall in a heap on the floor. I was just getting ready to get up and try to get him into a chair when Clara came in.

She was walking very straight, and she had this little grip in her hand, which she set on the floor just inside the door, and she looked at me and nodded, and then at Mr. Cincy.

"Clara," he said, and stopped.

"I'm ready," was all she said.

Mr. Cincy was standing on the darkened gallery when I guided the mule down the driveway and out into the street and headed him north toward the river. Neither one of us looked back, and we rode along for a long time in silence, Clara sitting on the seat beside me looking straight ahead, the only sound the mule's hooves in the dust and the crickets in the ditches and an occasional late bullfrog out in the darkness beside the road. The night was clear and just a little cool; the moon was coming up, a great ball of yellowish red just over the treetops. It wasn't until we had crossed the ferry and the mule had made the haul up to level ground on the other side of the river that she spoke.

"An early fall this year," she said, and I looked over at her, and in the moonlight I could see the paths of two tears down her cheeks. But she was still sitting straight, not moving. Then after a minute, she said, "It couldn't have worked out, could it," and it wasn't a question at all.

"I don't know," I said, clucking at the mule.

"I mean..." and she stopped, and reached down and opened the little grip and got a handkerchief out and wiped her eyes with it. "They would never let it, would they?" she said, after a minute.

"I don't guess so," I said. Then we rode along for awhile without saying anything, and I was thinking about "them," about Miss Emma and Mr. Earl, and whoever else she might mean by "they," and then, all of a sudden I said, "What do they matter anyway?" and I said it, I guess, sort of abruptly, because she turned on the seat and looked at me, and I glanced over at her twice, when I could take my eyes from the road in front, which was getting narrower and narrower now that we had left the main Green County road. It was darked now, too, in patches, where the moon was shaded by the tall white-oaks and cypress and hickory nut trees. She sat looking straight ahead, then, and didn't say anything for awhile. We were coming nearer the house; already I could hear the dogs setting up a howl.

"Phineas," she said, and I looked over at her and she wasn't looking at me. "Do you understand?"

"What?" I said, not wanting her to go on and at the same time wanting to hear it.

"That I love him?"

"You got a funny way of showin' it," was all I said, and she didn't say anything else until we got to the house. I pulled up to the front and she climbed down and stood there with the little grip in her hand and with one hand resting on the buggy; I could barely see her face in the moonlight. She seemed to swaller a couple of times. Then she said, and the words almost tumbled out on top of each other: "He understand, Phineas; he knows. We couldn't have each other at all the other way, he knows that, but he likes you Phineas, and you can help him, you can be his friend," and then she turned and ran up onto the front porch, and a yellow shaft of light flashed across the dusty, grassless yard and lit up for a moment the wheelless wagon sitting up on blocks, and then the door closed and she was gone.

V

IT WAS A long ride home that night, and I thought a lot about Mr. Cincy and Clara and all the rest, riding along behind the old mule, thought more, I guess, than I did all the rest of the forty years since then; even then, seeing the door close behind her, I knew somehow that that would be the last time I would ever see Clara; there was something final about it that didn't even need explaining or thinking about. And it was, it was the last time I ever saw her, because I didn't go to the funeral and Mr. Cincy didn't either. I didn't even know about her dying and all until a month after it happened, when Mr. Cincy told me, in what was to be the next to the last time he ever talked about her, at least to me, that she was dead and buried, and I had to find out from somebody else what happened; it was A.C. Logan, the fisherman who'd been at the funeral for Ben, who finally told me that she'd been carrying a child and had had an early birth and died before the old man could even hitch the mule to a wagon that he'd had to ride three miles to borrow from a Negro; and it wasn't until two years later that I found out where she was buried, and found out that Mr. Cincy had paid for it all, even to buying a whole plot to bury her in.

The way I found out was, in a way, peculiar. As I already said, I took, after all this, to visiting with Mr. Cincy, in his office and in the little house where he moved. (When Mr. Earl and Miss Emma left for Montgomery, which must have been about the time that Clara died, Mr. Cincy moved out of the big house and it stood vacant for about a year, until they sold it to a dentist from Baltimore, who had a heart failure and died two months after he moved in. There was a lot of talk then about it being a jinx house, and a lot of revived talk about Mr. Cincy and Clara. But then it died out; that's the way it did. A lot of talk right at first, and some people, of course, laughing at Mr. Cincy behind his back, then brief spurts of gossip from time to time, until even those stopped finally, until all that happened was forgotten by most. Every now and then there would be somebody who would bring it up, but most of the people in Hammond forgot everything except that there was something peculiar about Mr. Cincy, some story or other. He was never a town character or anything, because people forgot about it pretty quick; they just sort of ignored Mr. Cincy, was all, and he ignored them.)

But the time that I found out about Clara's grave was one late afternoon in the spring, during the first warm spell that we had that year; I was going to eat supper with Mr. Cincy and we had decided to take a walk along the river, and that particular day, with the days getting long, we walked farther than usual. I noticed after awhile that we were coming up near the cemetery; the sun was setting about them, but there was still plenty of light.

We walked into the cemetery and went along the road, under the great old oaks burdened with moss that lined both sides, not talking very much; we never did when we would walk. Mr. Cincy was puffing on his pipe, and when I would look at him the shadows from the trees would fall rhythmically across his face, and after about every fifth or sixth shadow a puff of smoke would drift up about his head, his hair already tinged with gray, to catch the sun briefly and then disappear, fade out, into the shadows up among the streamers of moss. After a while he stopped short and without a word walked over to a small plot and stood there looking down at it; I too walked up there and looked down at the stone, and it was a minute before I knew what I was reading: CLARA YOUNGBLOOD.

"It's *her*!" I said, and I looked over at him, but he just stood there, his pipe between his teeth and his hands locked behind his back, staring down. "How...?" I started to say, looking back at the grave; there was still some naked limerock pieces lying on top of the ground, I remember, and the grass hadn't yet taken full root. I wasn't over the surprise of seeing the stone yet, and I guess I gaped at him, because he smiled a weary little smile at me when he'd finally look, his mouth hardly moving behind the pipe. "You buried her here," I finally said, and he shook his head up and down, and looked back at the stone. "But you said —"

"I didn't go to the funeral, I wasn't there," he said. "They put her here, in this spot."

We stood there, then, not saying anything, and then I realized something, that Mr. Cincy had been here before, had been here many times, and I remember standing there and knowing, as I glanced at Mr. Cincy, that he had brought me here this one time, and that was to be it, that I wouldn't be back with him again, and I could see him coming day in and day out to stand and smoke his pipe and look from the stone through the trees toward the river as he was doing then.

"Phineas," he said. He looked up at me and took his pipe out of his mouth and then put it back. "Phineas," he said, "I still don't really know what to think. But it hasn't been very long, has it?"

"Nossir," I said.

Then he looked off across the river; the trees on the other side were black shadows then, and the cemetery was getting darker. "I think I understand what she meant now, Phineas," he said, and he turned and headed away from the grave, back towards home, and I sort of had to run a little to catch up with him.

VI

SO I STOOD there, near her grave, after they had buried Mr. Cincy all the way over on the other side of the cemetery, thinking about all that happened, and I could remember very clearly the way the little stone had looked almost forty years ago, the evening I stood there and heard the last words he ever said to me about Clara. And as I was standing there, it occurred to me that somebody who knew just a little bit about Mr. Cincy, who maybe didn't know about all those years alone with only that little stone, and whatever else he salvaged from it all, from her, which, I suppose, when you get right down to it, wasn't all that much to anybody but Mr. Cincy, who would probably wonder, if they knew about the other grave, Clara's, why Mr. Cincy had himself buried in that single grave all the way across the other side of the cemetery. Because you know he decided.

I guess Mr. Cincy had a long time to think about where he was going to be buried.

The Hunted

(First Published in "The Arlington Quarterly", 1970)

I

He had been told on more than one occasion that his face was one that looked peculiarly nineteenth century. "Like one of those that looks out at you from inside one o' them little ornate metal frames sittin' on tables in old ladies' parlors," his friend, Phineas Golson, had said, and he had snorted and shrugged. It was a long face, with high cheekbones and deep-set amber eyes, and a wide, clenched mouth; it glowed rugged and red, reddened from the sun he lived in and the whiskey he drank, and his tawney sun-bleached hair crossed his high forehead in a long flowing wave and curled about the base of his neck and behind his ears in little curly white ringlets.

"Yeah," was all he would say; he was a man of few words.

"Buck Haskell is a man of few words," Phineas might tell someone, "but huntin', now don't get him started on huntin', there ain't a man in west Alabama's a better hunter than Buck. Knows how to talk a good hunt, too, though you might not ever know it if you didn't bring it up when he'd maybe had one or two."

But there was usually a strained silence around Buck Haskell; he moved in a cloud of silence, and there was about him a tension that seemed to grow from some inner strength, a silent inner strength that was in the very way he walked, hunched slightly from the shoulders, his hands in his pockets, his strides long and sure. His movements were a part of his strength, and the smells of him were a part, too, the leather of his boots, the sour-sweet smell of the dried quail and squirrel and deer blood on the worn hunting coat, and the lingering sharp and sulphur smell of burnt gunpowder. People moved aside to let him pass and then watched him as he moved down the street, something like a battleship straining against the drag of half-steam; and he rarely spoke to people; people knew that he didn't see them.

He didn't have a regular job as a young man; he had once worked as a lumber grader at the veneer mill, but that hadn't lasted long (there had been a fight, the details of which were now long forgotten, but there was a Negro man named Threat Glover around town who bore a long, pinkish scar down his cheek that had been put there with a lumber hook; Phineas said it was a monument to Buck's only venture into industry). If anybody ever asked Buck Haskell what he did, he would say he was a land owner, which he was: he owned about two hundred acres, mostly woods and swamps, up along the river in Green County. He had a few tenant families who grew cotton and corn, and he himself had a small garden and a few scrub cattle and hogs that he kept for his own larder. He lived by himself in a rambling, unpainted part log, part plank house that had been built room by room by his grandfather and his father and himself, and he had the long, black iron crosscut saws that his grandfather and his grandfather's single slave had used to cut the wide floor boards hanging up on the outside walls of one of the outbuildings for anybody who wanted to look at.

There was about him a sense of pride when he showed them to anybody, but it was not in what he would say, or in the expression on his face; it was a part of the same aura of strength, the smells and the way he stood, pointing to them and then turning away to look off across a brushy pasture, overgrown here and there with clumps of Cherokee roses, to the ring of trees that circled his clearing. He seemed, somebody might observe then, *at home*, more than anything else. The house itself, even, seemed a part of him; the furniture was crude and the rooms were large and roomy, and there was no heat except for open fireplaces. And he kept it himself, except for an old Negro woman who came in and cleaned up once a week, doing all his own cooking and tending his fires and drinking whiskey in front of the fire at night, sometimes reading, by kerosene lamp, from one of the leather covered volumes that crammed a glass-front bookcase against one wall. (The books had belonged to his grandfather, who had gone to the University of Virginia before coming overland with his already aging and sick wife and his single slave to settle and make his way in the wilds of the Southwest frontier; the flush times had killed her quickly, but she had lived long enough to give birth to a son, Buck's father, and it had been he who had worked the place, killing himself and his wife, Buck's mother, so that Buck had been left to be raised by an old Negro man, the same single slave who had come from Virginia with his grandfather, who had lived to be 104 years old, according to his own calculations, before he had passed on in Buck's twenty-first year.) And he might surprise you when he'd come up with something he'd read in one of the books. "He gets hung up on things," Phineas said, "can't get em outta his mind. Like that business 'bout the ritual o' the hunt."

He had had to talk it out some when he'd found it in one of the books; it was something that had happened to him before, the picking up of a book and opening it and reading something that he knew he had known all along, seeing it right there before him on the page, something that he had almost taken for granted without even thinking about whether or not anybody else knew it or had thought it, too. It was a book about Indians, and there was a chapter on hunting, and he had turned right to that chapter and started to read, sipping at his whiskey, his windows opened to the buzzing, late summer crickets outside. And he had come to these words: "The young brave, upon the slaying of his first deer, is bloodied; that is to say, one of the older braves in the tribe, in a religious ritual, anoints the young brave's body with the warm blood of the slain animal. This, according to the primitive belief, made the hunter and the hunted one, and the young brave made a vow, then and there, to make his life worthy of the death of the animal. This was, in one sense, a justification of the kill, since primitive man felt that the animals which roamed the forest, particularly the deer and the bear, were sacred." Buck had stopped reading, the book lying open across his knees, staring at the cold fireplace.

"So that's why they do that," Phineas had said, "I always thought it was just a excuse to get a little drunker."

"It ain't that they know why they do it," Buck had said, "they ain't got any idea how come they do it."

"How come they cut off somebody's shirt tail if they miss one?" somebody else said, and Buck just stared at the man until the smiled faded from his face and he coughed and said, "That's inter*est*in', all right."

"Yeah," Buck said.

And after Buck had gone, the man said, "Thass bout the craziest thang I ever heard of," shaking his head, and Phineas had said:

"Not to Buck it ain't."

AND THAT FALL, when the leaves started to turn and the first rains beat them down and matted them on the woods' floor, the first days of Indian summer, Buck had entered the woods and they had looked different to him, different from all the other Octobers strung out behind him; there was an enchantment about it that even he had never felt before. The autumn breezes seemed gentler than before, and there was about the sky a deepness of pale blue that seemed endless in depth and at the same time crowding the topmost branches of the browning and reddening trees. He was just walking; he didn't even have his shotgun with him, though he wore the stained and torn hunting coat, its pale brownness blending into the forest as he went through the shadows and the dappled sunlight. Buck's eyes darted about, hearing the barking of a squirrel high overhead or the distant crashing of a deer as the animal heard his footsteps in the leaves long before he was within seeing or even scenting distance. He would pause before a stream, sitting on a log and staring into the clear, rippled water, and his mind would return to the page in the old, leather-covered volume, and he would see again the words; and as Buck looked around him, his eyes narrowed to penetrate the undergrowth, the sounds of the woods all around him. He felt that he was seeing, really seeing, the woods for the first time, because now he understood in a way that he had not understood before. He was a part of the woods, and they him, in a way that he had never before known.

II

HE KILLED eight deer and two wild boar that fall, all on his own land; everyday at daybreak he was in the woods, with cold biscuits and sausage wrapped in wax paper and tucked away in his hunting coat, and he trooped out at dusk, his legs moving then slower and more deliberately, to enter the house and drink his whiskey before the fire. The weather remained good; it was a dry fall, but there was enough night rain to keep the woods from being too dry; the nights were cold, and every morning there was frost along the path that led from his house to the woods, but the days were sunny and chilly, with high, fleecy clouds that moved slowly across the sky. Sometimes he hunted; sometimes he just moved through the woods, his shotgun slung over his shoulder, his eyes darting about, almost like a child on his first visit to the fair. Once he sat for four hours, without moving a muscle, watching four fat hen turkeys feed along a creekbank in a gulley before him; they never saw him.

One morning, after a heavy rain the night before, when the weather had turned much colder, Buck made his way down the path towards the woods, his heavy boots crunching the little frozen puddles that had formed. He was wrapped warmly against the chill of the day, and as he entered the woods the first rays of the new sun were playing over the sparsely leaved branches of the treetops. He walked steadily, strongly, going deeper into the woods, the undergrowth becoming thicker; once he stopped, and taking slow, careful aim he fired, the roar of his shotgun echoing around him in the still woods, and a squirrel, already dead before the sound of the gun died away, fell heavily to the ground, its body thumping dully on the damp matted leaves. Buck picked the squirrel up, feeling the warmth still in the motionless body, seeing the drops of blood glistening on the dull, grayish fur, and he shoved it deeply into his coat; the warm body bumped gently and comfortingly against his hip as he walked on deeper into the woods.

By noon he had crossed Rattlesnake Branch and was nearing the river; the pale sun in the clear sky barely penetrated the skeleton branches over his head, and it had no warmth; the damp groundcold crept up his legs, the leather of his boots growing stiff and brittle, and he felt it in the thin bones of his feet. He stopped once in a small clearing and had a sausage biscuit and a drink of whiskey out of a Listerine bottle that he carried in his coat. He went on, moving south, to where the land tapered off and rolled downward toward the thick river bottom.

He had topped the last ridge and was standing with his back against a tall pine looking off over the bottom when he first heard the sound. He cocked his head to the side and listened; it was laughter, a thick, almost masculine laughter that he somehow knew to be female. The laughter, faint at first, soon echoed around him, and his eyes darted in and out among the trees; and the sound grew closer.

"Nigger woman out here," he mumbled to himself.

He moved away from the tree and looked toward the sound, down a rock gulley that might have been a path, narrowing his eyes; then he saw her moving out of the woods, coming directly toward him. Buck stood staring at the woman; she was wearing a bright orange skirt and a black blouse with silver and green and gold spangles all over it, and her hair stuck out from her head in a thick, black tangle, like a sunburst around her face. He could tell immediately that she was a big woman, very tall and heavy, but as she came closer, her strong legs pumping, throwing her head back now and then to let forth a rumble of laughter, he could see that she was one of the tallest women he'd ever seen: well over seven feet tall as near as he could tell. Buck stood very still, watching her come up the path. "Nearer eight foot," he mumbled to himself, and she stopped, about twenty feet from him, and they stared at each other for a moment.

"What carnival sideshow you done excaped from?" Buck said, and the Negro woman's face broke into a broad grin and she threw back her head and laughed; he could see the muscles in her thick, brown neck straining with the effort. He watched her; he could now see that she was young, little more than a girl. "What you doin' out here, laughin' like a hyena for?" he said, and she looked at him; she came on up the path and reached his level, and he was looking up at her.

"Don't you know niggers laugh all the time, white man?" she said, grinning at him, her teeth strong and very white.

"I don't know nobody that laughs lessen he got somethin' to laugh at," Buck said. They stood staring at each other, the pale sunlight playing over the spangles that jiggled back and forth.

"You right, all right," she said, "'sides, I ain't no nigger."

"What are you, a elephant?" Buck said.

"I a Indian," she said.

"Shit," Buck said, and the girl threw her head back and laughed again; Buck could see the heavy breasts straining against the blouse, and the spangles dancing over them; he let his eyes wander over her body. "What you doin' on my land? You kin to some o' my niggers?"

"I stays here," she said.

"Where?"

"Rat down there," she said, pointing down into the bottom. "I ain't kin to nobody." Buck was standing with his shotgun slung over his shoulder, his amber eyes narrowed as he looked at her.

"How long you been livin' down there?" he said.

"Long time," she said.

Buck continued to regard her and she looked down at him; her eyes were deep brown, deeper than even her skin, and delicate, almost merry lights played in them, like the spangles that covered her upper body. They said nothing for a moment; then, only when the small sounds of the woods came back to him did Buck realize that for an almost imperceptible moment he had not been hearing them. He shook his head as though to clear it; she had not moved, and her eyes and her mouth still smiled at him.

"You a big 'un, ain't you?" Buck said, and he reached his free arm out and clasped his hand around her upper arm; her flesh was firm and warm. "Ain't you cold?"

"Does I feel cold, white man?" she said, grinning at him, and Buck just looked at her steadily. He followed her down the ravine, watching the sunlight glitter on the spangles; now and then she would laugh. "Whass so goddam funny?" he said once and she laughed again.

Her cabin was a one-room shack made of logs with a dirt floor and no windows; it was sitting in a small clearing beside a branch, and Buck stood looking around, his eyes darting about.

"How long have you been livin' here?" he said.

"Long time," she said.

The interior of the cabin was dim; there was a small fire burning on flat rocks in one corner, with a hole in the log roof for the smoke, and he stood looking around, his eyes gradually becoming accustomed to the dark; there was a pile of musty quilts against one wall, and he stood surrounded by the close, dank Negro smell that he had so long known. He reached into the folds of his coat and brought out the Listerine bottle and took a long drink of the whiskey; she was standing just inside the doorway, watching him, the grin still on her face. He handed her the bottle.

"Go on," he said, and she raised it to her lips and drank. "That where you sleep?" he said, motioning toward the pile of quilts.

She came across the room toward him and handed him the bottle, laughing to herself and watching him. Then they sat heavily on the quilts, her eyes visible and merry in the dimness; then, with a motion smooth and quick she lay back, hiking the orange skirt around the waist. "This what you been huntin', white man?" she said.

BUCK WAS slowly aware of the cold creeping through the quilts and into his bare legs; the quilts were rough and sour smelling to him, and he moved awkwardly. He turned his head and stared into her face, and she laughed, the laughter bubbling from her, her heavy breasts shaking with it; he could see her nostrils, straining and white rimmed, and he could smell her, her sex smell, her animal smell. "Goddam you," he said, "What are you?" Her laughter was all around him in the close little room.

Buck struggled to disentangle himself from the quilts and he groped about in the dimness for his clothes. His motions became almost frantic as the laughter became louder. He was clumsily thrusting his feet into his boots when suddenly the laughter ceased, and he looked at her; her eyes were wide and white in the darkness.

"Don't come back here looking for me," she said. They stared at each other for a moment, neither moving. "I'll be gone, cause I done got what I come for."

The little room was still and quiet; the only sound that disturbed the silence was the distant, high-pitched barking of a squirrel. Buck's eyes widened in his face, and he stared at her; his bare foot slid slowly into the other boot, almost of its own accord, and he backed slowly toward the door. His movements were stiff and his boots scraped lightly on the damp dirt floor. He continued to look at her, unable for a moment to break the spell, then suddenly he bolted around into the doorway. He ran awkwardly across the little clearing, breathing heavily, and he could hear her laughter begin again, ringing through the trees all around him, and he crashed heavily into the woods, running clumsily now, the groundvines and bushes grabbing at the loose laces of his boots. He ran blindly until he was no longer able to hear the horrible laughter, and then he had to slow; his breath came in pained gasps.

Soon he had to stop and lean against a tree; he breathed deeply of the crisp air, his head back. The woods around him were still. Slowly the color drained from his face; the amber eyes narrowed, and his breathing was smoother. He reached automatically into the fold of his coat and groped for the Listerine bottle; it was not there; he had left it.

Then he remembered the shotgun, too; he stood very still, his eyes steady, staring into the quiet, darkening woods. One lone cricket, the last of the year, began to chirp back in the undergrowth, and Buck, knowing how far he was from home, began to walk into the woods in the direction of his house.

The Iron Gates

(First Published in "Comment", 1969)

Let us roll all our strength, and all
Our sweetness, up into one ball
And tear our pleasures with rough strife
Through the iron gates of life

— *"To His Coy Mistress" - Marvell*

TO START with, Mr. Rhett Hunnicutt was a little man. And he always wore a bright red or yellow or blue tie, a wide one with a huge old-fashioned knot at the collar, and he carried a carved hickory cane; and he was a fast walker, some said the fastest walker in Hammond then or now or ever. (Once, when Miss Lila Hunnicutt was still living, and they had gone to Birmingham one day to shop, Mr. Hunnicutt got arrested for walking too fast down the sidewalk; they thought he must be a robber or something, getting away from the scene of the crime.) And he didn't drive a car, which is something that Miss Lila did, so that after she passed on he did nothing but walk to town and back, and out to the cemetery, and back to town, to play dominoes down at the courthouse all afternoon or sit on a bench in the sun in good weather and talk about banking (he was once on the board of directors of the Merchants and Planters) or cotton raising (one of the biggest events in his life then seemed to be when John O. Rowan and Son's Gin, every late summer, put the first bale of cotton in the park on the corner; he knew all about it) or even women. All the high school boys called him Rhett Funnybutt.

When they walked by him in the park, on the way to the drugstore, whether they were black or white or whether there was somebody, some lady maybe, nearby to hear, he might just holler out: "Hey boy, how's your pecker hangin'?" or something like that. And he'd laugh and slap his thigh and straighten the bright tie that covered up his whole front so that he looked for all the world like some kind of bright-breasted cedar thrush or something. And then he'd sit back with some of the others, Phineas Golson and maybe Hunter King, who was mayor then, and point out the women walking in and out of the bank across the street. Mr Hunnicutt didn't drink or smoke; he dipped some, and chewed a good bit, but he didn't drink. His only weakness, and he readily admitted it, was women.

Which was hard to imagine, in a way, if you had known Miss Lila; you could pass down Franklin Street any time of day and look in the Feed Store, through the dusty window, standing there surrounded by the smell of Nitrate and leather and the dry crisp smell of corn and hay, stand there and look in and see her at the desk, at least a foot taller than her husband and twice his weight. Perched on the high stool with her hat on, writing in the big ledgers that you knew had the same nitrate smell as the sidewalk, stand there as long as you wanted to and then pass on down the street and pass Mr. Rhett standing in the door and he would have something to say. But it was Miss Lila that you thought about. He had her beat walking, but she could hold her own with anybody else in Hammond, coming down the sidewalk ninety to nothing, her big hat flopping on her head, snorting like a bull. She was a teetotaler, about most anything. (Once she met Phineas Golson coming down the street puffing on a big cigar, and she walked up to him and snatched it out of his mouth and just stood there looking at him, her nostrils flaring, and Phineas just reached in his pocket and pulled out another one and said; "Awww, here, Miss Lila, have a *fresh* one.")

She had her own pew at the Presbyterian Church: the second one from the back on the right-hand side, and she was there every Sunday morning and every Sunday night, without fail, and up to the time when the new, younger preacher came to town, every Wednesday night at prayer meeting. She would fan through the summer with a Japanese Fan, one that her nephew had sent her from overseas during the First World War, and sit high in the winter with just a narrow, knitted ribbon-looking hat on top of her head for her sinuses; and twice a year, for over forty years, Mr. Rhett was there, too, Christmas and Easter, with a new tie on Christmas and a new straw hat or seersucker suit on Easter, standing there holding part of the hymnbook and moving his mouth (he couldn't have been heard anyway, next to Miss Lila) and mumbling along with the Apostle's Creed when it came time. (The children always watched to see him jump like a jackrabbit when Miss Lila started in on the Doxology.) Up until the time she died, she was there, and she passed on quickly, mighty quickly for a strong woman, most people said, but it was Phineas Golson who pointed out that it was her that decided when the time was nigh, not God; she'd always made the decisions, and she wasn't about to quit.

So it happened that Mr. Rhett sold out his feed store to Phineas's older brother, Mr. Sam, and retired to take up his walking full time and to play dominoes and visit the cemetery in good weather. He didn't seem to get any older; nobody knew how old he really was; some said seventy and others said eighty, and it didn't seem to matter to anybody, much less to him. He would come down Franklin Street, from Glynhurst, where he and Miss Lila had lived since 1914, tipping his hat to the ladies and stopping to talk with the children, and threatening the dogs with his cane. He wasn't above whacking them. One of the least curses brought on mankind by the coming of the automobile was that dogs turned on walkers, Mr. Rhett said.

It was in the late spring of what must have been his seventy-somethingth year that it happened. Mr. Rhett hadn't slowed down a bit, and nobody knew, really, where he was getting the ties, but they kept getting brighter and brighter and wider and wider. (Phineas told that he saw Mr. Rhett buying one off an encyclopedia salesman from Bessemer, but that was just Phineas talking.) And it was sometime after he'd decided that the one major weakness in his life was women. He talked about women all the time: the new nurse at the hospital where he went to visit Old Man Miller, who Mr. Rhett claimed to have held on his lap when he was a baby, and the girl who worked behind the soda fountain at Willingham's Drug Store; the high school girls walking home from school, and even his maid, who everybody knew was three days older than God and weighed over three hundred pounds. It was women that Mr. Rhett talked about.

Until the business with Mr. Carter, the caretaker at the cemetery, started. The men he played dominoes with were relieved a little bit, at first, until they found out that talking about Mr. Carter didn't cut into Mr. Rhett's talking about women any; it just doubled his talking time. What was happening, Mr. Rhett claimed, was that Old Man Carter was stealing flowers and potted plants off his wife's grave and putting them on others, that he was spending a small fortune to respect the remains of folks he didn't hardly know.

He went on and on about that, about how he'd hid in the bushes and watched old Carter pick up a pot of crawling ivy bought that day from Miss Lucy Stratford's shop and carry it off and put it on a grave half way across the cemetery, and about the time he'd bought some wax flowers at Willingham's, bright red and yellow ones that would last through the winter, carried them out there and the next day not a sign of them, not a sign of anything but old Carter hoeing up a flower border along the front fence, looking at him with his "goddam ghoul's eyes like oysters on cracked ice!"

"Old Man Carter don't care about no grave flowers, and you know it," Phineas Golson said. He let his domino rap real loud when it hit the table.

"What do you know? Answer me that. What do you know?" Mr. Rhett said. His collar with the big knot on it stood out from his neck and his Adam's apple bobbed up and down like an old turkey gobbler's.

"I know a hell of a lot better'n to spend my days spying on that old gravedigger," Phineas said. "Your play."

"If it's one thing I learned in business all my life, it's a man got to look out for what's his, don't nobody else gonna do it."

"Your play," the mayor said.

Mr. Rhett's domino hit the table with a sharp crack. He pulled out his old silver pocket watch and peered at it. Then he looked at Hunter King. "All right, play, goddamit!" he said.

HE WENT down the railroad track to the cemetery, because it was a short cut; he couldn't walk as fast, but he could get there quicker just the same. It was a beautiful day, early afternoon, and Mr. Rhett felt good and spry and like he was going to catch Old Carter once and for all. He was almost strutting when he went down the track, like a banty rooster, every now and then twirling the cane and whistling a few notes.

The first thing he could see when approaching the cemetery from this direction were the huge, black iron gates that the town had put there some thirty years before, with the iron pickets stretching away from it on both sides, sharp black spears holding back the privet hedge that seemed to grow at random, in spite of all of Mr. Carter's clipping and hoeing, now bright green with the new shoots darting through the fence overnight. Past the gates and to the right about fifty yards was where Miss Lila was laid to rest, with the double scroll tombstone that Mr. Rhett had bought in Tuscaloosa, one side reading LILA CULPEPPER HUNNICUTT, June 9, 1872-August 21, 1937, SHE WAS THE LIGHT OF MY LIFE, and the other side reading WILLIAM RHETT HUNNICUTT, with nothing in the space below it. It was on one of the prettiest plots in the cemetery; beyond it was a row of willows, then the slightly sloping ground where confederate graves were, marked by little tin battle flags put there by the United Daughters, and on beyond them was the river, lying sleepy and bright and hazy in the sunlight, the swamps on the other side looking still and lush in the distance.

Mr. Rhett paused, as he always did, at the iron gates, and stood for a moment looking at them. Actually, they were always closed and locked; there was a walkway to the left of them you actually used, and the road for the hearse and the cars came off Franklin street on the other side of the graveyard. They were about ten feet high, in the center, with black spikes tapering down from the highest point toward the heavy iron frames attached to the brick and cement columns on each side; there was an arch over that, with the words RIVERSIDE CEMETERY spelled out in iron letters, and it was repeated on small marble slabs in each column. Right in the middle, about eight feet from the ground, right where the gates came together and locked, was a shield with a large letter H on it, for Hammond, the town, of course, but Mr. Rhett always thought of it as standing for Hunnicutt.

It was while he was standing at the gates that he first saw Linda Mullins. She was over by the plot where Mr. Rhett knew that her Daddy was buried, and he figured that she was planting flowers; she was squatting down, running her hands in the dirt, and humming some song to herself; he could hear it, an almost not-tune, floating on the spring air like an organ in an empty church. He stood there for a moment and watched her.

Linda's mother ran a boarding house, and Linda helped out in the kitchen. Phineas Golson claimed that her mother kept her in a cage in the back room when she wasn't making her cook and wash dishes; it was a fact that she never seemed to go anywhere, hadn't for her twenty-five odd years, except to the picture show every Saturday afternoon, where she sat with all the children and watched the western and the feature and the serial all three times apiece before getting on her bicycle and tearing off home, her skirt hiked up over her thighs and her long, stringy blonde hair flying out in back of her head. It was Phineas, too, who told about her having fits up at the grammar school, scaring all the other children and the teachers half to death, up until the time that her Daddy died and her mama took her out of the fourth grade, where she'd been for four years, to help out at the boarding house. Where Mr. Rhett had eaten on the average of three times a week since Miss Lila had passed, and he had seen her. She would come in with her old fashion dress that looked like one of her mother's old castoffs on, with her hair pulled back and tied behind her head, to put a new bowl of potatoes or pork chops on the table, not looking at anybody, and whenever anybody said anything to her she would bob her head and tuck her chin and scurry out back to the kitchen. And she wasn't any ugly girl, Mr. Rhett could see that; her lips always looked pale and he could never really see her eyes, and her body looked like what Phineas said was a "croker sack full of dried out yearling bones," but she wasn't any ugly girl.

He stood there looking at her; her hair hanging loose down her back, and he could see her bony hipbones beneath the loose-fitted dress that was some kind of gray colored. He looked around; there was nobody else around at all, not even Carter. Mr. Rhett wondered where Carter was; then he said:

"Afternoon, Linda, how's your mother?" and she whirled around and stopped humming and just looked at him, reaching up with her knuckle to brush back her hair from her forehead. There was no expression in her eyes at all as she looked at him; he came on through the side gate and said again, "How's your mother?"

"Just fine," she said, then, and tucked her chin, pretending to look at the ground where she'd been playing, then off at the river, then finally back at Mr. Rhett.

"Mighty fine cook, your mother," he said, leaning on his cane. He straightened his tie with a quick flick of the wrist. "Yessir, fine as frog hair."

Linda said nothing at all; her face looked flushed and red, and her lips were pale. Mr. Rhett could see that her eyes were green, and he could see tiny veins in her cheeks that gave them a rougey look, and he thought of Miss Lila and her grave

"I came out to visit Miss Lila's grave, Linda. I come ever chance I get," he said, then he looked at the little stone before which she was sitting, with JOHNSON MULLINS written on it, which might as well have said MOON, because that was all, invariably, anybody ever called him as long as he lived, but now that he was dead, it was Johnson. She saw him looking at it, and she looked too, and then turned to him.

"My daddy," she said.

"Sho it's yo daddy," Mr. Rhett said. "Didn't I know yo daddy from the time he's knee-high to a hoppergrass?"

"Yessir," she said.

The way she always said "yessir" to everything irritated Mr. Rhett. He'd never known her to say anything but "yessir," so he said: "Long as I come out here to visit Miss Lila's grave you might's well go with me. You ever see it?"

"Yessir," she said, and Mr. Rhett cut his eyes over to her, thinking she was being smart with him, his little brown sparrowlike eyes sitting back from the bridge of his nose; he harumphed a couple of times and fumbled with his tie, a bright orange one with a lamppost and the old lamp-lighter painted on it in blue (he couldn't see the humor in Phineas's calling it a Parisian street scene, but Phineas would double over and have a giggling fit over calling it that).

"Well come on, then, girl," he said, straightening up and jabbing his cane in the dirt. She got up and fell in beside him, looking off at the river with her pale eyes but not seeing it, Mr. Rhett thought when he cut his eyes over to her. He glanced around and still didn't see Carter anywhere.

"Linda, you sho a pretty little thing," he said suddenly and she looked blankly at him until he saw a tiny smile somewhere about her eyes and she brushed at her hair with her knuckle again. The smile was gone as quickly as it had come.

"Well, here it is," he said as he pointed to the glistening tombstone. "Bought that scroll in Tuscaloosa, no need to tell you what I paid for it. I always said they wasn't nothing too good for my women, and Miss Lila was one of the best, yessirree."

The image of Miss Lila, sitting bolt upright in the church, or charging down the street with her hat bouncing on her head, jumped suddenly into his brain, and he thought about Phineas sitting on the bench in the park and the women that they had talked about, and it startled him so that he coughed.

Linda was looking from the tombstone to him and back again, a peculiar, questioning look in her eyes. "How old are you?" she said suddenly.

Mr. Rhett was speechless for a moment; he fumbled with his tie and glared at her, then startled himself again by whacking the tombstone with his cane. The sudden noise made Linda jump, too, and Mr. Rhett peered at her, his jaw working slowly, with two tiny drops of saliva, one at each corner of his mouth.

"Young enough," he said and arranged upon his face something that he hoped was a smile, somehow full of devilment, and Linda giggled and threw her head back and shook her hair and laughed. Mr. Rhett laughed, too. They both cackled away, their laughter ringing through the still cemetery, until they were both breathless and the laughter turned to gasps from Mr. Rhett and giggles from Linda.

Mr. Rhett slapped his hip and grunted, and Linda giggled again and sat on the tombstone. "Young enough," Mr. Rhett said again, and let out another cackle, but Linda just looked at him, her face now blank again. So Mr. Rhett sat down beside her. He cocked his head sideways, like a sparrow, and said:

"You go to the picture show last Saturday?"

"Yessir," she said, and pulled at a blade of grass, and stuck it in her mouth.

"Don't pull the grass outta the plot, Linda," Mr. Rhett said quickly, and Linda took the blade out of her mouth and threw it down.

"Smutt grass," she said.

"Ain't either," Mr. Rhett said, looking around the plot. There was a little plastic pot sitting at the edge of the low cement border, bright blue, filled with yellowish water. "I pay the association five dollars a year to keep smutt grass outta this here plot. Plus a nigger every spring."

Linda giggled, then. She was looking off across the river, at the swamps on the other side.

"What you laughin' at, girl?" Mr. Rhett said.

"Nothin'."

He could see her shoulder blades, like wings, pressing against the light shirt, and her shoulders were little knobs over her pencil-like arms. Her ear was uncovered by her hair, and Mr. Rhett could make out the tiny little hole where it had been pierced. He stared at her ear.

"Linda, I love you," he said, suddenly, and she seemed for a moment not to have heard. Then she turned around and looked at him, that same smile around her eyes; she looked as though she were about to giggle.

"I love you, Linda," he said again, and reached out and touched her on the shoulder.

She jumped then, and stood up; the smile had disappeared. Her eyes were like those of a mare when she's just smelled a first hint of smoke in a burning barn; they rolled at him for a moment, then away, then back. She took a step backwards, away from him; he was still sitting on the tombstone.

He fumbled in his side pocket. "Linda, I got a quarter for you to go to the show with," he said.

She was breathing very slowly; he could see her small breasts rising loosely under the shirt. The cemetery was still; Mr. Rhett thought he could hear the low cooing of a quail for a moment; he cocked his head, first to one side, then to the other, confused.

"What's the matter with you, girl?" Mr. Rhett said. "I ain't tryna hurt you. What's wrong with you, huh?"

Linda stood staring at him. He stood up, and with that she turned and ran. "Where you goin', girl?" Mr. Rhett shouted. "You come back here!" But she kept running, her skirt flying out behind her, the floppy canvas shoes making little dust clouds as she went up the walkway between the stones toward the iron gates. Mr. Rhett shook his cane after her, and it was just about then that she passed a clump of Cherokee roses and scared the covey up, about five quail that rose with what sounded like a deafening explosion of whirring in his ears; they passed right over Linda's head, it seemed like, and cleared the gates at the tallest point, headed for the vacant field across the road.

Linda didn't turn back one time. He watched her run through the little side gate next to the big locked ones, and hike the kickstand on her bicycle up with her heel and head off down the road away from him.

"Goddamit!" Mr. Rhett hollered. He turned away from the gates; Mr. Carter was standing on a cement slab about fifty yards away, with his hands on his hips, watching Mr. Rhett. Mr. Rhett shook his cane at him.

"What are you lookin' at, you oyster-eyed ghoul?" Mr. Rhett hollered. Carter threw his head back, then, and laughed; the laugh seemed to ring all around Mr. Rhett. Carter picked up a hoe off the ground and turned and laughed once again, then disappeared over a slight rise.

"And you bring them goddam flowers back, you hear?" Mr. Rhett yelled, but this time not quite so loud.

He whirled around and whacked the tombstone again with his cane, and jumped back because there she was, right in front of his eyes, Miss Lila coming at him snorting like a bull, a weeping willow tree that had picked up a little wind; he looked, after a minute, down at the stone, then toward the rise where Mr. Carter had gone.

Mr. Rhett stood there a long time, the slight breeze every now and then picking up and ruffling his tie like a tiny flag. Then he turned and walked slowly toward the big iron gates with the H on them.

NOT PHINEAS, or anybody else, said a word out loud when Mr. Rhett came down to the courthouse next day after that without his tie on. He sat there with his collar buttoned up and his cane over his leg, but without his tie on.

"Who'll bring in the first bale this year?" was all he said.

"Prob'ly Brighton King," Phineas said. "Your play."

"Suffer Little Children..."

(First Published in "Comment", 1968)

THE summer that he spent in Rose Hill with his Aunt Edna Earl was the first time he had ever really seen Jesus. He was eight years old, and he heard all about Him from Hess, his Aunt Edna Earl's wash-woman who came up the sandy, narrow dirt road early every Monday and Thursday morning to start the fire under the big black cast-iron washpot sitting in one corner of the chicken yard. That was the first time he'd ever really seen Jesus; he'd *heard* of another one occasionally during his first couple of years in school, and in Sunday School, when he each Sunday got another colored card with a picture of Jesus kneeling down in the garden, or walking along with sheep all around him, or riding on a white donkey while people were putting down green branches in front of him, or in Daily Vacation Bible School, when he had seen the whole town of Jerusalem made out of cigar boxes and round cheese boxes, built in a sandbox that stood up off the floor on legs, with even little wooden people standing around in it. But it was a different Jesus that Hess talked about. You couldn't see the other one.

He didn't feel just right in Rose Hill. The two hundred miles that he had come on the train from Mobile seemed to him to be ten thousand; the young corn in the fields and the dusty, sandy roads running between the ditches with high, red clay banks, and the houses with wide yards without grass, some of them with old cars sitting up on blocks in them, the few little stores along the highway with the little post office where his Uncle Semmes put up the mail, all of this held a peculiar fascination for him, as though he were not really there but was just dreaming of it. He hadn't particularly wanted to come, but it had seemed an already decided conclusion that this summer would be a good thing for him to spend a few weeks with his Uncle Semmes and his Aunt Edna Earl, who was his mother's sister, because Rose Hill was almost the country; and then there was his cousin Belinda, who was six years older than himself, and a boy named Baby-John, who was probably three or four years older and twice as big, with whom he played during the Saturdays when his family was there for a weekend visit. (His earliest memory of Rose Hill was of Baby-John and his brother Jack putting him on a flying Jenny down in the woods away from the house and spinning him so fast that he cried and then later promised them that he wouldn't tell.)

It seemed a bad summer from the start because it was the summer that his cousin Belinda "grew up"; he'd realized this when he'd gotten off the train, when his uncle Semmes met him and took him to the car where Belinda was waiting. He was carrying his brown leather suitcase that he'd gotten for Christmas, and it contained his shirts and blue jeans, and a whole carton of Doublemint that he didn't realize until nearly at the end of his visit had been put there by his mother because she knew he wouldn't brush his teeth, which he didn't. He had gotten into the back seat, and Belinda had turned around and said "Hiiiiii," with her head tilted to the side, and he had known then that it was the summer that she would grow up. She was a short, plump, blond girl whose hair looked like straw, and whose eyes were round in her round face and very deep brown; and that summer she always seemed to be on some kind of stage, flinging her hands around when she talked, and saying, "Oh, Martin," and sighing every time he said something to her.

So he ended up being alone most of the time except for Hess. His Aunt Edna Earl worked part of the day in the Post Office, and he didn't see too much of Baby-John, who rode a horse all day long. (If he happened to be in the yard, Baby-John would ride by going very fast and cut his eyes over at him to see if he was watching; he always pretended that he wasn't.) So it was really Hess with whom he spent most of the summer. Hess and the old black washpot in the corner of the chicken yard and the ironing board in the pump house where she worked all afternoon.

The first day he was there she had come into the kitchen, an old Negro with one gold tooth in the middle of her upper jaw, and a flat face surrounded by coarse, straightened black hair that stuck out from under a cap made from a rolled up, brown paper sack, wearing a shapeless old dress and some long discarded men's bedroom slippers, and had stood just inside the door looking at him and grinning.

"Lawd, Miss Ednerl," she said, after a minute, "Dis Mist Martin's boy?" and she laughed. "Ain't he gittin' fat?" she chuckled.

"He's visiting us all the way from Mobile, Hess," his Aunt said. "Martin, you remember Hess, don't you?"

"Yess'um," Martin said.

"Sho he do, Miss Ednerl," Hess said. And she reached up and took down a pink wad that was stuck on the paper sack hat and as she was putting it into her mouth, Martin saw that it was bubble gum, already chewed some.

That morning he had walked out into the chicken yard to watch Hess do the washing; she was tall and thin, and her back seemed to be crooked because she was always bending over. She was stirring the clothes with a peeled, wooden stick, and every now and then she would raise a piece of clothing on the end of the stick and peer at it, the steam swirling up from it, and then drop it back into the pot and stir. Martin watched her for a long time; she reminded him of a witch, with her bony face and long fingers, bending over the pot, and she kept mumbling and talking to herself, and the boy imagined that she was saying magic words over the steaming cauldron. He kept edging just a bit closer, in an attempt to hear what she was saying, when suddenly she looked up and saw him; he jumped.

"It say on the radio, you listen to the radio?" she said, after only a slight pause, all the while stirring clothes.

"Sometimes," Martin said.

"It say 'bout dese folks what got married, gwine take a trip, say dey gwine round de worl," she said, looking from Martin to the steaming pot. Martin just stood looking at her. "You gose to school?" she said, then she said, "Cose you do." Martin cocked his head to the side and she stirred in silence for almost a minute. "How dey gwine round de world, when de worl already be's round?" she said, looking at him. He stood flatfooted, watching the fire under the pot glitter on the gold tooth in her mouth. He didn't answer her. "How you reckon?" she said.

"I don't know," Martin said.

She rambled on some more about the married couple and then about other things, and Martin just stood by, listening when he could understand the mumble, and answering when she paused and looked at him, with one of her eyes slightly crooked, so that she looked like an old bird peeping around a corner.

Later, he helped her carry the baskets of clothes through the garden to the clotheslines, and helped her hang them, and all the time she talked. And then she went to sit on the back porch, in the shade, fanning herself with a brightly colored cardboard fan from the colored funeral home. "De Lawd made de heat, de Lawd made water to drink," she said, and Martin just stood there. "Fetch old Hess some water, chile," she said, sitting in the cane bottomed chair with her long skirt spread out over her thin legs. So he did, watching his Aunt Edna Earl take down the tin dipper from the nail where it hung just inside the kitchen door and fill it from the jug in the ice box, and he carried it out to her and watched her drink it, tilting her head way back when she drank so that her Adam's apple bobbed up and down with her swallows, and a thin trickle ran down the old brown cheek and dripped into the collar of her dress.

And he stayed with her all afternoon, down in the cool, dim pumphouse, while she ironed the clothes, slowly and carefully running the heavy black iron over the board and sitting the hot iron on a little pile of cedar branches. "Makes de clothes smell nice, chile," she said, when he asked her about the cedar branches, and he smelled the clear, sharp cedar smell that came from the hot switches. She would hum, snatches of songs and bits of rhythm that never seemed to fit into a real song. "What song is that, Hess?" he said, after she had been humming for awhile.

She stopped ironing for a moment and looked at him. "How do I know what song dat is?" she said, and continued ironing. He sat and watched her. After a few minutes she stopped ironing and looked steadily at him for a few seconds. "You saved, hon?" she said.

"What?" he said.

"You saved?"

He just looked at her, not knowing what to answer. "White folks get saved same as colored folk," she said, starting to iron again. "Jesus come to you, don't make no difference, black skin, white skin, all's the same to Him," she said, "done been to the river."

That night at the supper table his Aunt Edna Earl looked at his Uncle Semmes out of the corners of her eyes and said, "Martin's found him a friend, haven't you, Martin?" and his Uncle took a bite of cornbread and chewed. "That right?" he said. "Who?" Belinda said. "Why, he spent the whole day with Hess," his Aunt said. "Hess?" Belinda said, and she sighed and rolled her eyes over at Martin and then back to her mother. "Really, Mama," she said, "what happened to Baby-John?" His Uncle said, "Yeah, I thought he already had a friend." His Uncle took a big bite of lady peas and another bite of cornbread. "Baby-John," Belinda said, with disgust, "that creep!" "Belinda," her mother said. And then she looked at Martin. "You *were* with Hess all day, weren't you, Martin?" she said.

The tone of her voice worried Martin. It was almost as though she were accusing him of doing something wrong, like when she'd caught him going without his underpants the first week he'd been there. He hesitated and looked at his cousin, whose round eyes were upon him. "Yes," he said, then.

"With that crazy old thing?" Belinda said. And she sighed.

Martin looked at his Aunt. The look in her eyes was like the tone of her voice. He looked down at his plate, and, for the first time since he'd been in Rose Hill, he felt a twist, a pain, of homesickness.

OF COURSE HE wondered about the being saved and the being crazy. When Hess came again, he sat on the swing on the front porch and watched her come up the road, walking slowly, bent over at the waist. He sat very still, and he thought she would pass on by and go on around to the back of the house, but when she was even with him, she stopped and tilted her head towards him; she had on a brand new paper sack, with just a few wrinkles. "What you up to, chile?" she said. He sat very still, looking at her through the shrubbery; he thought he heard her chuckle. "You ain' speakin' to colored folks dis mornin'?" she said. He didn't answer, and she laughed out loud then. "Let me git on back home and git me a tap stick, cause I sees me de bigges' ole cane-cutter jackrabbit sittin' in his clump of Cherokee roses, actin' like he ain' dere." And she laughed again, and went toward the back of the house, and Martin sat in the swing and watched her disappear behind the house.

After a while, after he knew that she would have started the fire and would be stirring the clothes, he went around back and climbed up in the chinaberry tree and watched her. He was about twenty yards from her and in back of her, and he hadn't seen her turn around, so he was shocked when she straightened up and said, without looking at him, "Fust time I ever seen a jackrabbit climb a chinaberry tree," and then she looked at him and grinned, the sun glinting on the gold tooth when she did.

He didn't say anything for a minute. Then he said, "Hess, are you crazy?"

She threw her head back and laughed. "Crazy like a fox, I is," she said. She started to stir the clothes again, chuckling to herself. "You crazy, chile?" she said.

"No," he answered.

"What make you think ole Hess crazy?"

He didn't answer her. Instead he climbed out of the tree and went over to her. She was bent over the pot. "Hess?" he said.

"What, hon?"

"What did you mean about being saved?"

"Lawd, chile," she said, "dat what on yore mine? Don't you know 'bout de Lawd?"

"Jesus?" he said.

She lifted a limp and water-heavy sheet on the stick, and then plunged it back into the pot. "When you gits saved," she said, "Jesus comes up to you, He say 'Blessed art dou,' and you gits to singin' and shoutin' and carrin' on, and He say 'Go out and spread my word 'mongst the worl'.'"

He watched her for a moment. "You mean you saw Him?"

"Sho," she said. "Ain't you never seen Him?"

"You can't see Jesus," he said. "He's everywhere, but you can't see Him."

"He errywhere, all right. But you looks hard enough, chile, you see 'im. You go right up and tetch the hem o His garment."

THAT NIGHT he was sitting in the swing with Belinda. The yellow bulb on the porch was burning, and one or two bugs were fluttering around it. They weren't supposed to flutter around yellow bulbs, but they did anyway. Distantly, and sounding very far off over the crickets and the bullfrogs along the drainage ditch across the road, where Martin could see, in the moonlight, the trailing branches of weeping willow bushes like a girl's hair, he could hear the sound of somebody's piano playing an old song that Hess would hum, and he listened quietly for a few minutes. Every few minutes Belinda would sigh, as though bored; she seemed determined not to talk.

Finally, he said, "Belinda?"

"What," she said, with a sigh, and she crossed her arms in front of her.

"Are you saved?"

She didn't say anything for a moment. Then she turned and looked him squarely in the face. "What a dumb damn thing to ask a person," she said. She said "damn" all the time now.

"Well, are you?"

"Aww, look," she said. "You don't go around talking about things like that." She seemed to squirm slightly in the swing, so that it creaked. "Let's swing, come on," she said.

"Because Hess —"

"Hess!" she said. "Hess, Hess, Hess! Damn old nigger," she muttered.

Martin sat very still. Belinda pushed at the swing, but his feet dragged on the floor. "If you not goin' to push, then get out!" she spat at him. And he could see her round brown eyes, framed with the straw-like hair, glaring at him out of the darkness.

It was the same look that her mother had, his Aunt Edna Earl, now, when she watched him come up on the porch and get the dipper down and get Hess some water out of the jug. One day she had said, "Why don't you go over and see what Baby-John's doin'?"

He hadn't known what to say. "It seems to me that you'd get tired, Martin, just standin' around talking to Hess all day." She was sitting at the kitchen table shelling peas, and she wasn't looking at him. Then she did. "What do you talk about all day?" she said, her hands poised over the bowl.

Martin said nothing for a moment. "Nothin'," he said. "Things." She went on shelling the peas, and Martin slipped out the door; she didn't look up from the bowl. Martin ran down the garden path to the pumphouse, and burst in on Hess. "Hess!" he shouted.

"Chile!" she said. "Don' come in here startling ole Hess like dat."

"Hess," he said, "I want to see Jesus."

"Hush up talkin' like dat," she said. "What you running round her for shoutin' bout you wanna see de Lawd."

"But you said —"

"You see 'im. He come to you. What you think, I gone say he down by de mule lot rat now, if you c'n ketch 'im?"

HIS VISIT wore on and the nights became longer. He took to going to his room right after supper, and he would sit on the edge of his bed and look out the unfamiliar window, at the stars, and the way the pale, silver light of the sky lingered on the dusty new cotton across from the garden, and he would hear the lonely rattle and then steady hum of the pump out in the pumphouse; it would run for a little while, and then the silence would return, and slowly, the crickets. Some nights he could hear a far-off piano playing old hymns, sometimes light and joyous, sometimes sweetly sad in the darkness. And he could hear the voices in the old house, sometimes Belinda's whining, sometimes his Aunt Edna Earl, and, at times, the voices were talking about him; most of the time he couldn't hear the words, but he knew. Once he did hear his Aunt ask his Uncle what he thought was the matter with him, and he heard his Uncle say, "Awww, he's just homesick. Let him alone." So then there were just days with Hess and nights in his room. Sometimes he'd walk the mile down the sandy road to Hess's house, and she would be sitting on the front porch of the little shanty dipping snuff, and he would sit with her, dangling his legs over the edge. Once, when a little Negro girl about his age came around the house and stood looking at him, her eyes round and her finger in her mouth, Hess had said, "Go on an' play, chile; can't you see me and dis white boy talkin'?"

And then one night he heard his Aunt talking long distance, and he knew that his visit was going to be over before long. He could tell by his Aunt's voice, the way she shouted, "Hello, Hello" into the phone a couple of times, that she was talking long distance, and to his mother. And so he knew.

SO IT WAS the last week that he was to be there that his Aunt and Uncle's church had the night revival services. And they let him decide whether or not he wanted to go. They had a preacher from up at Hammond, and a man to lead the singing who came all the way from Meridian, Mississippi, every night. The family went off together, and soon, on the night air, he could hear the singing, the shrill voices coming out of the darkness from the big, wooden frame church sitting on top of the next hill.

The next day was not Hess's day to come, and he didn't go to her house. Instead, he spent the whole afternoon walking in the woods. And at supper time, he announced to his Aunt and Uncle that he wanted to go to church that night.

"Well, good," his Aunt said. And his Uncle gave him a dime to put in the collection plate.

The inside of the church was very large and not too bright. He had been before, to that church, but it was always in the daytime, in the morning, when the yellow and blue and red windows picked up in the bright sunshine; now the colors were dull and lifeless, and he could sense the darkness behind them, heavy and oppressive; and it was hot, not like the heat of the sun, but stale and damp, like a dark cloud, and the walls were a drab, paste-like white. They sang the first song, and Martin could see Mrs. Elsie Taylor, who ran the Ladies' Sewing Shop, and who always smelled like mouthwash when he went in there with his Aunt, singing in the choir, and he watched the way her nose would almost touch her chin when she closed her mouth, and he could see Mrs. Boozer, the preacher's wife, whose white hair and the way she had it fixed, and whose straight-line mouth, made him think of the picture of George Washington in his home room back in school, which seemed far away, out of some old time that he had lost contact with forever. All the choir stood very straight, and their mouths moved all at once, as though they were all pulled by some string held by some giant off in the woods behind the church, and they looked very serious.

And then, after a while, they had a long prayer, and Martin kept stealing glances up at the preacher from Hammond; his name, as he had heard his Aunt say, was the Reverend Claude Wallgood, and he was big and fat and parted his thin black hair down the middle of his head and wore little unrimmed glasses that seemed to strain to cover his eyes; and he had on a light green suit that had big half-moons of dark green sweat under both arms. He had his head back and his eyes closed, and Martin looked around him, at all the bowed heads, and he saw Mr. Biddle, who ran around the Shell Station, already asleep with his chin on his chest. And then Martin looked back to the pulpit. And that's when it happened.

Because there, standing just to the right of the Reverend Wallgood, and back just a little bit, was Jesus. Martin, startled, looked around at the bowed heads once again, and then back up, and He hadn't moved. He was standing there, in the long white robes, with his dark hair down to his shoulders, and he was looking at Martin. Reverend Wallgood still had his head back and his eyes closed. He paused in his prayer for just a second.

"I knew you'd come," Martin said, and his voice rang loudly in the church, and he felt his Aunt's hand grasp his knee. "It's Jesus," he whispered to his Aunt.

"Martin!" she hissed, out of the corner of her mouth. She kept her head bowed. The preacher's voice started up again.

"I see him!" Martin said, and his Aunt's hand tightened on his knee, and the preacher visibly faltered, and there was a stir and a murmur in the section where Martin and his Aunt and Uncle were sitting. The preacher was looking toward him. "It's Jesus, see?" Martin said, jumping to his feet and pointing, and the Reverend Wallgood turned and peered over his shoulder and turned a blank face to the boy. Jesus stood silently, a glow-like smile on his face. "Hess said I'd see you!" Martin shouted, and started out into the aisle, and his Uncle grabbed him. "Martin!" his Uncle said, and Martin struggled against him, and his Uncle's grasp tightened on his arm.

"But...but," Martin gasped. Everyone in the church was watching them now; the preacher's mouth was hanging open, and there was a buzzing going from pew to pew. "The young Davis child, from Hammond...Edna Earl's nephew, you know. Of all things! What did he say?"

And then his Uncle was on his feet and pulling him up the aisle. He struggled for a moment, and tried to look back, toward the front of the church, but then he gave up and allowed himself to be pulled up the aisle. But he didn't start to sob until his Uncle dragged him past Belinda, where she was sitting with some other girls her age, and he saw her face, and her eyes, and read there the hatred that she had for him, and the terror as she looked at him and quickly looked away.

His Uncle was hurting his arm as he opened the door of the car and pushed Martin into the back seat; he was crying quietly now, and his Aunt got in and left the door open so the light would be on him. Her hat was crooked on her head. "Your mother will certainly hear about this, young man," she said. "The very idea!" She was very mad.

"But I saw Him, Aunt Edna Earl, honest I did," he said, between sobs.

"No more of that? Where did he get such ideas?" she pleaded of his Uncle, who was sliding under the wheel.

"From that goddam crazy nigger," his Uncle Semmes said.

"I might have known," his Aunt said. "I warned him. I tried to get him to play with Baby-John, but no! Now this. What must Reverend Wallgood think? And all of them?"

"He's your sister's child, not yours," his Uncle said, pulling into the road.

"Semmes," his Aunt said. "Not in front of..." and she nodded her head toward him in the back seat. "Hush now, Martin," she said.

He tried to stop the sobs. "I saw Him," he gasped, and he was thinking of Hess, and about how she had told him that he would, that he could.

"Of all the nutty things," his Uncle muttered, shifting into third.

"Just wait until his mother hears about it," his Aunt said.

And Martin sat silently in the back seat; he felt the darkness of the night closing in around him. As they rounded a curve he looked back, but it was already too late to get a last look at the church.

Glad My Eyes

(First Published in "Somewhere In All This Green and Other Stories", 1999)

I

D.O. Prants woke up one summer morning and looked around the bedroom and saw an Angel standing near his bed. He immediately knew that it was the Angel of Death, come to check him out, to run a kind of preliminary assessment. And he knew just as immediately that he was going to sign up to play softball, was going to do it that very day, before it was too late, and he didn't give a damn whether his wife Mayfrances liked it or not.

The Angel was a young man with a hooked nose, and he smiled at D.O., a kind of cocky grin. When D.O. switched on the light the Angel disappeared, but D.O. knew better. He closed his eyes, but he was even more wide awake that way so he opened them again. Mayfrances was snoring gently beside him, and he fitted his body against hers, getting as close to her ample hips as he could.

The orange sun was just coloring the sky outside the window, and it was like a thousand other mornings when he'd waked up with his feet already hitting the floor, but this morning he just lay there looking up at a faint water stain on the ceiling that looked vaguely like a bird in flight. He was fully awake now and the Angel had withdrawn, leaving a faint unpleasant odor and a morning chill. It seemed that every last ounce of energy had gone out of D.O.'s body, and he wished he could close his eyes and roll over and sleep some more, sleep way into the morning the way he used to do as a young man, but he was completely awake now. The house seemed as still and quiet as the inside of a tomb. He heard the distant gurgle as the automatic coffee maker kicked on, he filled it every night right before he went to bed, and he knew he would soon smell the coffee as it drifted through the morning air. Reluctantly, he got up.

Mayfrances found him on the back deck, looking at the sunrise, sipping from his favorite mug, a deep navy blue one that said NOT OVER THE HILL BUT ON TOP OF IT on the side in orange letters. He was lost in thought, not even aware of her when she walked out there, and she stood looking at him, at the way his wrinkled bermuda shorts cut into his expanding belly. She knew that she had changed shape over the years, just as he had. He was completely gray, even to the sparse hairs on his chest and the private hairs down below, but her hair was still as black as a crow's wing and she wore it in two buns at the back of her neck, one under each ear like Olive Oil in the funnies.

"I've decided I'm gonna play," he said to her, and she didn't answer him. She had her own mug, a white one that said HOTLANTA in bright red letters that Darlene, their daughter and only child, had sent her last Mother's Day, and she blew on the surface of her coffee, not looking at him. She wore her ruffled silk dressing gown, a pale pink. Then she sat on the glider and it rocked gently back and forth, and she was concentrating on not spilling her coffee. It was an ongoing argument that they had had for years, and it had always ended in a draw. Just like their marriage: it had been a forty-five year draw. D.O. wanted to play on the Baptist Church softball team, and Mayfrances wouldn't let him, because she knew he only wanted to play against the Episcopalians, who were their biggest rivals.

D.O. went to the Baptist church, whenever he went, which wasn't very often, and Mayfrances was an Episcopalian who saw church attendance as an obligation, which was another reason for their draw. They had been married on Saturday, May 13th, 1950, and the next day was Sunday, and D.O.'s young bride had dragged him off to services at Trinity Episcopal Church. The preacher —

they called him a priest — was a chubby little man all decked out like a bird, chanting and motioning in the air, and them following along in a book — Mayfrances had kept jamming the book right up under D.O.'s nose — and all the kneeling and standing and crossing themselves like you never hoped to see. D.O. thought it was an embarrassing show, and he'd never been back.

"I don't want any argument, either," he said. "This time I'm gonna play." Mayfrances just looked at him over the rim of the mug. "You hear me?" he said. He wanted to tell her about the Angel, but he didn't. He couldn't talk to her about something like that. It was too personal. It would make him too vulnerable, give her too much of an opening.

"I didn't say a word," Mayfrances said. She was a tall woman, almost a head taller than D.O. Her shoulders were narrow and her chest was flat, and her body sloped outward toward her hips, which were wide and heavy and plump.

"You didn't have to," D.O. said.

He had made up his mind. *I'll show her and the Angel, too,* he thought. Hammond had had the city league going for at least fifteen years, and he had always wanted to play, and he was finally going to. By God. He stood looking toward the east, toward the elm tree in Maud Green's back yard, the streaks of clouds in the new sky like some mad painter's hectic and careless brushstrokes. He was aware that Mayfrances was looking at him, her stare burning a hole in his bare back. He needed to get on, eat his cereal and get dressed and get on out there and open the store, but he just stood there. Finally, she said, "When you get locked onto somethin', D.O., you are as stubborn as a snappin' turtle."

D.O. stood there leaning on the railing, thinking about Darlene over there in Atlanta. She was their only child, and she was the darling of D.O.'s life, had been when she was a little girl in pigtails and then when she was growing up and being a teenager and then graduating high school and going to chiropractic school over in Atlanta, where she had decided to set up her practice. She was successful. She might have gotten her brains from her mother but she had gotten her shrewdness and her ambition from him. He missed her terribly.

MAYFRANCES didn't like to cook much in the summertime, so for supper that night she served stuff she'd bought at the Deli out at Food Fair. D.O. ate a fried chicken breast, green beans, mashed potatoes and gravy, and fried squash out of a white, styrofoam container. He settled back, satisfied, little knowing that the next few minutes would change his life forever.

"They make good cornbread out there," he said, sopping the last of his gravy.

"They sure do," Mayfrances said.

D.O. closed the lid and patted his belly. "Well," he said, "I made the team."

"You what?"

"I made the team. I talked to the Wayne boy this mornin', he said I could play tonight. We play the second game, against the Episcopals at eight o' clock." Dexter Wayne was the youth director at First Baptist, a pale boy who doubled as the softball coach.

"The *Episcopalians*," she said. "Not the Episcopals."

"Whatever," he said.

Her lips were like two thin lines across her face. He had said that on purpose. He was so mean and stubborn about her church, had been from the start. She remembered a conversation they had had shortly after they were married, when she had tried to get him to go to inquirer's class. "No thank you, I don't care to inquire," he had said.

"Why don't you want to go to Trinity?" she had asked. "Just give me one good reason."

"All right," he had said. he had thought for a few moments. "The hymns."

"The hymns? What's wrong with the hymns?"

"You can't sing 'em. They drag on like a record runnin' at the wrong speed. And they're gloomy. Like that one we sang that day I went. 'Dark and cheerless is the morn!' Jesus Christ. What kind of hymn is that?"

"That's not all it says," she said. "Look here." She had a prayer book with a hymnal in the back that her parents had given her when she confirmed. "Look here, see? 'Joyless is the day's return, *Till thy mercy's beams I see.*' See? That's God. Lord Jesus. It's just dark till you see God. Then it goes on," she read. "'Till thy inward light impart, Glad my eyes, and warm my heart.' See? It's joyous. Anybody can sing that."

"You call that joyous? Jesus Christ!"

"Well, what do you call joyous?" she asked sharply.

"I don't know. Something like...I don't know."

"What?!"

"Well, 'Up From the Grave He Arose! Something like that. 'In The Garden!'"

"Up from the *grave*?"

"'In The Garden!' 'In The Garden!' All right?" And he had stormed out of the house, rattling the screen door behind him.

"I don't want you to play," she said now.

"I don't care what you want," he said.

There was a long silence, and she just looked at him across the table. Her slender fingers rested on the red formica tabletop. She pushed the styrofoam container that had held her salad away.

"You're determined to embarrass me, aren't you?" she said thinly.

"No, Mayfrances —" He could see that her eyes were misted with tears. Her jaw worked slightly, as though her tongue had found a tiny bit of salad behind a tooth. Her eyes continued to fill with tears, and he thought that surely she was overreacting. Maybe even putting on an act. He had to stick to his guns. He wanted to feel superior to her; he felt justified and self-righteous. He let the silence grow large between them. Finally she spoke, and her voice was as dry as sand.

"And all my friends from *my* church will be there. You want to humiliate me."

Her eyes were sparkling with moisture now, and in spite of his sense of victory it pained him to see her like that. It always had. But he wasn't going to give in to her again. She did not answer him. She sat very straight. She sighed deeply, a long drawn out breath. He knew it was a preparation for some pronouncement, and he braced himself. He was not prepared to compromise.

"This is about a lot more than softball, ain't it D.O.?" she said. "We both know that."

He did not answer her. He sat very still.

She went on, her voice flat. "I'm sorry that I'm not enough for you, never have been. Your life was over when Darlene left home. You've made that plain. I'm sorry I..." Her voice trailed off, and he stared at her.

"Come on," he said. "You're makin' too much of this."

"No, this is a lot more!" She was quiet for a moment, and he did not know what to say to her. He was beginning to be confused by her tone, by her stillness. Yes, he missed Darlene. What did she expect? He wanted to tell her about the Angel of Death that lingered in the corner of their bedroom, but he was afraid she would laugh at him. He wanted to tell her that when he awoke in the dim early morning and sensed it there he could roll over and snuggle against her body, her warmth, and he would feel it begin to fade. But he would always make sure that he was not still hugging her when she awoke. Sometimes she would elbow him if he was. He wanted to ask her if she knew he hugged her in those gray hours before the dawn, if she was ever secretly awake, too. He could not make his tongue work. A strong sense of alarm began to vibrate deep down within him, and he did not understand why. It was as though he were trembling inside, and he felt little twinges, like the flexing of a kitten's paws, around his heart. She spoke slowly, enunciating each word clearly, as though she were speaking a foreign language: "Don't you think I'm scared about my life, too?" she said, almost whispering. "Don't you think I worry about the dark night of *my* soul?" He was shocked. Had she seen the Angel, too? He did not know how to answer her. "I have too much to account for," she said, "too much to pay for."

"I'm not following you," D.O. said. He could not imagine what Mayfrances had to pay for. She had never done anything in her life to have to pay for. He narrowed his eyes, inspecting her closely. He was afraid it was a trick, a way of talking that was designed just to get the best of him. She had a college degree, taught public school. He just ran a store that sold rubber boots and overalls. He had always known that Mayfrances thought he was not quite good enough for her. He had started out selling on the road, working eighteen hours a day selling anything he could find to sell, and he finally saved enough money for a down payment and bought his store and then looked around for a woman to marry, to share his life with. And he had made his store into a money-maker, enlarging it over the years and adding more and more products, so that he finally made almost as much money as she did in her teaching job. He felt that she had always lorded her salary over him.

She just sat there. She did not move. The sense of alarm was quicker now, hammering away right behind his eyes. He had been prepared for anger, for nagging. For stubborn, unyielding resistance. But not for this. His tongue was dry. This had all seemed suddenly to turn into a nightmare, a conversation that had started with him telling her he was going to play softball, something as simple as that, and now he found himself plagued with a deep fear and he had no idea of what. "Be serious, Mayfrances," he said. "For God's sakes..." His voice trembled. He had no idea what was bothering her so. He could not put his finger on it. "What in the world are you talkin' about? Lots of men play softball. Come on."

She looked away, out the window, then back at him. He saw tears squeeze from her eyes and run undammed down her cheek. "Please tell me you won't play," she whispered, and he could barely hear her. "Just do that for me." He had thought her pleading would thrill him, but instead it pained him to see her hurting so. He did not know what to do about it, short of agreeing not to play. And he could not do that. He would never do that.

He waited. He could hear the ticking of the old windup clock she kept on the shelf over the stove. The late, dusky sunlight was yellow in the house. It was past six-thirty, and he knew the first game had already begun. He thought of all the other men running about under the lights, tossing the white balls back and forth, scampering about on the green grass of an endless summer evening.

"Please," she said again, as softly as a sigh.

"No," he said. This was one of her crazy spells, he told himself. This was just her way of convincing him not to play. "I'm gonna play. I'm gonna play, Mayfrances. By God I'm gonna play!"

There was another long, hollow silence. "All right," she said. She just stared at him.

He laughed then, uneasily. He squirmed on the slick surface of the breakfast nook chair. He tossed his head and patted his belly. He knew that something was dead wrong. He knew that their lives, at that moment, were even more badly out of kilter than he had ever suspected. He laughed again, and it sounded faint and substanceless in his ears.

She paused. He waited expectantly.

"What?" he said impatiently.

"Darlene is not your child," she said. Her voice was flat, matter-of-fact, and he was sure he had not heard her right. But he couldn't say a word for a few moments. Finally he uttered, again,

"What?" and his voice was high pitched, squeaky, incredulous. He shook his head in violent denial. Then he calmed himself, taking a deep breath. He shrugged. He laughed out of the side of his mouth. He rolled his eyes around. Her words had gone right by him, bounced off his forehead. "You better run that by me again," he said. He grinned. Then he thought of the smile on the face of the Angel, a mocking smile.

"I said, Darlene is not your child." The words stung him fiercely. Her eyes were cold. He knew that he could not be hearing her right and at the same time he knew that what she was saying was as absolutely truthful as anything he had ever heard in his life. She wanted to hurt him, to get back at him. She had been planning this for years.

"You're crazy," he said. "Of course she's my child. Whose else is she if she ain't my child?" His tongue felt swollen in his mouth. His words echoed in his own ears like he was in a cave and someone else was saying them.

"You didn't know him. He was just somebody passin' through."

"Somebody passin' through?! Jesus H. Christ."

"It was a man named Matthew Hornsby. He worked for the state department of education. One of those times when you were gone off on one of your weekend hunting trips." She sniffled. "I never saw him again. I'm sorry."

"You — You're sorry?!"

"Yes."

"Wait just a goddam minute. You tell some cock and bull story like this and then you just sit there and tell me you're sorry? Who is this Matthew Hornsby? Huh? I'll kill him. You were a virgin when we got married."

"What's that got to do with it?" she asked.

"Just that you don't do shit like that. You never did."

Her words tumbled out as though a dam had burst and she couldn't stop them. "Only that once. Twenty-five years ago. And I've had to live with it over the years. Every day that I looked at Darlene or thought about her, which has been every day, every minute of my life since she was born, I've had to live with it. And I know the Angel, when she comes in the night, I know what she wants. She's been there hovering over me every night for twenty-five years. She wants me to confess, to repent." *The Angel? She?* His mind raced frantically. She went on quickly. "I know what she wants, and I have to tell you, you see, I have to tell you so that —"

"Wait a minute. The Angel?"

"Yes," she said, "the Angel."

She has seen it, too. My God, she has been seeing it for twenty-five years! She had never mentioned it to him in all that time. They had both seen it and they had never mentioned it to each other. He was stunned. He sat very still. He could not believe that this was happening to him. He knew she was telling the truth. She would never make something like that up. It was a truth that he had never thought even in his wildest dreams that he would be able to accept, and yet here he sat; it was something so beyond his imagination that he could never have thought of it in a million years, and it could not possibly be true. But he knew it was. His breath came in gasps, and he was sweating. He could feel his dinner like a cold lump in his belly. When he spoke, he whispered. "Why are you tellin' me this now? Just because I want to play softball. Because I want to beat the Episcopals?"

She did not answer him for a long time. They sat in silence in the darkening room. Finally she spoke. "We've lived a lie a lot longer than the twenty-five years that Darlene has been on this earth," she said. "You know it's true, D.O. Neither one of us has known how to love the other. We haven't done like you're supposed to. And now it's almost over."

He could not move. He sat there as though glued to the chair. His whole life seemed to pass by then, projected on the reverse sides of his eyes, his early years on the road, his meeting Mayfrances at the Wisteria Cotillion, their first house, Darlene's birth and her young life... His chest felt swollen, and tears welled in his eyes, stinging them. He looked at the woman across the table from him and knew finally and totally how little, how slightly, he had known her. In all those years of his life. He wanted to reach out to Mayfrances, to hold her, but he could not. His arms were as stiff as old boards.

III

THEY HAD no jersey to fit him, so D.O. stood in the batter's box in his white T shirt, in his *undershirt* as he knew Mayfrances would know. He felt even more naked than that, because he imagined all the other men on the field, all the people in the stands — men, women and children — all knew their shameful secret, had known it for years, had known him for the fool that he was. The lights were blinding to him, the red dirt of the infield reminding him unpleasantly of a raw, opened grave. He felt slow and clumsy, and the bat was much heavier than he remembered them to be.

The Baptists were leading the Episcopalians 13 to 1, in the sixth inning, and Dexter Wayne had put D.O. in to pinch hit. D.O. had sat fuming in the dugout during the game, sitting stiffly in a state of shock over what Mayfrances had told him, feeling anger beyond belief at the injustice of it all, the insult of being made to sit on the bench while all the others had fun, all these demons raging in his brain like devils let loose in a storm. He could have declined to go into the game. He could have changed his mind. But he would not allow himself that. This was what he wanted, and he would have it. The game itself, on the field, seemed to move much faster than he had anticipated, and even now as he stood looking around with the bat on his shoulder he had trouble getting his bearings. He sensed impatience from the Episcopalians' catcher, an auto parts store owner named Luke Preston, and Simon Hart, the umpire, an old friend of D.O.'s who ran a dry goods store downtown.

"Anytime you're ready, D.O.," Simon said, and D.O. heard Luke laugh

By God I'll show you, D.O. thought. He looked into the stands. He saw Mayfrances sitting there, all by herself near the end of the bleachers. D.O.'s eyes shifted to the people in the stands; they seemed to be talking among themselves, paying little attention to what was going on on the field. He was startled when Simon said "STRIKE ONE!" The pitcher, a fellow that D.O. did not know, had quick pitched him. He was grinning. Everybody began to laugh. The people in the stands began to laugh, too.

"I wasn't ready," D.O. said.

"You're in the batter's box, D.O.," Simon said. "Heads up."

The seconds pitch was floating toward him, soaring high over his head, and he gritted his teeth and took a mighty swat at it, his aluminum bat swishing through the air, missing the ball by two feet. He lost his balance, grunted, and sat down in the red dirt, flat on his ass. The laughter rolled over the field like thunder. Laughter at *him.* He could see Mayfrances sitting very still, staring at him. He could not see her eyes. He was glad that he could not. He was glad that Darlene was not there. Thinking of her he felt a stab like a dull knife had been driven through his chest. What Mayfrances had told him could not be true. There was no way that Darlene was not his daughter. Darlene would always be his daughter.

He struggled to his feet, dusting off the seat of his khaki pants.

"Oh and two, D.O.," Simon said.

"I know it, goddamit," D.O. said.

"Hey, listen to that! I thought we was playin' the Baptists," Luke said. "He cusses like a whiskeypalian."

"Shut up and play ball," D.O. said.

He swung the bat over the plate, measuring the pitcher. The man wore horn-rimmed glasses and he still had the stupid grin plastered across his face. The whole infield was hooting and hollering, having the best time, and D.O. could still hear the peals of hilarity from the bleachers rippling and moving across the field like breezes across a wheatfield. The pitcher tossed the ball, and D.O. fixed on it with his eyes. It wavered, seemed to jerk around as it started its downward flight toward him. He could see it so clearly he could detect the specks of red dust clinging to it between the seams. He swung. He could tell he had hit it hard from the satisfying way the bat smacked the ball. As he dropped the bat and began to run toward forward first, he could see the ball lined over the shortstop's head, rising, darting toward the gap in center field, and his legs felt heavy and dull. As he rounded first, his breath catching in his throat, he saw the outfielders' backs as they chased the ball. His breathing became labored as he lumbered toward second base, and his eyes darted into the stands, seeing Mayfrances sitting there, alone. She sat apart, away from everyone else, as though in some sort of cyst, and he realized, almost with giddiness, that he had expected to see her Angel sitting there with her. He was aware of a blinding light that preceded him around the basepaths, and he knew what it was. He could see it clearly now, understand it at last: he had confused his own Angel of Death with her Angel of Mercy. It was almost as though his vicious swatting of the ball had clarified it all. The expression on the Angel's face — not a hooknosed boy but a hooknosed girl — had not been a grin but a benevolent smile! After all! And as he ran he began to hear the subtle rhythms of that hymn that he hated, dragging like the wind resistance that tore at his pants leg and slowed his running, and the words flickered through his brain like some crazy mantra that kept time with his panting breathing: *Glad my eyes! Glad my eyes! Glad my eyes! And warm...And warm...My heart!*

He continued around second. His sweat was in his eyes now, burning them, making everything unfocused, and he felt himself slowing down, as though he were dragging a heavy load, and he thought, *I'll stop on third, I'll be satisfied with a triple, I showed em, Glad my...Glad my...* But he didn't stop. His blood seemed to hammer in his brain as he rounded third. His toe hit the bag and he tripped, and he felt himself begin to go down even as he continued to run, and he tried desperately to keep his balance as he danced and staggered down the baseline toward home plate. He pitched forward and skidded on his face and his belly, and he felt his head hit the hardpacked dirt, and everything went dark. *Jesus H. Christ,* he though. He could not breathe. He was numb. He could hear the shouts and hoots of laughter, louder now, but soon fading in his ears as though he were drifting further and further away from them. He was only faintly aware of someone touching his shoulder with the ball and Simon Hart saying, "OUT!"

IV

WHEN THE game was over, all the noisy children and teenagers and adults — the Baptists and Episcopalians alike — went home. Dexter Wayne drove home to his wife, Kelly, who had stayed home because she had cramps. And Dexter, like Simon Hart and Luke Preston and the new young priest from Trinity, whose name was Bernie Crease, and practically everybody else who had been there told, amid much laughter, the story of D.O.'s hit and of his falling down on the way to home plate. It was a story well received by Kelly Wayne and by Father Crease's wife and whoever else it was told to. It was a story likely to become a part of Hammond lore for a long time.

And later that night, as the pale and ghostly summer moon rose over the softball field, long after the lights had been doused and everyone in town had tired of telling the story and laughing and had gone to bed, D.O. and Mayfrances Prants sat in the aluminum and wooden bleachers. They would not now have cared about the laughter even if they'd heard it. Because they sat side by side, close together in silence, as close together as they could get, and they were holding hands like young lovers.

Birmingham: Mother's Day, 1961

(First Published in "The Hermit King and Other Stories", 2010)

MARTIN, DOC AND MOLLY'S ONLY SON, lived in a home for retarded adults in an Atlanta suburb. He was forty two years old with the mental capacity of a four year old. As Doc was driving Martin back to the bus station in downtown Birmingham for his return to Atlanta after a visit, he was surprised to see the streets unusually crowded for a Sunday afternoon. Doc wondered if it had anything to do with this being Mother's Day, maybe a parade or something. The holiday had been the reason for the timing of Martin's visit this time. He was to stay a month, but after only two weeks Molly decided she had had enough. "I just can't stand him, Bennie," she said, calling Doc by the name she had met and married him under. "Everywhere I go in the house there he is. Sneakin' up on me. I can't hear him when he walks. He sneaks. I look up from whatever I'm doin' and there he is, not two feet from me, looking at me, and my heart jumps up in my throat. He makes me nervous! And he looks at me like everything is my fault!" She dissolved into tears, randomly spaced sobs wracking her body like little electric shocks. Doc knew exactly what she had experienced.

Doc heard Martin mumbling to himself in the passenger seat. Though Doc was ashamed to admit it even to himself, he too was relieved that Martin was going back early. Doc's son's attention span was so short he couldn't watch television or go to a movie or anything like that. He couldn't read, of course. He would simply stand there, at your elbow, gazing at you curiously, waiting for whatever was next. This went on during every waking moment. They had once bought him toys suitable for his mental age, and Martin had gone into a temper tantrum and broken them all. Every time Doc took him fishing Martin wound up with a hook in his arm or hand; once he had fallen out of the boat and almost drowned. Molly had given up years ago, but Doc still struggled to find something to entertain Martin.

When Doc glanced over at him Martin grinned broadly, showing two missing teeth, one on the top and one on the bottom. It gave him an off-center, jagged look. There were times when Martin seemed almost normal, when Doc would actually try to talk to him like to another adult, and on those occasions, after all this time, Doc's heart would soar briefly with expectation only to plunge quickly again into hopelessness and despair when he took a closer look at his son.

"What did you say?" he asked. Curtly. Abruptly. Sometimes you had to treat Martin like a disobedient child.

Martin looked away, out the open window. He mumbled again, his voice all but lost in the street sounds beyond the open window, but Doc clearly heard Martin say: "I need me a hot woman." Doc decided to ignore it. He had no idea where Martin might go with that idea. Martin had had a couple of girlfriends that Doc knew of in more than twenty years he had been in Chattoochee Village. All the Villagers were sterilized, one of the conditions for admittance, so that there would be no consequences of "dalliances" between them, and there would be "dalliances," Doc and Molly had been informed in their initial interview with Dr. White; after all, the doctor had reminded them, the Villagers were physically all adults. No consequences? Doc glanced at his son again. When Martin and his last girlfriend broke up, the boy (Doc could not help thinking of him as a boy) had beaten his rival so severely with a mop handle that the man was hospitalized for two weeks.

Martin was slight of build, only five feet four, and his stoop made him seem even more physically stunted. He had always walked like an old man, hunched forward, his overlarge head preceding him wherever he was going. Though Doc's own hair had turned white in his thirties, Martin had not a single gray hair on his head. But in the last few years, Martin had developed a middle-aged paunch that rode just beneath his high belt line. The rest of his body was thin, his narrow neck pushing his face toward whatever he was looking at as though, Doc would think, he were nimbly curious or about to make a piquant observation. Until Doc looked into his flat, passive eyes, a kind of brownish gray, and saw that there was nothing in there.

The closer to the bus station they got the more crowded with cars and pedestrians the street became. Doc stopped the car at a red light. He and Martin both looked at the crowd of people, mostly men, milling in front of the station. He had a vague memory of some big event happening today, that he had overheard two men discussing in hushed tones in the waiting room of his optometry office, but he could not recall for the life of him what it was.

Doc wondered if he'd ever find a parking space. He thought of all the times he'd carried Martin's suitcase any distance. Martin, when he came home to visit, packed practically everything he owned in it. Doc had vowed to himself that he wouldn't lug the suitcase at all this trip. It was like carrying a suitcase filled with bricks. Martin would not carry it himself. He would simply refuse to pick it up and would walk off and leave it. He had lost suitcases in the downtown Atlanta bus station numerous times over the years, and each time they had to outfit him with an entire new wardrobe and set of toilet articles, which he rarely used anyway. Doc and Molly saw it as a useless and extravagant expense, but they had to do it, even though Martin would wear the same clothes every day until his house parent at the Village made him bathe and change. This time, Doc planned to make Martin carry his own suitcase.

Martin grinned at all the people out in the street. Crowds excited him and he clapped his hands, two quick raps. "Goin' to church," he said. "Gonna say the Apostles' Creed."

"No," Doc said, "they ain't goin' to any church." The men looked rough and mean, the kind Doc always tried to avoid. They wore blue jeans and work clothes. They looked like steel-workers from out at Fairfield. Some laughed loudly with their heads thrown back; others scowled and frowned at each other. There were all moving toward the bus station. Police cars were parked all along the street, and Doc could pick out cops' uniforms in the crowd. "I don't speck these fellows are regular church goers, son. Looks to me like they're lookin' for a beer garden that's open on Sunday."

Doc had an uneasy feeling about the crowd. He knew it had to do with what the men had been talking about in his waiting room. He had paid little attention at the time, and now he wished he had listened more closely. As he eased through, passing in front of the bus station, he knew the parking lot in the back would be full. He would have to park on the street. This was not the best part of town. It was over close to the section of downtown where all the troubles had been going on, where the unrest was. The Negroes; Reverend Shuttlesworth and all. There were no colored people at all living out where he and Molly lived, in Center Point, so Doc didn't pay a whole lot of attention to the stories when they came on the television news. He didn't have the time to watch television much.

And he rarely read a newspaper. He had dropped that habit when he had taken his second job: he worked at night for a place called Deluxe Cleaners, on Roebuck Parkway, collecting bags of dirty laundry in the dorms of a junior college near their house and delivering in return bulky bundles of fresh clothes wrapped in brown paper. It sometimes took him most of the night. He had been doing that for fifteen years now, though he never stopped to count. He would have been surprised to realize it had been that short a time, since he felt as though he had been doing it his entire adult life.

Doc had to go three full blocks beyond the bus station to find a parking space, and then he had to parallel park. Their old 1952 Chevrolet two-door coupe did not have power steering and it was a struggle. He left the front end protruding slightly into the street. He knew he didn't have to feed the meter on Sundays; maybe sloppy parking was forgiven, too. Anyway, he thought to himself, every policeman in Birmingham was back there at the bus station.

When they were on the sidewalk, Martin said, "I want a Krystal Cheese."

"You just ate," his father said. "Right before we left the house."

"I want six Krystal Cheeses," Martin said, "with some French fries."

"No," Doc said. He unlocked the trunk and opened it. "Get your suitcase, son," he said. He knew what the reaction would be even before he said it. Martin just stood there, looking around, gazing up at the buildings around them. "I said, get your suitcase, Martin. I mean it!"

Martin gave no indication he had even heard him. If the boy was going to pack so much into his suitcase, then he should have to carry it. If he had to carry it he would learn his lesson, Doc thought. But Martin could not "learn" any lesson. How many times over the years had Doc presumed that he could, only to realize that the boy made no connection at all between cause and effect? Doc had mostly stopped trying, but his patience was thin today.

Doc could feel the beads of sweat popping out on his forehead. "You pack it so heavy, you carry it," Doc said angrily. "I'm not touching it." Martin just stood there. He shaded his eyes from the afternoon sunlight and peered up the street toward the bus station. "I mean it, Martin," Doc said, almost shouting. "Get the goddam suitcase out of the goddam car!"

Martin took a step or two toward the bus station, as though Doc had not said a word.

"Martin, I swear..." Doc began. He tried to quell his anger, to keep himself calm. "Look here, son," he said, his voice trembling, his breath short, "if you don't tote your own suitcase I swear I'm gonna get back in the car and leave you here, right here. And you'll never see me again." The boy looked at him with an odd and curious expression in his dull eyes. He looked hostile. Frightened, but defiant as well. He made no move toward the car and his suitcase.

"Get it out!" Doc said. "Now!"

"No," Martin said. He turned and started up the sidewalk.

"Goddamit!" Doc shouted. Martin kept walking. "Goddam you, boy!" Doc yelled to his son, bellowed to his departing back, as Martin was now loping steadily toward the bus station, his gait both awkward and determined. The boy walked purposefully, not looking back. His belt, which he had bought himself on one of the villagers' periodic trips to a department store in Dunwoody, had a ridiculously large silver buckle shaped like a horseshoe. The belt was several sizes too big for him and the silver tipped end hung and flapped beside him as he strode. Martin seemed not to be aware of the excess length.

Then Martin stopped and looked back at him. Doc slammed the trunk and went around to the driver's seat and got in. He tilted the rear view mirror. He could see Martin standing there, watching him, waiting for him to catch up with him with the suitcase. "Goddamit," Doc muttered. His chest felt oddly hollow, and he was light headed. He started the car and ground it into gear and pulled out into the street. He adjusted the mirror again and watched Martin grow smaller and smaller, standing alone on the sidewalk. "I'll just show him," Doc said aloud.

Doc couldn't believe what he was doing. He was proud of himself, but his hands were shaking and his knuckles were white where he gripped the steering wheel. He made a right turn and went several blocks and turned back left. He began to tremble all over. He thought he was going to pass out in the traffic, mostly big trucks that rumbled all around him now that he was on First Avenue North. Up ahead he saw the Sloss Furnace belching smoke across the viaduct. He saw in his mind's eye the forlorn, hunched figure of Martin on the downtown sidewalk. Doc's mouth was dry and he could not swallow. "Jesus," he muttered. "Jesus H. Christ!"

Then he was in the billowing, acid gray smoke that drifted into the open windows and around him like shredded clouds, and he could smell the hot sulfurous burning. He caught glimpses of the bright red molten iron as it was being poured, the hot crimson that would light up the night sky so brightly that it could be seen all the way from where they lived. He could feel the loud metallic clanging of the foundry vibrating in his bones, felt it burning in his blood. He was crying, the tears running unobstructed down his cheeks.

His vision was blurred. His heart was constricted in his chest, a tiny knot no bigger than a plum. As he passed through the smoke, he felt that he was disappearing, that the other end of the viaduct would take him straight down into the bowels of the earth. He came suddenly out into the clear spring air.

He could not see clearly when he got off the viaduct; he had to pull to the side of the street and wipe his eyes. He sat there for a long time, the engine rattling. It serves him right, he thought. He remembered the bus ticket sticking out of Martin's shirt pocket. He remembered all the policemen. And it was then he remembered what the men had been talking about: bus loads of colored people, coming into Birmingham. "Freedom Riders," they scoffed.

Doc eased back into the Sunday afternoon traffic, his hands quivering on the steering wheel. He turned off First Avenue, going south. He would double back, finding his way through the unfamiliar streets. He had to get back to the bus station, because something very bad was going to happen. He knew that. The sun was high, the air coming through the windows muggy and damp. Doc was so tired it was an effort to keep the car steady.

He could not remember a time in his life when he had not been tired. Even when Martin was over at Chattoochee he dominated their lives. He called several times a week to complain about the place, about the food or his new counselor. There seemed to be a tremendous and continuous turnover on the staff, which Doc could understand. Sometimes Martin would call and then refuse to say anything, He would call collect to pout silently, the phone company clicking off cash money by the minute.

It took everything he and Molly could scrimp from the basics to keep Martin at Chattoochee Village. Doc's income from his optometry practice would have been sufficient were it not for Martin's expenses. His office was in a strip of shops in Roebuck Plaza. It was a narrow space to begin with, and he shared it with a dentist who drank all day and — for all Doc knew — inhaled his gas too since by the end of the day he was always totally drunk. Doc would never have let the unpleasant man work on his teeth, but the dentist paid half the rent on the place.

He and the dentist had a sign out front with a big white molar and a big blue eye on it. Doc spent his days giving eye exams to the blue collar people who lived in the area and selling them less expensive frames than the fancier chain optical companies that kept moving in. It was because of them cutting into his business that Doc had to take the second job at night. Over the years Molly had had a series of jobs: as a minimum-wage aide in a nursing home, waitressing at several restaurants in the area until her legs and feet could no longer stand the punishment, selling tickets in the booth at the Roebuck Plaza movie theater. She now worked downtown in the women's clothing department at Pizitz and at night she did alterations, both for Pizitz's men's and women's departments and for Deluxe Cleaners.

Doc's anger had subsided now. It was replaced by a familiar sense of helpless disappointment that only heightened his fear and worry for his son. The disappointment was always with him because he knew that his life had been wasted, that it had never really been his own. He could be considering retirement now, like other men his age. He could be looking forward to resting after what could have been a long and fruitful career. But there was no way, because of Martin. It had not worked out that way at all.

Doc always felt a terrible and persistent guilt when he thought about how simple life would be without Martin. He found himself wishing, not for the first time, that the earth would open up and swallow Martin, or that he would get on the wrong bus and wind up in California or Alaska or somewhere, that the boy could somehow simply disappear from their lives, painlessly and quickly. He considered briefly turning back around and leaving Martin to his own devices. Maybe something terrible would happen to him. Maybe he would get in the middle of whatever was going to happen at the bus station, with the colored people on the busses. Doc knew now the men collecting at the bus station were Klansmen, and they played rough. They were there to meet the busses.

The two of them had gone to church together that morning, because Martin always insisted on it. They went to the Presbyterian church Martin had grown up in, over in Woodlawn. They went without Molly. Molly would not go any more at all, and, truth to tell, the church had gradually lost everything meaningful for Doc as well. He had tried to maintain his beliefs, but he could not. He could neither understand nor believe in a God who would create Martin, who would make of his and Molly's lives such an empty and unrelenting journey. Better that Martin had died as an infant, during that brief interval of order and peace for them all.

Doc wiped the sweat from his brow with his finger and flicked it out the window. There is no spring anymore, he was thinking. We go right from the deep freeze of winter to the blistering of summer. He thought of the hallways of the girls' dormitories he was allowed to enter because of his second job, stepping off the elevator and shouting "Man on the hall!" The hallway would be deserted, but as he worked his way along, picking up the white bags of dirty laundry, girls would appear. Crossing the hallways in slips and transparent nightgowns, some even in only panties and bra. Or coming from the shower with just a narrow towel wrapped around them, sometimes a plump breast and a nipple peeping out at him, all of them cutting their eyes at him and giggling. Every year, with new girls, it was the same.

He didn't tell Molly about this experience. She would have a conniption if she heard about the college girls. She did not believe in sex for older folks. "My god, Bennie, it ain't fitten'," she said to him one night longer ago than he could remember. "That's for the young 'uns. I ain't got the energy left over for that!" On those few occasions when he had tried again —awkwardly, fumblingly, after one of his visits to the girls' dormitory — she had become angry and had spat at him that he was nothing more than an animal. The only time they slept in the same bed now was when Martin was home for his infrequent visits. Martin slept in the other bedroom, Doc's room, then. Doc snored, and Molly had complained that it kept her awake. Molly snored, too, but Doc didn't tell her that either.

He tried not to think about Molly too much anymore. It broke Doc's heart that he had had to watch Molly grow old and faded so quickly, the luster of her hair and eyes replaced by a bitter tongue. He could not bear to recall the mere days, the briefest of moments, when they, innocent twenty year olds, had brought their new baby home from the hospital. Molly was still pretty then, not wearied and worn down. She still smiled and laughed; she was as fresh as a morning breeze in the springtime. They were happy, almost delirious: a family, exciting and comfortable and nourishing for each other. At the time Doc had been certain that it was all a tiny glimpse of heaven. And then they found out the fact, the truth about their son.

Doc saw the street in front of the bus station was blocked off, police cars parked diagonally across it. He sat there, trying to figure out what to do, the car idling. Where in the hell was Martin? In the bus station, Doc thought, of course. Then he saw a man with a big camera, a newspaper photographer from the looks of him, being chased by two men, who caught him on the sidewalk next to where Doc was parked. They began to beat him with bicycle chains. They picked up his camera and hurled it to the sidewalk, smashing it.

This was serious business, all right. Doc got out of his car, leaving it right there, very near where he had parked earlier. He watched the two men sprint back toward the bus station. Doc opened the trunk and got a tire iron. He could hear shouting in the distance, a roar, almost like a ball game. He saw Martin's suitcase there in the trunk, and his stomach gripped on him. He thought he might be sick.

He loped down the sidewalk toward the bus station, carrying his tire iron. A policeman stood on the sidewalk just outside the door. He pushed it open for Martin. "Go git 'em, buddy rubba," he said, grinning. Inside the bus station was chaos, pandemonium. He saw another policeman.

"My son," he yelled to him. "I'm lookin' for my son. I got to find him!"

"Little feller? With a red necktie?"

"Yes! Yes!"

The policeman pointed toward the boiling crowd. The screams and shouts were deafening, echoing from the tile floor and the high, rounded ceiling. There were people on the floor, bicycle chains whistled through the air. There were cries of pain, cries of anger. Doc waded in. "Let me through!" he exclaimed, "I got to find my son!"

"Them folks ain't no kin to you," one of the men said to him, laughing.

"Let me by!" Doc yelled, pushing the man out of the way.

And then Doc was face to face with an elderly Negro man. The man's eyes were wide, his mouth open. He was praying, the words faint, incomprehensible. He looked at Doc but Doc could tell he didn't see him. Doc didn't see Martin anywhere. Panic seized him and a white hot rage filled him to bursting. The intense anger came on so suddenly that it caught Doc by surprise. He forgot momentarily where he was. Then he swung the tire iron and hit the old man on top of his head. He heard the dull thud. He saw the blood begin to spurt as the old man dropped to his knees and then fell sideways to the dirty floor.

He came back to himself with a rush. "My God!" Doc blurted aloud. "My God!" He looked at the old man, motionless on the floor. Someone bumped Doc from behind, then he was jostled from the side. Hot tears sprang to his eyes. He thought surely this was some nightmare and he would awake. But he could smell the bus station, smell the rank of the bathrooms, the stink of sweat and blood.

He tossed the tire iron to the floor. His tears blinded him. He floundered, turning, groping back toward the door to the street. He could not comprehend what he had done, could not even call the old man's face back up in his memory. And yet he could still see his eyes.

He pushed out the door into the hot sunshine. The air revived him. He looked around frantically. There were sirens now, more policemen arriving. Doc turned back toward the bus station, but he was blocked. "Nobody goes in," said a policeman.

"But my...my..."

"Nobody. Sorry."

Doc staggered off down the sidewalk toward his car. He knew he looked drunk, but the policemen on the street paid no attention to him. His head was splitting with an ache so profound that for a moment he could think of nothing else, not even Martin, not even the old Negro he had hit. He prayed that the old man was not dead. He prayed that Martin was somehow all right.

And then, through the fog that shrouded his head, he saw him. The boy was sitting on steps of the church near where Doc had left the car. Doc squinted in the afternoon sunlight. Martin sat calmly peacefully, eating something. When Doc got closer, he recognized it as a Moon Pie. The boy sipped on a Coke; he did not see Doc. He did not even look up when Doc passed. Doc plodded on to the car, feeling the sweat run in cool rivulets down his sides under his shirt.

Martin would be with him forever. Martin would continue to be like a shadow at his elbow, like a shade of himself. His son: waiting expectantly for the simple clue of Doc's next move, for the direction of his most casual and innocent word.

An Encounter with a Friend

(First Published in "Inlet", 1976)

THIS happened at Heidi's Motel in Brewster, New York.

They were the first people to check in. It was early afternoon, but it was very hot, the first very hot day of summer; the manager of the motel, who spoke with a thick German accent, was drinking a sweating bottle of Miller High Life. She was young and quite pretty and small; he was short, with a paunch, and long sideburns and thick, dark hair. They asked for the same room they'd had last year, overlooking the pool and rose arbors, and of course they could have it. They spent the afternoon at the pool; the water was very cold (it had been 45 degrees two nights ago, the manager had told them), but it was stimulating. They felt very good, and had their drinks by the pool. Then they drove up Route 22 to an Italian-American restaurant and had pizza and beer. They drove back to the motel feeling contented and refreshed; most of the long drive was over, and tomorrow they would be in their cabin in Vermont.

They decided on a game of shuffleboard; it was a beautiful night, starry and cool. They played several games, he winning them all, amid much laughter. They had been playing about half an hour when they noticed the boy standing quietly back in the shadows.

"Hello," she called out. There was no answer, and the boy stood very still. "Come on, play the winner," she said, laughing.

The boy edged out of the shadows. He was probably thirteen, medium height and dumpy, adolescent heavy-hipped. He seemed very shy and awkward.

"Good evening," he said, almost formally.

"Wanna play the winner?" she said.

"I suppose," the boy said. He hesitated; he seemed unsure of the sincerity of the invitation. "I mean, I wouldn't want to..."

"No, come on," the man said, "we'll have a tournament."

The boy seemed to brighten a bit. "Say, I could keep score for you. I have my own system for keeping up with the minus scores."

"Great," he said.

So they played on, the man winning and then playing the boy. Gradually his shyness seemed to diminish, but he played badly, awkwardly. "The last time I played shuffleboard was aboard ship, and I slid two disks overboard," he said. They all laughed as one of his shots flipped on its side and rolled off across the lawn toward the pool.

The woman then played the loser and the man kept score. There was much laughter and joking. The woman told the boy that she taught Junior High School English, and the boy seemed very pleased. He was looking at them eagerly, his eyes sparkling in the dim light. He went about the game with great gusto, laughing loudly at his shots. It was growing late, but they were having so much fun they kept playing. They were all startled by the voice from the terrace above them.

"Two minutes!" it said, sharply, and they all looked up. They could see the woman in the dim light; she was standing very straight, looking down at them. Even in the dimness, they could see her red hair, but they couldn't tell her age. They looked at the boy. He seemed embarrassed.

"Excuse me a minute," he said.

"Sure," the man said. They watched him shuffle up the incline and around to the terrace where the woman was standing. They couldn't hear what the two were saying, but gradually they realized the boy was begging.

"March!" they heard the woman say.

"But —"

"March, I said!"

"Come on, let's play," the man said softly. They began to arrange the disks.

"Good night," they heard the boy's voice call down to them. "I certainly had a good time."

"Good night, enjoyed it," they said. They watched the boy trudge slowly up the hill beside the woman.

"Must be his mother," the woman said.

"Yeah, it *is* late," the man said.

They didn't finish the game; the man was leading twenty-three to minus-ten when a mosquito got the woman just at the corner of her left eye. It was badly swollen by the time they got to bed.

The next morning they overslept; the motel manager had forgotten to call them at seven-thirty. When they entered the little coffee shop about nine, there they were. They could see that the woman was quite old, with flaming red hair, sitting very straight and looking dourly around her. Her face was pale with powder. The boy seemed very excited, and he grinned broadly.

"When we didn't seen your car we thought you'd gone already," he said.

"My husband had to go out and get some medicine," the woman said, smiling. "I got an awful mosquito bite last night after you went in." He continued to grin at them. "Maybe we should have been good fellows and gone in then, too," she said.

The older woman looked haughtily at them, then looked away. "Eat your breakfast," she said.

They were the only people in the coffee shop. They couldn't help but be aware of how the woman kept correcting the boy, his table manners, the way he sat. Several times he looked over at them, his eyes eager. They could tell he was very embarrassed. The woman and the boy finished their breakfast first; as they passed the table on the way out, the woman nodded curtly. The boy stopped.

"Goodbye," he said.

"Goodbye," they said. "Have a nice trip."

"The same to you," he said, then he ran to catch up with the woman.

Their table overlooked the parking area, and as they ate they watched the boy load the car, the woman standing by, fanning with a lacy handkerchief, giving him orders. It was a long black Cadillac. They watched in silence for awhile.

"That must be his grandmother," the man said, after a minute.

"I wonder where his parents are?" the woman said.

"I don't know," the man said. "He sure seemed lonely, didn't he?"

They continued to eat in silence. Then they watched them get into the car. The car moved slowly out of the parking lot and into the highway, the old woman sitting erectly behind the wheel. They finished their meal. They were smoking when the woman reached across the table and took his hand. They looked into each other's eyes.

"I love you," she said, softly.

"Very much," he said.

Somewhere in all this Green

(First Published in "An Anthology of Bennington Writers", 1978)

RALPH Fosque's old blue Buick slung a rod on Interstate 65, just as he passed a sign that said: CLANTON EXIT, 1 MILE. Things like that happened to Ralph Fosque. He had driven all the way from Wheeling, West Virgina, to Clanton, Alabama, without one knock or flat tire or sputter, only to have the old blue Buick sling the rod as though it could somehow read the sign. It was a once-elegant car; it had a radio antenna on the back that had once gone up and down when you pushed a button on the dash. It didn't matter that it didn't work any more, since he had sold the radio to a friend for ten dollars seven years before and had put a tape deck in. It was playing Barbra Streisand's "Greatest Hits" when the rod slung. When he coasted to a stop on the apron of the highway, Barbra Streisand was singing *"People, people who need people"*.

"Shit," Ralph said.

He got out and raised the hood and waited for a cop to come along. He leaned against the car and smoked a cigar and listened to Barbra Streisand singing *"People, people who need people"*. He wasn't in any hurry. He didn't know what he was going to find in

Clanton, anyway. He hadn't seen his daughter Martha in twenty-two years. And she didn't even know he was coming. Two boys went by in a Pontiac convertible with the top down, and the passenger toasted him with a can of beer. Sterling, it looked like. "You, too, son," Ralph muttered around his cigar. "You too." He stood there, watching the puffs of gray smoke go towards the cloudless, deep blue Alabama spring sky. He hadn't been in Alabama for over six years. He didn't think they made skies that blue in West Virginia. A huge transfer rig roared by, and he felt the wind from it whip his breeches against his legs. He watched the back of it disappearing down the Interstate toward Birmingham. There were two red arrows painted on the back, one pointing left, the other right. Written under the left one was:

PASSIN SIDE

Under the other was:

SUICIDE

"Shit," Ralph said, looking up and down the highway, wondering where a cop was. He saw an Alabama State Trooper car coming the other way. He saw it slow down, then speed up. He just stood there, puffing on the cigar. Pretty soon he saw it coming over a hill in his lane. It coasted to a stop behind him, and a young trooper got out. He wore a white ten-gallon hat and a silver name plate that said: Armistead Hunnicutt, Cadet.

"Got trouble?" Armistead Hunnicutt said, coming up to him.

"Naw, I'm homesteadin'," Ralph said.

The trooper looked at him. After a minute, he said, "What ails this heap o' junk?"

"Slung a rod," Ralph said.

"Where ya headed?"

"Clanton."

"Good thing," the trooper said, looking at the car. He kicked the left rear tire.

"Son, there was a time when I coulda bought an' sold the entire fleet of the Alabama State Troopers," Ralph Fosque said.

"It ain't for sale," Armistead Hunnicutt said. "I'll get somebody to come out from Clanton and tow this thing in."

"You do that."

"You stay in the car," the trooper said. "Don't be standin' around on no Interstate. First thing you know your ass'll be a grease spot outside Chattanooga."

A BOY WHO looked no more than fifteen came out in a tow truck to get him. He was from a Shell filling station, and Ralph could tell he didn't much know what he was doing, but he just watched. The boy looked like a rabbit. His skin was very pale white and his eyes were pinkish-looking. Ralph watched him fool with the chain. He decided he was an Albino. They had Albinos in Clanton.

"You write that on there?" the boy asked.

"What?"

"On your license plate, there," the boy said, pointing.

Ralph looked where he was pointing. The tag said: WEST VIRGINIA, ALMOST HEAVEN.

"They come that way," he said.

"Well, I'll be goddammed," the boy said. He scratched his head. He looked from the tag to Ralph and back. After a minute, he said, "Our'n says HEART O DIXIE." He worked at the chains.

"I'll be goddammed," he said again, after a minute.

RALPH FOSQUE bumped along the dirt road, looking for James Knox Polk Avenue. He was now driving a 1951 Dodge pickup, painted a bright orange, that he'd traded the owner of the Shell Filling Station even for the Buick. At least, almost even; he had the tape deck and the stack of tapes on the seat beside him. He had looked it up in the phone book: Roy W. Letson, 15 Polk Avenue. Nobody knew where it was. "Polk Avenue?" the owner of the Shell Station had said. "Ain't no such animal, least as I know."

"Here it is, right here, in the telephone book," Ralph said.

"Me, I live in Highland Riverview Estates, myself," the filling station owner said. He turned away. He had on a neat-looking brown shirt with a black clip-on bow tie. He was very clean. He didn't look as though he ran a filling station. "Whyn't ya ask Joe

Boy over there, anyhow," he said, pointing to a policeman who was standing watching the boy who looked like a rabbit fill the orange pickup with gas.

"Where the hell is Polk Avenue?" Ralph asked, coming up to the policeman named Joe Boy. Joe Boy took his cigarette out of his mouth and looked him over. He wore his gun slung low on his leg like Randolph Scott.

"Why might you be wantin' to know?" he asked, and Ralph just looked at him.

"I heard that's where they keep the Albinos," he said.

Joe Boy looked puzzled.

"What?" he said.

"I heard all the way up in Wheeling, West Virginia, that you got a lot of Albinos in Clanton, Alabama, and I come down here looking for 'em."

Joe Boy scratched his head.

"You with the circus or somethin'?"

"Son," Ralph said, sighing, "I'm lookin' for my daughter and son-in-law, Roy and Martha Letson, and they live on Polk Avenue, according to that phone book of yours, so I'm askin' one of Clanton's finest how to get there. Now is that a crime?

Joe Boy looked him up and down. He looked for a moment as though he wanted to grin but was afraid to. "Whyn't you just say so in the first place?"

RALPH STOPPED the truck at an intersection and looked around. The sun was very bright, and there was lush greenness everywhere. The whole world was made out of sunlight, kudzu, and honeysuckle. The sandy, rutted roads curved away from where he was, gentled in quiet, dappled afternoon light. Down to the left was a chinaberry tree and a mailbox. He sat there a moment, the motor of the orange pickup rumbling and sputtering. The gear shift lever jumped around like it had the palsy. He was at the center, so no choice could be wrong. He turned toward the chinaberry tree and the mailbox.

R. LETSON, the mailbox said. The fence sagged, and the gate hung on its hinges. The yard was sandy and a rusty 1949 Mercury was sitting on blocks beside the house. It had a FOR SALE sign in the back window. Ralph cut the engine and sat looking at the house. A black cat sat on the porch rail looking at him. They looked at each other for a few minutes. "Hey there," Ralph said to the cat, after a minute. The cat just looked at him. "Tell me," Ralph said, "can a man smell honeysuckle so long that he gets to where he don't even know he's smelling it? Tell me that. Up in West Virginia, why, a man don't ever get used to the smell of coal dust. But honeysuckle?" The cat just looked at him.

He got out and slammed the door, and at that the cat jumped down and ran under the house. Ralph waited after he knocked, and in a minute Martha opened the door. She stood there, looking at him. She squinted her eyes in the afternoon sunlight. "This is your daddy, Ralph Fosque," he said. She just looked at him, much as the cat had. "From Wheeling, West Virginia," he added. They just stood there, awkwardly.

"Hello, Daddy Ralph," she said, after a minute. "Won't you come in?"

HE WAS SITTING at the table, drinking a mug of coffee. The kitchen was full of cooking dinner smells. "I just said to myself," he said, "why, Ralph, you don't need no appointment to see your own daughter, why, just pop in on her, go right ahead."

She stirred something on the stove. "Twenty-two years," she said. "That's a long time." She had on a plain blue dress without sleeves, and her arm was lean and tanned, strong like the branch of a sapling, and her hair was straight and blonde and her eyes were steady and green as new clover. "That's a long time," she said again.

"What's time?" he said. "What good did it ever do anybody to count time?"

"A year is a year, and twenty-two of 'em is twenty-two of 'em," she said, looking at him, brushing a strand of hair that stuck to her damp forehead.

"That shore is a fine lookin' cat you got out there," he said, smiling. "Better be careful you don't chunk him on the fire with the coal come winter."

"You come all the way from West Virginia to talk about cats?"

"I come to see my daughter," he said, " and meet my son-in-law."

"Hah," she said.

He sipped the coffee. "Things reach out to you, honey," he said. "Years, miles, don't make any difference. I'm gettin' on. A man twenty-five, he wakes up in a hotel in Detroit, not known how he got there, why, he just pulls on his britches and goes. A man my age, he gets to layin' there, wonderin' how he got there. First thing you know, he gets to thinkin' about this little towhead girl takin' a bath in a washtub on her granmaw's back porch. He gets up and looks out the winder, expectin' to see honeysuckle and muscadines, and he don't see nothin' but concrete and neon signs, and somethin's wrong. Cause that little towhead girl is there, just the same. Don't you see?" He sat there, cradling the coffee mug. She didn't answer him. She put the spoon down.

The baby cried in the next room. She looked at the man, her father, and he looked back at her. His face was alive and tired at the same time, craggy as a petrified stump. "Law," he said, and grinned. "Is that a granchile?"

"How many you think you got?"

"More'n I can keep up with, that's the God's truth," he said, grinning at her. "Seems I spent half my life keepin' up with the wives and chirren, much less gran' chirren."

"And women," she said. "Just women."

"*And* women," he said, nodding his head. "And there never was a one I didn't love." The baby squalled. "Law, he's got lungs on 'im. Or is it a she?"

"A she," She went into the next room and came out with the baby. She rocked it in her arms. "Hush now," she said. The baby stopped crying. Ralph sat there at the table, looking at Martha holding the baby. He looked at the tilt of her head. "We named her Mary, after Momma's momma," she said. She was looking at the child with her green eyes; Ralph sat there watching her, taking all of her in, the strong bare feet on the linoleum floor, the leanness of her body. She was quiet-looking. She rocked the baby in the smells of honeysuckle and slow-cooking greens, the clean used life smell of the house. It was full of the scents of hundreds of afternoon thundershowers and thousands of hickory and oak and coal fires, and baby smells. "A towhead girl takin' a bath in a washtub on her granmaw's back porch," Ralph said. "Old Mary Durrett. She was some woman, wasn't she?"

"She sure was," Martha said. She put the baby in a yellow plastic infant seat, and little Mary looked around. She looked at Ralph with large, darkish eyes. She smiled at him.

"I'll never forget the day we buried that old lady," Ralph said.

Martha poured herself a cup of coffee and came and sat at the table. She sipped it and looked across the table at him. There was some of the same harshness, the chiseled quality, in her face. For a moment he thought he was looking at old Mary Durrett in the flesh. It was the eyes. The woman eyes. He could sense, almost feel his daughter's power.

"How old are you now?"

"Thirty-two." She sipped the coffee. Her hands around the cup told him that no one could hurt her. He remembered old Mary's hands, gripping the handle of a churn, on that same back porch. She looked up at him. "Ain't you gonna ask me about Roy?"

"What about him?"

"He ain't here."

"Well, where is he?" He looked at her; the eyes held in whatever it was: anger, heat.

"He's gone," she said.

"Where?"

"I don't know. Just gone." They sat there at the table; he looked at the yellow salt and pepper shakers, the red plastic top of the table. He could hear the ticking of a clock, and a distant mockingbird, somewhere in the privet and Cherokee roses piling and reaching to the back of the house. The smell of new-cut alfalfa on his daddy's farm, forty years before, was in his nostrils, yet he knew it could not be. He had not been to Brookhaven, Mississippi, in he couldn't remember when, and the stone over his own mother's grave was so worn that nobody could read it, and the plot was full of smut-grass and weeds. When she spoke, he was startled.

"When I was carryin' her, Mary, what I used to think about more than anything else was that I was carryin' what would someday be somebody's grandmother. Most folk would think that was silly, I reckon, but it just seemed like it was, well, that that little thing wasn't just somethin' that would be and then all of a sudden go. You know what I mean?" He just looked at her. "I mean, Daddy Ralph, it's like grabbin' onto something that you know can't hold you up and then you find it holds you up anyhow, you know what I mean?" She looked at him, and then cut her eyes down at the table. "Ahh, shit," she said. "I don't know."

Ralph looked at her. "Yeah, I reckon," he said. "Yeah, I think I do know what you mean."

"Roy can't help what he is, no more'n you could help what you always were." She sipped the coffee, and smiled. "But that don't mean I have to let it beat me. Either one of you." The room was still and quiet.

"Look over there," she said, and they looked at the baby. It was sleeping. They sat there with no sound but the ticking of the clock. After a minute, Ralph stood up.

"I reckon I best be goin'," he said.

"Won't you be stayin' for supper?"

He stood looking at her. For the first time in his life he had found a place where there was no room for him, no room at all. And he didn't have to let that beat *him*, either. He'd be damned if he would. "I got a long drive," he said. "I'm on my way to Florida. I'm meetin' another fellow in Clearwater. You know, a land deal and all that."

She smiled. "Okay," she said.

She stood on the porch, holding the baby, watching him crank the orange Dodge. The cat had come back out and was watching him, too. The engine roared into life, sputtering, and the gear shift jerked and whipped around and he pounded on the clutch. He leaned out the window. "I'll see you, hear?" he yelled, and she waved.

RALPH PULLED into the Shell Station and the boy who looked like a white rabbit was standing by the pumps.

"We've done closed," he said.

"I don't need nothin' but directions," Ralph said. "How do you get to the freeway headin' south for Florida?"

"You goin' right," the boy said. "Just keep on goin' the way you goin', you'll see the signs." He put his hands on his hips. "I done brought that Buick o' your'n offa Mr. Hunter," he said, grinning. "I'll be the onliest feller in Chilton County with a license plate that says WEST VIRGINIA, ALMOST HEAVEN!"

"Well," Ralph Fosque said, "that's mighty nice. You take care of that thing, it's a good car."

"Yassur," the boy said proudly.

Ralph let the clutch out and the pickup scratched onto the gravel and headed into the highway. Pretty soon he got to the freeway. He got into the southbound lane, and soon he passed a sign that said: SHORT ROUTE TO FLORIDA — VISIT FORT WALTON BEACH. He rolled the window down and let the fresh air blow in his face. He started to hum, an idle, tuneless, meaningless humming. The sun was setting and the sky was streaked with yellows and oranges, oranges that almost exactly matched the color of the Dodge pickup. He cruised along, looking at the green rolling hills that reached out to him and invited him. He heard a horn blast, and two boys passed him in a Pontiac convertible with the top down, going very fast. One of them gave him the finger. Ralph grinned.

"You too, son," he said. "You too."

The Night of the Yellow Butterflies

(First Published in "Arete: The Journal of Sport Literature", 1985)

DOYLE could remember the first night he had dreamed of the yellow butterflies. It was when he'd first heard of the college coaching job and decided to go for it. He usually dreamed of spiders and deserted, silent baseball fields. That night he started awake and lay in the hot, quiet, cramped little room, thinking of the swarm of yellow butterflies in his dream. It was a still night; even the crickets were quiet, and Doyle lay there feeling anxious and nervous. It was seven and a half months since he'd had a drink of whiskey.

DOYLE was employed by the Hammond, Alabama, Recreation Department, and he knew he was little more than a janitor except in the summers, when he coached the Hammond Rebels in the semipro Black Belt League. He was standing, leaning against the dugout, watching his team take infield practice on the red-dirt infield. They practiced twice a week and played on weekends, a double header on Saturday night and single game on Sunday, usually clearing expenses and beer money after paying for the lights. He watched Sammy Jackson, fluid and smooth at third, field and throw a bullet to first; Sammy's arm was still awesome, even at 47 years old, and he could hit. He'd played six years in the Yankee organization, making it as high as Triple A one year, when he'd broken an ankle sliding and lost whatever speed he'd had. Sammy had his own television repair shop now, doing real well. Doyle smiled, watching him lope toward the plate, field the bunt and wheel and throw to second; the ball cleared the pitcher's rubber by maybe two inches and the second baseman, a high school kid named Gerald Saunders, fielded it cleanly just as he crossed the bag. Any runner from first would have been out by three feet.

Doyle's mind was wandering: he was thirsty, but he limited himself to two beers a day now. No matter how much he concentrated, he couldn't get his mind off that coaching job over at Sumter State. Being a college coach. Being the coach of the Sumter State Teachers College Angels. He hadn't even finished high school, but he knew that didn't matter, not to Jack Cotton, and that's who mattered, Jack Cotton.

"Well, well, well, there he is. You know, somethin' just tole me I'd be meetin' up with Doyle Sprayberry one-a-these-here hot afternoons." Jack Cotton wiped his mouth with the back of his hand. The other men at the table grinned; the window air conditioner in the roadside beer joint hummed. They all knew him. Everybody in West Alabama knew Doyle, or knew of him, at least everybody who had anything to do with baseball. And everybody knew Jack Cotton, who owned half of Greene County, and who was chairman of the executive committee of the Sumter State Board of Trustees. Cotton practically had the soybean market for West Alabama cornered, and the name of the new baseball stadium at Sumter State was JACK COTTON FIELD. "Didn't spect it to be in a beer garden, though," Cotton said.

"Just a cool one now and again," Doyle said, and Cotton nodded and squinted at him.

Doyle casually sipped the ice cold Budweiser. He had needed nothing more than Jack Cotton's greeting to him to know that Cotton knew about his application for the coaching job. And the talk that afternoon was about a three-car wreck up near Eutaw that had killed six people. The only mention of baseball was when Cotton looked squarely at Doyle and said, "That Black Belt League team a yours is gonna win the state series this year, ain't it, Doyle? Didn't miss it by much last year."

THERE WERE two semipro leagues in Alabama, the Black Belt in the South and the Sand Mountain in the North, and every year the two pennant winners met in a playoff series, the best of seven. It wasn't such a big deal, except to the people who followed the teams and the men like Jack Cotton, who bet the big money. Last year, Doyle's fifth pennant for Hammond, the series had been played for the first time in Rickwood Field in Birmingham, the last week in August, and they'd actually made some money. The Rebels had lost in six games to the Gadsden Tigers. This year had to be his year. He had a pitcher named Buddy Koch, a Jewish kid who'd just graduated from high school, who could throw at least ninety miles an hour. Doyle hoped the scouts wouldn't discover him for at least another year. And his center-fielder, Calvin Burton, had a few good years left in him; Calvin, a farmer from out near Gallion, was the best center-fielder Doyle had ever seen, outside the majors. He was so fast that nothing could get by him, and he was Doyle's leadoff man. Last year, in 47 games, he had fifty one doubles and had stolen fifty-one bases, including home three times. And there were others, enough to build a team around. A good team, for a man who knew baseball, and Doyle knew baseball. He chewed on a matchstick, watching the routine ritual of infield practice.

IT WAS when Doyle was alone, in the early evenings, that he most missed his drink, because that's the only time he ever allowed himself any more to miss his family. His wife. He rented a room from a widow, and it opened onto a cinder alley, and Doyle would sit on the stoop, his breeches pulled up to get the breeze, and pass the time on those evenings when he was home. The last time he'd heard anything about his wife, she was living in Lake Charles, Louisiana. Both his kids would have finished high school by now, and Doyle didn't know where they were or what had happened to them. His wife had finally told him that it was the booze or her, and the booze made up his mind for him. When Doyle thought about his life, his short baseball career, it was hard for him to know if the booze had been a part of the cause or an attempt at a cure. He had thought at one time that he'd had it made, and he'd had good reason to. One of the things that give him pleasure to think about, sitting in the doorway picking up what little breeze there was, was the fact that he was listed in *Ripley's Believe It or Not*. Doyle, as a young pitcher, had compiled the best won-loss percentage ever in all of organized professional baseball: in the summer of 1949, pitching for the Selma Cloverleafs in the old Class B Southeastern League, he had compiled a record of 26 wins and no losses. It was a feat that had never been duplicated. 26 and 0. The next year, after moving up to AA Ball, with the Chattanooga Lookouts in the Southern Association, he'd won 3 and lost 8. He lasted half the '51 season, going one and one, but his one victory was a no-hitter against the Mobile Bears, when he allowed only one batter to reach base on a walk, and he didn't remember the game very clearly because he had pitched all nine innings dead drunk. The only time he could get the ball across the plate, throw strikes, was when he was drunk. He had been scared to death he'd bean somebody and kill them on the spot. But he was still there, right in *Ripley's Believe It Or Not*. Anybody who wanted to could look it up. He wished he had a nickel for every beer he'd won on that one. Once, when he went with a bunch of other fellows up to Townsend, Tennessee, to dismantle an old log cabin for a rich man who claimed it had been built by one of his ancestors, who wanted it brought down to Alabama so he could put it back up on his farm, he and the other men had driven over to Gatlinburg to see the sights, and they'd gone to the Ripley's Museum, and there he was, a drawing that didn't even look like him, some pitcher in a uniform that didn't even look like Selma's, but there was his name, Doyle Sprayberry, all right. 26 and 0. He didn't pay for a beer or a plate of brook trout or a steak on the whole trip.

DOYLE stretched and prepared to go in, now that the evening was cooler, and he could sleep. He would think about the season ahead as he drifted off to sleep. He stood up, wishing he had a good stiff drink. The last time he'd had DTs had been in a hotel room in New Orelans, and he'd thought he would die. He never wanted to go through that again. He'd read about people having the DTs years after they quit drinking, all of a sudden, right out of the blue, and he wondered about that when he saw his old stray dog, Dropo, walk by down the alley with a yellow butterfly on his head.

JACK Cotton liked to watch the games sitting in the folding chair behind the screen between home plate and the Rebel dugout. He could sit with his buddies and sip bourbon out of a bottle in a brown paper sack. This night he was wearing a blue Dodger cap.

"Hey, Doyle, got to get somethin' going, babe," Cotton yelled at him, and Doyle nodded. They were trailing the Grove Hill Red Sox 1-6 going to the top of the seventh. Doyle was pitching Percy Meroney, a lefty who usually played first base; Percy was overweight, and he loved to chew on the stub of a cigar which he carefully stuck on a ledge under the roof of the dugout before they took the field. Once tonight he'd forgotten it and taken the mound with it jutting out of the corner of his mouth and the umpire had gone out and yelled at him and made him throw it away. Percy had thrown it over toward the Grove Hill dugout because they'd been giving him a hard time all night. Everybody knew Percy would throw a spitter when he thought he could get away with it.

"Hey Percy, Percy! Whooo, Percy, throwin a bacco ball tonight, Whooooo," they yelled, "Hey, hey, hey, look out now, Hey Blue, check that ball, see if it don't say Tampa Nugget on it!"

Doyle watched Percy come in with his round house curve, and the batter grounded sharply to young Saunders at second; the boy handled it nicely and threw the runner out. There was some scattered clapping and cheers. A pretty good crowd for early in the season. Doyle leaned back against the screen, chewing on a toothpick.

"Doyle," Cotton said, "I tell you. The team needs somethin'."

"Yeah," Doyle said.

"Well, listen here," Cotton said. "Listen. I's talkin' to Doc Day just this morning. You heard about that boy down at Sweetwater? High school boy?"

"I heard some," Doyle said.

"Nigger boy," Cotton said. "A first baseman. I forget his name. Anyhow, from what Doc and some others say, the boy can do most anything. And that's what you need, you need somebody to make somethin' happen, right?"

"Right," Doyle said.

"Well, I tell you what. I'm gone loan you a truck, tomorrow, all right? Tomorrow, no sense in puttin' things off, and you drive down there and get him. I already got him a summer job lined up out at the veneer mill. If he's workin', tell 'im we'll pay 'im a little more than he's gettin'. If he ain't got a car, we'll find 'im some place to stay. All right?"

"All right." Doyle said. "But hell, he ain't but one player. Besides..."

"Besides what?" Cotton said. "So he ain't but one player. That's a start ain't it?"

"Reckon so," Doyle said.

Sammy Jackson hit a bases loaded triple in the bottom of the eighth, but he died on third, and the Rebels lost 4-6, which put them two and two on the young season.

DOYLE GOT to Sweetwater early in the afternoon, and he didn't remember driving down there. But that was nothing new for Doyle. For years and years, that happened to him. He'd be driving down the road, say going south toward Opp, then all of a sudden he'd be tooling along, south of Opp, and he couldn't remember driving through the town. Finally he told somebody about it, he didn't remember who, and the fellow told Doyle not to worry about it, it happened to everybody, especially when they got tired.

He found the boy at the combination baseball-football field out behind the deserted school building. He was alone, tossing chert pebbles into the air and hitting them toward the outfield with a broomstick.

"Keeps my eye sharp," the boy said when Doyle walked up. Doyle had been watching his smooth, natural left-handed swing as he walked down from the school. The boy was big, six four or so, well over two hundred pounds. Some of the pebbles shattered, some went zinging out of sight toward the row of pine trees four hundred feet away.

"Good swing," Doyle said. "Wait a minute." He grabbed a handful of pebbles and walked about fifty feet away. "Here," he said, and sidearmed one. The boy swatted it neatly over Doyle's head, whinggggg, like a twenty-two. He connected with every one Doyle tossed. Mostly line drives. One missed Doyle's ear by about an inch.

"You adjust good," Doyle said. "Can you hit a curve ball?"

"Shit," the boy said. He hadn't grinned yet. Sullen, Doyle though. Sulky. All right, better than a goddam clown.

"What's your name?"

"Easter."

"Easter what? That your first name, or what?

"No," the boy said. "Luke. Luke Easter."

Doyle narrowed his eyes at the boy. He was standing easily, looking off at the trees. "You jokin' me, boy?" Doyle said.

Easter looked surprised. After a minute, he said, "What you mean, jokin'? I ain't said nothin'."

"You only just stood there and told me your name was Luke Easter. Luscious? Luscious Easter?"

"What about it?"

Doyle scratched his head. For some reason he thought of his dog Dropo, with the yellow butterfly. "Listen," he said, "you throw left or right?"

"Right," Easter said.

"Uh-huh," Doyle said. "Well." He squatted on his haunches and pulled a long stem of smut grass from the ground and stuck it between his teeth. "Well," he said, again. "What kin are you to Luke Easter?"

The boy looked puzzled. "I *is* Luke Easter," he said.

Doyle spit the smut grass out and squinted up at him. "*The* Luke Easter, I mean," Doyle said.

The boy glared. *He's a mean one,* Doyle thought.

"I'm the only Luke Easter I know," he said.

THEY DROVE back north toward Hammond, mostly in silence. Once, Doyle said, "You never heard of Luke Easter, played in the majors?"

"Naw," the boy mumbled.

"You *must* be *some* kin to him, name like that. He 'uz one a the first blacks to play in the majors, come up with Cleveland in forty-nine. I never seen him play. Don't know where he was from, nor what happened to him. But maybe he's from Alabama, maybe, huh?"

The boy said nothing. He just watched the dusty cotton fields passing by outside the window.

"You don't know, huh?" Doyle said, after a minute.

"All I know," Easter said, "is you get three strikes. Three. And thass all. Thass all the strikes, thass all I know."

Damn, Doyle thought. *This one's a talker.*

THE NEXT night, after Doyle had gotten him a room and settled him into his job at the veneer mill, Easter started at first base and Doyle hit him clean-up. "What the hell?" Sammy Jackson said, and Doyle said, "Easy now, less just try 'im and see what happens." Easter went four for four, a triple, three singles, six runs batted in, and the Rebels beat the Greenville Giants 11-0 behind the two-hit pitching of young Buddy Koch, who pitched his first shut out since high school and got drunk for the first time in his life after the game.

THE REBELS went on a tear. That weekend they went down South and swept a doubleheader from the Linden Red Devils, 10-1 and 14-2, and then went on to win their next five straight. Percy Meroney hadn't been happy giving up first base, but he was now part of the starting pitching rotation. With the Rebels scoring that many runs, Doyle figured, Percy couldn't do a lot of harm. They won his next two starts 16-13 and 9-8. Jack Cotton was happy. Sammy Jackson, hitting in the number three spot now, was hitting .438, and Easter was hitting .640 through his first eight games with the team. And the Rebels were 10 and 2, leading the league by 2 games.

"Lookin' good, Doyle, Lookin' good," Cotton said from his folding chair behind the screen. He winked at Doyle. "You swing your weight, I'll swing mine," he said.

"Is that a promise?" Doyle said.

"Now, Doyle," Cotton said, "you know I don't make promises."

DOYLE, to celebrate, had raised his daily quota to a six-pack, and sometimes his stomach bothered him a little. He wished whiskey didn't make him crazy; it didn't bother his stomach like beer did. Maybe he'd let down and sip a little, but he held off, because he was worried. "That's your problem Doyle," his wife used to tell him, over and over, "you worry all the time. *Specially* when things are goin' good. You worry, then. And that ain't no fun." The boy, Easter, was something, but there was just something about him. He was so quiet. And when he did talk, he didn't talk to anybody but Doyle, and then he mostly talked in riddles. And he didn't seem to have a family or anything. Nobody from down around Sweetwater seemed to know anything about him much at all. He'd only played high school baseball that one year, and that was about it, as near as Doyle could determine. One night, during batting practice, he'd handed Doyle a new baseball.

"Look at that, " he'd said.

"What?" Doyle had said.

"That," Easter said, pointing to the baseball.

"What about it?" Doyle said, turning it around in his fingers.

"Don't you see how perfect it is?" the boy said. "It don't have no beginnin'," he said, "and it don't have no endin'."

ONE DAY Doyle stopped by the library down in the city square and got the *Official Encyclopedia of Baseball* down off the shelf. "Might know you'd be the first one comin' and grabbin' that thing," Miss Mamie Jowers said, chuckling. "Thass the brand new one, just come in this morning, right hot off the presses, as they say."

"Thanks," Doyle said. He flipped it open, flipping through until he found the right page. He sat down at a table. "Luscious 'Luke' Easter. BL TR, 6'4-1/2", 240 lbs., b. Aug. 4, 1921, St. Louis, Mo., d. March 29, 1979, Euclid, Ohio." Doyle felt his stomach sink and then turn over. *1979!* Just the past spring. All of a sudden he remembered something, remembering reading it in the paper. It came back to him in a rush. Luke Easter had been a bank guard or something like that and he been shot and killed in a hold-up. And it had happened on March 29, just the past spring. Doyle scanned Easter's statistics; his career in the big leagues more or less paralleled Doyle's in the minors. Easter had been a rookie with Cleveland at the age 28. All those years in the Negro leagues. He looked again. March 29, 1979!

EASTER was sitting by himself at the end of the dugout, and Doyle sat down next to him. Doyle had a half-filled pint of bourbon in his back pocket, and it made a gentle clunk on the bench. "How you doin'?" he said.

"All right," Easter said.

"Listen," Doyle said, after a minute, "I been meanin' to talk to you."

The boy said nothing.

"I been talking to Larry Peevy down at Sweetwater, he's an old friend o mine," Doyle said. Peevy was the high school coach down there. "He tells me you just appeared, just showed up one day and went out for the team. But you didn't graduate or nothin'. He check for me. There ain't any record of you bein' in any classes. He said you was just there."

"Yeah, I played ball."

"Uh-huh," Doyle said. "Listen —"

"Lemme ast you somethin'," Easter said. Doyle waited. "Do you think it's just a accident that there's *three* outs in an inning?"

"Well..." Doyle said.

"And three bases. And there's nine innings, and nine players on each team. Divide that nine by three and you come out three, so that every man can come to bat a minimum of *three* times in a game. Tell me, is that just a accident?"

"It's the way the game's played," Doyle said.

"That's what I say," Easter said. He stood up; he was on deck, and he started to swing a couple of bats, and Doyle watched him. He got out a fresh matchstick and stuck it in his mouth. He watched Easter stroll to the plate and line the first pitch over the right field fence.

"Another one for Leroy," Sammy Jackson said, next to Doyle. Leroy Seales was a little boy who lived in a white house just beyond the right field fence; he had a dog named Major that he'd trained to chase baseballs and fetch them back under the house, where nobody could get at them. Leroy sold them back to Doyle by the dozen count.

DOYLE didn't mention a word to anyone about all his confusion about the two Luke Easters. Nobody else seemed to notice it, not even Alston Elledge, who wrote up the games for the Hammond Times and was the official scorer. Alston was quite a baseball fan, and he knew a lot about the game, and there was no way he couldn't have heard of Luke Easter, but he didn't let on if he had. Doyle didn't like Alston a whole lot, so their conversations were limited anyway, but a conversation they'd had recently bothered Doyle. Some scout, who claimed to be representing Kansas City, showed up one night with a radar gun to clock Buddy Koch's fast ball, and he sat up top with Alston. Bull Willingham, the Rebels' catcher, had taken to wearing an inch and a half thick sponge when Buddy pitched, and that night Buddy gave up one hit, a little infielder dribbler that was one of those accidental shames, because Buddy was throwing so hard. They couldn't touch him, and the ball was always popping out of Bull's mitt halfway to the mound. After the game, Doyle stopped Alston. "How fast was he throwin'?" he said.

"79 tops, and that was the first inning," Alston said.

"Shit," Doyle said "Somethin's wrong with that little sumbitch's gun."

"I don't know," Alston said.

"Hell, Alston, you saw him. He was throwin' at least ninety."

"Maybe I saw it, maybe I didn't," Alston said. "Anyhow, it don't show in the boxscore."

"What the hell are you talkin' about?" Doyle said.

"Just what I said, you see it, you know it, you can believe it or not."

Doyle squinted at him. *What the hell?* he thought. "How you like my first baseman?" Doyle said.

Alston glanced at the score book. "Three for five," he said and bustled off, like he was headed for some important appointment or something. He also had not seemed to notice that there was a yellow butterfly sitting on his right shoulder.

DOYLE knew he should start worrying more the first morning he woke up with that dry, familiar ache, and fixed himself a quick drink first thing. But this time he was going to handle it. Things were going too well for him. Things were not right. Nothing was wrong, but things were not right. In Andalusia one night, Sammy Jackson was thrown out at the plate trying to score from second on a short single up the middle. The score was tied at the time, and neither team got any more runs, but when the game was over, the Rebels had won, 3-2. "Somethin's wrong somewhere," Doyle was saying to McInnis, the other manager; "look at the scorebook again."

"Quit bitchin', Doyle, you won," McInnis said.

"But Jackson was thrown out at the plate, it was, look, look here," Doyle said, grabbing the book. "In the third inning, right here."

"Yeah, but Saunders scored on the sacrifice in the sixth." Doyle looked at the scoreboard. There was a run up there, top of the sixth. He looked at the scoreboards again. "Well, it ain't in here."

"Sure , it is," McInnis said.

"Look, goddamit," Doyle said.

"I already looked, I don't need to look again."

"Well then, to hell with it," Doyle said.

THEN one day Bull Willingham mashed his finger; he was a mechanic during the day and Doyle's only catcher.

"Don't worry," Easter told Doyle. A skinny kid named Peter McMillan showed up at the ballfield that night, fully dressed in a Rebel uniform, and caught a perfect game, and Doyle never saw him again.

"Hey, listen," Doyle said to Luke. They were standing down the right field line. Doyle had been hitting fungoes, and Luke was just watching. "Listen, I know your secret." He peered at Luke, but nothing showed on his face.

"What you mean?"

"Just what I say, I know your secret. You're Luke Easter."

"Ain't I told you I is?"

"Listen," Doyle said, leaning closer. "Tell me, how come nobody ever remarked about the McMillan boy, asked where he come from or where he went?"

"How come you astin me?"

"Cause you know, that's why."

"I done tole you what I know."

"Yeah, three, three, three, I don't want to hear all that again."

"All right," Luke said.

AT THE end of July they were eight games out in front, and the way they were going nobody could catch them. Doyle felt good about that, but still uneasy. Jack Cotton sat behind the screen, and every time Doyle looked over that way, he got a big grin and a thumbs up sign. ("Did you ever wonder about where that McMillan boy came from?" Doyle had asked Cotton one night, trying to be casual, and Cotton had said, "What McMillan boy?")

"I hope the hell you ain't plannin' on quittin', or leavin' me," Doyle said to Luke.

"Naw, I ain't," he said.

Doyle looked hard at him. The light in the dugout was dim, the players on the field pale figures dancing about. Doyle was a little drunk. He could hear the buzz of the crowd, one of the big crowds they were attracting now. "You think we gone go all the way?"

"Yep," Luke said. "You can count on it. All the way."

"All the way to Sumter State?"

"Like I say, you can count on it. Believe it or not."

Doyle squinted at Luke Easter in the dimness. He took a sip from his bottle.

"Look yonder," Luke said, pointing, and Doyle looked out toward center field. The whole outfield was aswarm with yellow butterflies, but nobody else seemed to notice.

THE NIGHT of the yellow butterflies was one of the largest crowds to ever watch a Black Belt League game in Hammond. The Rebels beat Tuscaloosa, 5-1, to clinch the pennant, and later went on to beat the Cullman White Sox four straight in the state series. Doyle Sprayberry, the next spring, coached the Sumter State Teachers College Angels, and his first baseman was a kid named Luke Easter.

But that night, the night of the yellow butterflies, two old men who'd been watching baseball all their lives were talking as they walked home from the game.

"They sho nuff *used* to have crowds like that," one of them said.

"Good ball game, *good* game," the other said.

"But that was a big crowd. Lots of people out there. Only other crowd I can remember that big was one, oh, musta been back around, let's see, years ago, back around 1949 or so. Everybody went to the games then, wasn't no TV or nothing, and there was this fellow travelled around all over, called hisself The Great Muscontoni, or somethin' like that, and he'd go around to see these ball parks, you know, and what he'd do, is he carried this coffin around with him, and he'd make a big to-do and all, and during the game they'd bury him out in center field and then dig him up at the end of the game. The Great Muscontoni, that's what he called hisself. Anyhow, he come here to Hammond and sho nuff, had a big hole dug way out against the fence in center field, you know, went through this whole rigmarole and ceremony and long about the fourth inning they buried him. Well sir, when the game was over, they dug the sonofabitch up, and the damn fool was deader'n hell."

"No kiddin'," the other old man said. "Well, I'll be damned."

"It was somethin'," the old man said, walking through the shower of yellow butterflies.

Old Wars and
New Sorrow

(First Published in "The Sucarnochee Review", 1974)

TO THE other curates, even to the Rector at St. John's, Mrs. Bridges was a chore; to Simmons White she was a duty and a care. In a ninth floor room overlooking Government Street, she lay in her tall bed like a queen: Mrs. Ward Bridges, oldest living communicant of the Parish, wealthiest. She had entered the room almost fourteen years ago, claiming a heart condition, and though the doctors had found nothing wrong with her, had remained there ever since, a monument, a curiosity, so that passersby on busy Government below pointed out the windows of her room to visitors as routinely as they pointed to the azaleas lining the boulevard or to Bienville's statue in the park.

"So, young man," she had said to him on his first visit to her. "*You* are that new curate at St. John's." She sniffed, peering down at him, her lips smacking slightly, little discs of rouge on each cheek. She wore a lacy bedcap. "Father White, I believe it is," she said.

He chuckled nervously. "Well, *Mr.*, or just Simmons, will do all right,"

"Hmm," she said.

"Actually, I do prefer Mr. to Father, if you don't mind." He smiled.

Her expression didn't change. She lay with her arms folded in her lap. "Well, I *do* mind, but never mind," she said. She looked away, out the broad windows. Workmen were methodically putting up bunting for Mardi Gras in a steady, drizzling rain. "Rain, you see," she said, suddenly, "ugly, winter rain, I do not miss. Rain has not touched my head in a number of years. I suppose you know that. But I have a lovely view of Mardi Gras, a much better view than I ever had in the old days, even when we rented a room in the Battle House. I was always much too drunk to see a parade by the time it came by. Several times they were gone before we even knew it."

Simmons chuckled appreciatively.

"You find that funny?" she said, swinging her head slowly around to face him again.

"Well..." He shifted uncomfortably in the hard, hospital chair.

"'Hmm," she said. "Yes, I suppose you would." She glared harshly at him. "How old *are* you?" she asked bluntly.

"I...well, I'm thirty one," he said.

"Hmm," she said. "Hmm." She smacked her lips. "Well, you have two years left before they crucify you." She cackled softly, her eyes watering; he could see her yellowed dentures. He tried to laugh with her. His smile, self-conscious and rigid, felt frozen on his face. "Now...now," she said, gasping for breath. "that *is* funny, wouldn't you say?"

"Moderately so, I suppose," he said. Her laughter stopped abruptly, and she squinted at him. Her expression returned to her original waiting gaze. He had no intention of letting her bully him. John Porter, his rector, earlier that day, had been enigmatic about her. "Don't get the idea that we're, that anyone's courting her for her money," he'd said, sitting behind the desk in his study, wreaths of gray smoke from his pipe curling about his silvery hair. He shook a match out and tossed it into an ashtray. "All that is, well, taken care of. Look at the memorial plaque on that Flentrop organ, for example, next time you're in there."

"I've noticed," he said.

Porter puffed on his pipe; he was handsome, fiftyish, given to herringbone tweed jackets that made his clerical collar look like a turtleneck sweater. Rumor in the Diocese was that he would be offered the Bishopric of Louisiana but would turn it down to stay at St. John's, the largest and richest Parish in Alabama. "There are, of course, some members of the vestry who think that's what we're doing, catering to an eccentric old woman in the hopes she'll leave us a bundle, which is fine with them, but actually, and I want you to understand this, we are visiting her, on *her* schedule, because she is sick."

"But I thought you said there was nothing wrong with her, that..."

Porter regarded him over the expensive pipe clenched between his teeth. "Wouldn't you say that a person who cuts herself off from all real human contact for fourteen years is sick?" he said.

"Well," Simmons said, thoughtfully. He cleared his throat. "There *are* historical and traditional precedents."

Porter laughed. "Mrs. Bridges is no nun, Simmons," he said, "which I'm sure you'll find out soon enough."

HE SAT there, curiously inspecting the old woman. Her face was open, simply waiting. She reminded him of the collective faces of a congregation, preparing themselves for the sermon. *Speak to me if you like,* her face said, *say whatever you wish to say; I may listen, I may not, it matters not a whole lot in the long run anyway but I'll be polite.* When he didn't speak, she turned back to the window, her jaw working rhythmically. "Moderately so," she muttered, a whisper.

How old are you? he wanted to ask.

"If they used the same sort of stuff, crepe paper and such, that they used when I was younger, it would be bleeding all over the place in this rain," she said, suddenly.

"Beg your pardon?"

"The workmen," she said, motioning toward the window. Her watery eyes fixed on him again. "It *is* getting close to Mardi Gras, you know, or don't you use the same calendar anymore? Or does it have a different name? Or perhaps you've done away with it altogether?"

He smiled. "I just didn't follow what you said."

"Oh?" She pointed to him; her gestures seemed exaggerated, grotesque. It was her posture, the hospital bed, the quiet. "It was the reference to bleeding, wasn't it?"

"Mrs. Bridges, I —"

"Paper bleeds, Father White, just like people," she said.

He stiffened. "*Mr.* White, if you don't mind. I'm nobody's father."

"You are the Vicar of the Father of us all," the old woman said. She was rigid in the bed, glaring at him, "you sniveling, prissy little son of a bitch."

Simmons' mouth parted in shock. They stared at one another for a moment, then the old woman smiled. She cackled again, softly. "Got you with that one, didn't I?" she said. The smile faded from her face. "You, my dear young man," she said, "are a priest of the Anglican Communion, and as such, are addressed as Father. Though I must admit, as the years pass, and the parade of young wet-behind-the-ears seminarians that passes through the room grows longer and longer, it does seem a bit ludicrous, at least from up here."

Simmons chuckled. "Well, I certainly didn't expect a lecture when I dropped in to see you," he said.

"Oh? What *did* you expect?"

He coughed. "A friendly chat, I suppose," he said.

"Didn't ole Pretty Boy Porter prepare you for me?" she said.

"We talked about you, yes," he said. He wanted to be straightforward, honest. He waited.

She smiled at him.

"Well," she said, after a minute, "It was a lovely little chat, wasn't it? Do come again."

THE MARDI GRAS celebration had begun, with the first parades. Simmons had to search for a parking place; he finally wedged his Volkswagen between two larger, shinier cars, into a space that was really not a space, on a narrow side street near the hospital. The cobblestones were shiny with drizzle. The weather people were promising a wetter than usual spring, and in Mobile that meant very wet indeed. As he walked along, hunched against the dampness, he was thinking of Clem Whitten, another curate at St. John's. Clem's "beat," as he called it, was the waterfront. He claimed to have been thrown out of more bars than anyone else in Mobile, and he had once wound up in jail; many of the older and most loyal communicants had been outraged, and the Bishop had had to be called in. It had been handled quietly, mainly because when Clem did bring in the drunks and prostitutes, he took them to the Church of The Holy Comforter, a crumbling, ancient red brick and exquisitely beautiful little church in the slums near the docks. The Rector there was an alcoholic who had once been Rector of All Saint's Church, the second largest parish in the Diocese.

"So, you've drawn old Bridges," Clem said, sitting slouched on his couch, sipping a beer. The remains of a sent-in pizza lay in their grease-spotted box on the coffee table. "That one's a case for the books." He belched; Clem wore little rimless glasses and a baggy gray sweater, and his slightly graying hair was cut long. "It should be good training for you, Simmons," he said. "You look the type, you'll get a little church up in the Black Belt or the Delta and spend your afternoons coddling old ladies who get all teary-eyed over the 1928 Prayer Book and who don't know or understand a shittin' thing about it in the first place." He belched again and took another drink from the can.

Simmons crossed his legs, then uncrossed them. He didn't especially like Clem; he reminded him too much of so many men he had known in seminary, the easy cynicism, the nonchalant liberalism. Simmons had a dogged stoicism toward Clem; he tolerated him because he was the voice of what he had heard with deadening regularity for fifteen years.

"She *is* interesting," he said, searching in his pockets for his cigarettes.

"She is dead," Clem said. "Kyrie Eleison, Christi Eleison, Kyrie Eleison." He made the sign of a cross wearily in the air with the beer can. "*Life* crawls in the gutters of this stinkin' town, life's a dollar-and-a-half bottle of Red Dagger wine, a five dollar blow job in a doorway. Life is what's left after some poor bastard's had the shit kicked completely out of him, Simmons, but what would *you* know about it?"

SIMMONS sat in the sterile, gleaming, brightly lit hospital room. They could hear the sounds of the bands, the shouts and squeals from the parade below them.

"You keep coming here out of duty," she said, suddenly, an edge of bitterness in her voice.

"No, I come here because I want to," he said. The question made Simmons uneasy. In his quiet moments, his habitual hour of meditation before sleep, he had been troubled by doubts about his motivations toward her. He found her room a refuge.

"Wouldn't you rather be down there, in all the excitement, getting nicked in the forehead by a piece of hard candy thrown by some drunken member of the Junior Chamber of Commerce all dressed up in a clown suit?"

He laughed. "No," he said, chuckling, "no, I wouldn't. Actually, I'm afraid I get a bit bored by the parades."

"Ahhhhh," she said. "But Father, aren't they a celebration of life?"

The word pierced his forehead like a hot needle. *Life*. The word echoed behind his eyes, in Clem's high, sharp voice. *What would you know about it?* The sounds of the bands, the Mardi Gras, were distant, tinny, far away.

"They have..." he said, almost stuttering. "They've lost much of their meaning, over the years I mean." He shifted in the chair. The textured plastic bit into his thin buttocks. He glanced slyly at Mrs. Bridges; the old woman was smiling at him, knowingly.

"We have a great deal in common, you and me, Father," she said, "up to a point." She lay, her arms crossed in her lap, with a contentment that was almost maddening to him. "Of course," she went on, "that's something, life I mean, that I've resigned from. I lie here, and my most comforting moments are when I can imagine very vividly that I'm lying in my coffin." He realized that he was gaping at her, astonished. "Didn't you know, dear, that I've received Extreme Unction, nine and a half years ago, to be exact, and I'm simply waiting, waiting for my heart to crack. Growing a bit impatient, I must say!"

"But," he said, "but there's nothing wrong with your heart."

She sighed, she turned and looked lazily out the window. "Must I hear the same old hymn?" The room was quiet except for the muted parade sounds. "Hopefully this will be the last Goddamned Mardi Gras I will have to endure. I long for Ash Wednesday." She sighed again and lay her head back on the pillow and closed her eyes. He started to speak, to say something. He had no idea what. It was as though he were sitting with a corpse. She went on: "My family came over on the Mayflower. They actually did, though I know that if everyone who claimed *that* were telling the truth the little vessel would have sunk a hundred feet off the coast of England. And my family spent all those years, generations and generations of the faithful heart, laying up for themselves treasures on earth, and I'm all that is left. I'm the last." She opened her eyes and looked steadily at him. "We never had children, by choice. Mr. Bridges was an idiot, I could not have borne his idiot children into this world. Have you taken the vow of chastity, Father?"

Simmons' first impulse was to blurt that it was none of her business. He sat in momentary confusion. His cool, thin fingers rubbed his eyelids. "Yes," he said. His hands trembled.

"Good," she said.

"It was not an easy decision," he said.

"Of course not. Very few decisions that matter at all are easy. Except, of course, for that mass of crazy people down there," she motioned to the window, "who think they are alive and are deluding themselves into thinking they're celebrating that fact." She sighed and lay back. She lay propped, her hands folded, the old fashioned make-up powdery in the harsh, fluorescent lighting. He sat staring at her. She was like a statue. After a minute, she said, without opening her eyes, "I'm tired now. I must sleep."

THE CARNIVAL around him seemed to spin inside Simmons' head. People shoved and elbowed; children fought over bits of brightly colored hard candy that showered over the crowds and rolled and bounced on the sidewalks and in the gutters. A gaudy green and gold float was going by, a king and queen of some sort, of some ball, perched at the rear, girls in long, antebellum dresses surrounding them, waving at the masses lining the parade routes. High school bands, between the floats, played cacophonously, Sousa marches clashing with peppy versions of popular tunes, snare drums rattling in different cadences. Simmons pulled his lined raincoat tighter around his neck. Over everything hovered the distant, murky smell of the bay, mingling with greasy hot dogs and popcorn, damp wool, unclean bodies.

On and on, day after day, the parades moved toward their climax. Simmons knew that he was seeing them with new eyes. He could remember being brought as a child the two hundred miles to see them, to sit on his father's shoulders and gape at the wondrousness of it all, the color, the excitement. Now the costumes looked tawdry, the pathetic bands with their banners proudly proclaiming their origins merely tacky. He had not understood their meaning then. And later still, as an adolescent, he had marveled at the mystery, the strange reverence that would shade his mother's voice when she pronounced it: *Shrove Tuesday*. "Today, Simmons, is Shrove Tuesday." They would go to the Parish Hall and stuff themselves with pancakes, cooked by the men of the parish, grinning and red-faced in their aprons, jokes about the bottles kept out of sight in the kitchen. Afterwards, his father would get drunk, and his parents would argue deeply into the night, he lying under the blanket, hearing their muffled voices in the front of the house. And then there was church, always, the next day. The kneeling, exotic mystery of the ashes. The somber strangeness of the service always frightened him. Then, as a teenager, it embarrassed him, and he loudly gave up cigarettes when he did not smoke, gum when he disliked chewing it anyway.

As a young man, the priesthood had seemed to him a natural and comforting calling. His father had died when he was in high school, and his mother was embittered and selfish, refusing to understand his love of books, the fascination that poetry, that words, that ritual itself held for him. He found great comfort in the aesthetics of his church. He had no close friends, had never been fond of girls, and his mother was suspicious of him.

"I don't think it's natural at all, it ain't healthy," she'd said to him.

"I think Father would be proud of me," he said.

She snorted. "Your daddy was never proud of nothin' but his own self, all his life, God rest his soul." He turned away from her; he had meant — by "Father" — the priest who had presided over his confirmation.

Simmons thought that the happiest day of his life had been the day, after four years at a small college near his home, that he'd gotten the letter of acceptance from seminary. Merely the idea of being a priest had sustained him through all his adult years. The idea made him feel secure, and safe.

HE MOVED through the crowd, one hand jammed into his pocket, the other holding the coat at his chest. He wondered, momentarily, if he were subconsciously covering his collar. No one paid any attention to him. The delirium of the celebration seemed to increase around him. He felt repulsed by it, apart. Isolated from the harsh laughter, the noises, the joy of these beings that surrounded him. He longed for a quiet cigarette, a stiff drink. But he wouldn't go into a bar; there would be people there. He thought of Mrs. Bridges, lying propped up in her bed, gazing down upon the spectacle below her, the frenzy of which he was a part, the benign, contented smile on her ancient face. Had he been alone, at that moment, he would have wept. Simmons abruptly moved away from the parade, back toward his car. Down a narrow, dim side street, he passed an old Negro man, drunk, urinating against the wall of a building. "Hey Mistuh," he said, "Hey, you got a few dollahs you could let a old man have? Huh? Hey Mistuh." Simmons walked faster, away from him. The voice followed him. "Hey. Hey Mistuh."

SIMMONS KNELT behind the altar rail, his head bowed. His eyes were fixed on the gray carpet before him. The huge old church was chilly and dank, and the afternoon sun barely penetrated the clouds, a thick, obtuse light behind the two-story-high stained glass windows. The priest's voice droned on, the collective voices of the Communicants joining him now and again, and Simmons mumbled the responses into his chest. "Behold, I was shapen in wickedness, and in sin hath my mother conceived me. Thou shalt make me hear of joy and gladness, That the bones which thou hast broken may rejoice." The words, in Simmons' ears, were dry and faint as in a dream. The church was three-quarters full, and against the silence behind the service Simmons could hear muffled coughing, the squeaking of the kneelers under shifting knees. "The sacrifice of

God is a troubled spirit: a broken and contrite heart, O God, shalt thou not despise." Simmons hunched in prayer; his body, his shoulders were tense; he knew he would tire of the kneeling, but he could not relax. He prayed for the soul of Mrs. Bridges. "Glory be to the Father, and to..." He crossed himself. "As it was in the beginning..." John Porter's voice was rounded, practiced, echoing in the high rafters and beams. "Lord, have mercy upon us. *Christ, have mercy upon us*. Lord, have mercy upon us."

Simmons' mind would blank, and then return to the liturgy; it was by turns strange and unfamilar, and then there came the ashes; he sensed the Priest moving down the row of curates. Stunned and rigid, he felt Porter's thumb on his forehead, pressing hard, the black cross: "Remember, O man, from dust thou art, and to dust thou shalt return." He bowed low, crossing himself; his eyes blurred. He could see Porter crossing to the acolytes, the back of his plain, unadorned white cassock. He swallowed, hard, almost a gulp, and he sensed Clem Whitten, next to him, sneak a look at him.

Then they began to come down, moving quietly down the aisles, damp shoes shuffling, and Simmons remained kneeling, locked in place as though in a vise. The other curates had risen, accepting the silver patens of ashes from the acolytes, lining up behind Porter. Simmons could not move. An acolyte, a hideously fat little boy with new pimples, stood in front of him, holding the gleaming silver saucer of ashes out to him the boy smirked, suppressed a grin. Simmons could not remember his name, only that his adolescent hips were awkwardly rounded and girlish under his cassock and he was whiny and petulant, spoiled, detested by the other young people in the church. Simmons shook his head at the boy, glaring at him. Then the boy grinned, hesitated; he crossed back to the altar, replaced the paten and went back to his place, kneeling, staring across at Simmons, who knelt alone as Porter and the other curates moved down the altar rail. "Remember, O man... Remember, O man..." Businessmen in flannel suits, teenagers in jeans and sweaters, women dressed in every-day, some holding children, wide-eyed and innocent. Old men and women whose bones popped as they knelt. Some unkempt, unshaven, smelling of booze and the early spring dampness of the outside day. The black crosses went on and on.

Simmons' heart raced; his chest constricted, and his forehead ached. He could not quiet his trembling. His brain, his mind, was not his to control. Images of his past besieged him, his loneliness as a child, the coldness of his intellectual training, his utter failure to know compassion, to even understand what it was. His senses were so acute that the words of the service still echoed in his mind, and he could smell the people, their human stench. *Thou sparest when we deserve punishment, and in thy wrath thinkest upon mercy. I had not thought death had undone so many.* He choked back a wave of nausea. "Remember, O man..." The illusion of fire consumed the images in his mind's eye, and Simmons felt himself wafted away, soaring, drugged with his own saliva collecting in his throat; he swallowed, and his mouth was as dry and brittle as a wafer. The wine, he knew, would be vinegar; and the damp air would scald his body with a fierceness that he had never known. He knew, in that moment, the depths of his own sin, and his body shook with the terror of the knowledge; he had forsaken, and he would know no mercy. He had not understood, *which passeth all understanding.* From the cold, detached refuge of Art; of Dante, of Eliot, with an act of will that took all the strength he possessed, he forced his mind back into the church, felt the thin kneeler beneath him, the sheen of perspiration beneath his robes, felt the heat of his clasped hands. And he saw, with the clarity of a fine photograph, the image of the hospital room, hovering high over the noisy and lively crowds in the streets, the masks and their wafer-candies.

IN THE Sacristy, after it was over, speaking was only in hushed, hesitant whispers. There was none of the usual post-service joking, no playful remarks. Porter looked curiously at Simmons, but he said nothing, and Simmons knew, could easily predict, that he would be summoned for a conference, a chat. No one spoke to him. He disrobed hurriedly, not meeting the eyes of any of his fellows, and got his coat. He felt oddly apart from them, removed, as though he had been made privy to some knowledge forever closed to them. His communion with them up to now had been false, a charade on his part, and he did not know if he could discuss it with any of them, dissect it with any other human being. His tongue still tasted faintly of the wine, and he buttoned his coat, hesitating for just a moment, then went back up the hall, out through the Chancel. He stood for a moment, looking at the bronze cross over the altar, the old wooden railing worn smooth by thousands, maybe millions, of hands.

He stood for a long time, in the silence, looking at the image of his salvation. He had never been, was not now, complete enough to truly pray. One day, perhaps, he would be strong enough to be. To die, and to live. Then he went up the center aisle, through the Nave, savoring the quiet emptiness of the church, toward the heavy, carved wooden doors.

Outside, the chill startled him. He stood on the steps for a moment, lighting a cigarette. The somber sky had started its drizzle, and he pulled the collar tighter around his neck. He started down the damp sidewalk. An old man sat hunched on a bus-bench at the corner; Simmons could see that his frazzled overcoat was tied with a string, was torn and dusty. Gray whiskers unevenly covered his chin. He was smiling, stumps of blackened teeth. A greasy, black cross was scrawled crookedly across his forehead.

"You got a little money for some wine, Father?" the old man said. His voice was hoarse, a spectral whisper. Simmons fumbled for his billfold and gave the old man two crumpled dollar bills.

"Bless you, Father, bless you," the old man said, grinning, sly, satisfied. His eyes were joking, cunning and crafty. He snickered.

Simmons moved quickly and awkwardly away from him; he stood for a moment on the corner. Blocks away, over the still-leafless trees, he could see the hospital rising into the mist.

Passin' Side/
Suicide

(First Published in "The Alabama Literary Review", 2002)

G LORY SANDERS is a friend of mine. She's a drunk like me, only she calls herself a "grateful recovering alcoholic". She hauls me to the AA meeting in the basement of the Episcopal church over in Talladega every Thursday night, and when she gets up to talk that's what she calls herself. Glory runs the Water's Edge Bait Shop on county road 20. Glory has been around the bases a few times. She's been there and back, as they say.

I'm sittin' in the little back room café at the Water's Edge, that looks out over the lake. I'm drinking coffee and she's behind the counter, leaning on it, smoking a cigarette. Glory's always telling me to get a job. That's what everybody says to me, get a job. "You need to get a job," she says. "You need to go to a meetin' every day, ninety meetins in ninety days." I tell her I ain't the meeting type. They made me swear when I was leaving the treatment center that I'd go to at least three meetings a week. I raised my right hand up and swore to God, knowing right then I wasn't going to do it. No way. But I figured they wouldn't let me out if I didn't say it.

"When you going to —" Glory begins. She's leaning on the counter.

"Don't start," I say.

"Jesus, Robert," she says. "I'm just tryin' to..."

She don't finish. She calls me Robert. She knows I don't like for people to call me Bob, but she always used to call me Bob before I went to treatment. Now she calls me Robert. Glory was there the night the cops took me in, after that fight at the Silver Moon Café. She goes around with the cops on Saturday nights, looking for drunks she can save.

"I'm a honorary deputy," she says, "on a mission of mercy." They put me in the county jail and then took me to a psycho ward on the top floor of Brookwood Hospital in the city. The windows had bars on them. After a few days they gave me a choice: thirty days in jail or thirty days at a treatment center out in Warrior. I thought it was a no-brainer.

Glory was waiting for me when I got out. "I'm your sponsor," she said.

"Like hell you are," I said.

There's a television in the café. Me and Glory are watching So You Want to be a Millionaire. Half way through the program she says, "These people are dumb."

"Dumb as a post," I say.

Glory is looking at me funny. "What are you, forty-four? Forty-five? What?"

"You got it right," I say.

"What?"

"Both."

She looks at me like that explains something to her. She turns back to the TV set. I have two birth certificates. I guess I'm two different people. One of them says I was born on April 9, 1936. On that one my mother's name is Annabelle Pleasants, and the father is listed as "unknown." I am Robert Pleasants. On the other one, dated April 6, 1935, my mother's name is Annabelle P. Fosque, and the father is Ralph Fosque. On that one my name is listed as Robert Fosque. "We was never married," my mother told me. "It was the fifties, you had to do that." "Do what?" I asked. I was about ten years old at the time she talked to me about it. "You know," she said. I didn't know. But I didn't say anything. "He was a real bastard," she said, "you're better off not ever knowing him."

"I don't give a shit," I said, and lit up a Camel. I kept them rolled in the sleeve of my white T shirt.

I have always gone by the name of Robert Pleasants. It has never made two hoots in hell to me that I've got two birth certificates, two names.

"Shit," Glory says, her eyes on the screen, "the next time I see forty-five it'll be a hunnert and forty-five!"

If you ain't a drunk, you don't know what the Big Book is. Unless you're married to a drunk, I guess, or living with one. It tells you all you need to know about recovery. It's the AA Bible. It lays out the twelve steps for you, right there. Glory keeps after me, and I'm on step nine. Sometimes I do them half-ass, but I try to do them. "Seek out those people you've hurt with your drinking and make amends to em," Glory says. "Just one'll do. It'd take you the rest of your life to find 'em all. Just one. Find 'em and..."

"... And what?"

"Say you're sorry. Ask 'em to forgive you," she says. "It ain't easy."

"Shit." I say.

I think about Jolene. She would have to be the one, I guess. She was too young for me from the start, but she was something wonderful I just couldn't let alone. I could tell her mother thought I was trash. She didn't like me from go. They lived in a little white-washed frame house over on the other side of Pachuta, near Bay Springs. Jolene worked at the Ritz Twin Theater in Pachuta, selling tickets. I thought I might like to spend the rest of my life with Jolene, and when I thought that it scared the hell out of me. She would get off at eleven and we'd drive out to the quarry in my pickup and spread a quilt and make love under the moon. She was sweet as the inside of a ripe pineapple. Salty and juicy as a plum in June. She was not even yet twenty, but she was wise. She knew what she was doing.

"Why you come sniffin' round me, old man?" she would say, running her fingers over my bald head, giggling. I'd root like an old hog, and she'd squeal like a piglet. Lordy. I get horny just thinking about it.

"We thought you was in jail," Jolene's mother says, when she finally gets to the door. The front yard has old tires painted white half buried in the dirt on both sides of the front walkway. There's one of these old bottle trees in the front yard. I knock and knock. When she opens the door she just stands there looking at me. Her name is Sheila. Her expression don't change at all. Her eyes droop like wilted blossoms. She's got on a pair of red shorts and a T shirt that says SHUT UP AND PITCH. She props herself against the door jamb with one arm. She's got her other hand on her hip, the fingers of that hand holding a long thin cigarette with a little string of smoke rising straight up like the thing is hanging from the ceiling. Just stands there, like that, until all she says is, "We thought you was in jail."

"Nope," I say. "Jolene here?"

She don't say anything, but her lip curls down. She looks tired enough to've been digging ditches. She's skinny as a preacher bug but she's got this little belly, like half a soccer ball. It looks like it don't belong on her, like she borrowed it from some fat person. She's a lot closer to my age than Jolene is.

The living room smells like cigarette smoke and used up butane. It smells like cooking grease and dust. One great big old vinyl recliner. One of those console televisions that you don't ever see any more, that sits on the floor. There used to be a sofa with an old blanket thrown over it, but it's gone. I could smell coffee. These folks drink a lot of coffee, I remember.

"She ain't here," she says, after she's already motioned me in.

"Where she at?"

"She's gone."

I look off out the side window. There are two lawn chairs out there, with the yellow and white webbing faded and broke and hanging down. There is a Snapper lawn mower and a charcoal grill, both gathering rust. I see clumps of crabgrass in the yard. I remember then how the grass smells when the sun's been on it a while. How the sun makes you smell the dirt, the earth. Ever since I got out of treatment I think about things like that.

"I ain't got no significant other," I told my counselor, when I was in the treatment center. His name is John Berry. He's a drunk, too, sixteen years sober. They want me to invite somebody to come for family week. They tell me I need to.

"You must have somebody," John says.

"No. You got the information right there." I point to this clipboard he's drumming his fingers on on his desk. It's the long form I filled out when they first admitted me. He holds a ball point pen in the fingers of his other hand. They are delicate and slim, like a woman's. He's all man, though, a wiry son-of-a-bitch. He don't let you get away with nothing. You can't shit him. I have tried, the whole time I've been here. "Mother dead. No sisters and brothers." I say.

"What about your father?"

I laugh. I have told them every story in the book about my father. I told them he was a black man, working in my mother's yard. I told them he was a Gypsy, passing through. That he was this rich doctor in Mountain Brook. That he played ball for the Yankees. I passed the time thinking up shit to tell them about my father. I told my therapy group my father was George Wallace. Half of them believe me. They had burned up so many brain cells they'd believe anything.

"Okay," he says. "But there must be somebody." I think of Jolene. It's been about a year then since I've seen her. I sit there seeing her in my mind's eye. She ain't what you'd call a knockout, but she's a pretty thing. Her mouth is too big. Her eyes are too close together. But she got great hair, and legs. She's got legs so great they're prettier than eight miles of new road. You never saw better legs than Jolene's got. What got me, though, was how she always knew what I was thinking, and it made her laugh. She would look at me — she has these really black eyes, like marbles — and I would be thinking of something funny to say and she'd be already laughing. Like that.

"No," I say. "there ain't nobody. Period."

"Okay," he says.

"You got yourself a loner here, John-boy," I say. "I can take care of myself."

"Yeah," he says, "right."

Me and Jolene were easy together. We could just sit for a long time without even talking. "You're old enough to be her father," her mother said to me.   "So?" I said, and Sheila cut her eyes at me. Her droop-tired eyes. Jolene's daddy is a welder, works at TCI in Birmingham. Him and me used to drink beer together. We'd smoke some weed, visit the craps game down at Zorba's corner. Named Sid, and he's restless as I am. He works all the time, ain't hardly ever at home. "I ain't never thought of myself as old," I said to her, "as old enough to be anything."

"Jolene wants a life, a family," she said.

"I ain't standin' in her way, am I?" I said.

She told Jolene I'm a sorry one. Jolene laughs about it. She puts her hand on my arm and holds it there, leaves it there. She just looks at me. Her eyes smile at me.

I am at the Silver Moon Café, a few months before the night of the fight that got me sent up to treatment. They call it a café because you can get a hamburger or a platter of greasy fried catfish and hushpuppies, but it's mostly a night club and dance hall. It's got big plate glass windows overlooking the lake. It's got a long bar against one wall and a bandstand and a dance floor. Country bands play here, nobody you ever heard of, and it's always packed to the gills, specially on Friday and Saturday nights. These cowboys and their women come out from Birmingham, and good old boys from out in the county wearing their caterpillar hats and great big silver BAMA belt buckles. College kids come out here sometimes, looking for trouble. Or for women. Same thing.

I'm flying high. Soaked to the ears. This woman, Jesse, is here. She's got eyes so green it sets your teeth on edge just to look at them, married to a mechanic at one of the shops over in Talladega. Her jeans've been painted on and she wears cowboy boots and a little frilly white blouse. You can see her nipples from here. I've danced with her before. It seems like the whole world is loud and drunk and high and happy. The band tonight is called Naked as a Jaybird, and they play all these great old Eagles songs.

I sit and drink my beer and stare at Jesse, until she starts to stare back. I can see those green eyes glowing through the smoke. I don't see her husband. She's with these two women I've seen here before, both about forty, at least ten years older than she is. The three of them get up and dance together, and Jesse keeps looking over at me. I'm breathing smoke and beer vapor, and the band is whacking out on "Take it Easy." Overhead lights spin. Beer signs make these melting drops of colors on the wall across the room. It feels and looks good. Just right.

I'm glad I'm here. This is one place I'm supposed to be, right now, in the whole world. I'm just about to go over when somebody grabs my arm from behind. I turn around and it's Jolene. She's smiling, happy. Laughing. She's got a long-neck Rolling Rock in her hand, waving it in time to the music.

I think: What are you doin'? Checkin up on me! I say, "What the hell are you doin' here?!" I'm thinking, She thinks she owns me. Just let a woman...just let a woman.

I say it real ugly like. "Well? You don't own me, woman," I say.

The grin just disappears from her face, falls away like a lightbulb blowing out.

"I'm sorry," I say, "I don't know you." I say it hard and nasty. "I was just fixin' to dance with somebody," and I walk off and leave her standing there. As I walk over to Jesse, I can still see Jolene's eyes, the way they looked. They are like a little child's that you've disappointed, let down. Jesse sees me coming and stands up. Her body looks fluid, like I would drown in it. I look back and Jolene is gone.

That was the last time I saw her. I think about them eyes now, full of all that hurt, standing here in the living room with her mother. "Well," I say, "you gone tell me where she is, or what?"

"She don't want to see you," she says.

"Now how do you know that?"

"I just do," she says. She's tapping a filter tip cigarette against her thumbnail. "You want some coffee or somethin'?"

"Black," I say. When she goes to get it, I stand there smelling her cigarette smoke. I can taste it in my throat, scalding and spicy, the warm way it swells out your chest. I gave them up. When I got out I just threw my pack in the Coosa River. I figured without booze, I didn't want cigarettes. I want one now, but I won't ask her for one. I'm tense, tight like the skin of a drum.

Sheila brings me my coffee in a blue mug. There is a picture of Jolene on the table in the corner, in her high school cap and gown, that tassle thing hanging down beside her face. She is smiling her easy smile. It's as natural as a breeze, that smile. I realize I ain't seen Sid in months. The house has a feel like he ain't in it anymore. I don't ask.

"I want to tell her I'm sorry," I say. I blow on my coffee, sip it.

"Ha!" she says, "I already told her that." She don't look at me. She sits down in the vinyl recliner. When she brings her cigarette up to her lips I can see her hand trembling. She shakes her head. I can see where her hair is parted on the top, ragged, like when she combed it she was in a hurry. "Sorry is as sorry does," she says.

"I'm serious," I say.

"You think I ain't?" She looks up at me. She's got tears standing in her eyes, and I can see she's really pissed at me. She's really upset. She looks at me like she hates me. "You come in here...You come in here..." she mumbles. Her shoulders slump, just collapse and fall. "I have made my peace, and then you..." She drags on the cigarette and sucks the smoke deep, then blows it out like spitting.

"She's dead," she says then. I don't hear her for a moment. The word goes right by me. Then it comes back around and hits me in the back of the head. My knees go weak.

"What?" I say.

"You heard me," she says, her voice rising to a shriek, "she's dead! Dead! You want me to spell the word for you?" She stands up and turns her back on me. I can't move. I just stand there holding the mug, and I have forgot how to move my arms. I don't know what to say. I don't know what to feel. I think she must be lying to me. I can see the bones in her shoulders, under the thin cloth of the T shirt. I know she ain't lying to me. My mouth goes dry.

"What...what...?" I manage to say. She doesn't answer. I find my voice, but it sounds hollow in my ears, like an echo. "A car wreck, or what?" I say.

"No," she says. "She was pregnant." She turns back around to face me. "She was pregnant, with your child, and she —"

"Wait a minute," I say, "wait a minute now —"

"With your goddam baby, and she wouldn't...she wouldn't..." It feels like the floor moves under my feet, like I'm gone fall, right there. "I tried to get her to have an abortion. I tried to talk to her, make her get rid of it, but no. No! She wouldn't listen to me. 'I'm gonna have it,' she says. 'I want this baby,' she says." She is just looking at me now, her eyes narrow slits. I can see her tears track down her cheeks. She breathes real deep. I'm just hanging there, like in midair. I can't take it in. She looks like she wants to say something else. I can see her brain working behind her eyes. It's like I'm watching a television show or a movie. A long ash falls off her cigarette and she notices it and grinds the butt out in a glass ashtray that's already full. She starts tapping another on her thumbnail.

She takes another deep breath, then another. When she starts talking, her voice sounds calmer, but still tight and dry. "She was staying with my sister out in Center Point," she says. "She got a better job working at Rich's in Century Plaza Mall. Everything was fine, she said. She would come out here and I never saw her so happy. I kept tellin' her she didn't know what she was gettin' into. She didn't care. 'Don't worry Mama,' she'd say, 'I'm happy.' She said she wanted to be a single mother, was looking forward to it. Then somethin' happened. One day she started bleedin'. She was eight months along, and they figured the baby was coming early, so they took her to the hospital. Took her to Medical Center East. Somethin' was bad wrong. The doctors said the baby was dead. They had to operate on her to get it out."

She stops. I can feel my heart beating in my ears. "What happened?" I ask. My mouth has gone completely dry.

"Somethin' went wrong with the anesthetic," she says. She opens her eyes wide. She looks at me like I'm pond scum. "She had a reaction to it. She had these convulsions... She... went into a coma. She never woke up," she says. "And then she died. And I never got to say goodbye to her, and she was all I had, all I ever had."

I don't say anything. I don't think there is anything to say. There is nothing I can dredge up from inside me that would matter at all. She starts to cry, then, just stands there sobbing, and I can see her pale eyes go all opaque, like she's not seeing me any more at all, like she's totally all alone in the room, in the world.

I drive around. There is a lump of cold in my chest. I get on the expressway and drive all the way to the Georgia line, to Tallapoosa, then turn around and come back. Something is burning and smoldering in the back of my brain. I see five thousand billboards advertising whiskey and beer. Every one is like a mouth full that I can taste, and I swallow, and it's only air. I play the radio, but I don't hear it. It's like I keep dozing off from time to time, and I worry that I'll drive off a bridge.

Like I jerk back awake and I'm surprised I'm driving down the road because I've been dreaming. I've been with Jolene, smelling her skin, smelling the soap she used to use. Shampoo that made her hair smell like fresh berries. Then I just feel her there next to me in the truck, sliding over, fitting herself around the gear shift lever, getting close. She's warm. Comfortable and quiet. I miss her now, something terrible.

It gets dark and I'm on the back roads, all the way up in St. Clair County, and I just keep driving. I can't think of anywhere I want to go. And I can't think of any reason to go home. Then I'm on County Road 20, and I can see lightening bugs twinkling like stars between me and the lake. I have shut the radio off long ago, and I pull off and shut the engine, and all I can hear are the crickets and the tree frogs, and off in the distance the deeper burping of bullfrogs at the edge of the water. There's no moon, and the night is dark as pitch.

I try to cry. Grief for Jolene burns the back of my eyes like acid. But the tears won't come. I feel dry as sand. Grief for that child. Our child. I remember the look in her eyes that night at the Silver Moon. That look is burned into my mind. I know I can't ever forget it. If I have Jolene in my memory, I have to have that look, too. Those eyes. And Sheila, too. I see the shiny tear paths on her face. I see the hatred in her eyes.

I don't know how long I sit there alongside the road. I start the truck and drive on. I feel drained of strength, like coming off a ten day binge. I see the neon sign for the Silver Moon up ahead. The clock on the dash say it's a little after midnight and the parking lot is full. I park half in the ditch and get out. I can hear the music, distant, the stomping of feet and laughter, and the bullfrogs, coming from somewhere a long way away from where I am.

I'm walking toward the front door. The crowded parking lot is dank-hot, smelling like sweat and tar and motor oil. Then I see them, these motorcycles, seven of them, pulled up in a row, gleaming black and silver in the dim neon light from the sign. There are four Harleys, two BMWs and a Triumph. It's a motorcycle gang from Woodlawn, in Birmingham. I've seen them before. They've been out here before, with their tough-mouth women and their tattoos and their leather pants. They wear curly beards. They're mean, real bad-asses. They carry knives.

In the pale light I'm looking at the first hog in the line. It must be the leader's. It's an expensive BMW that gleams like a freshly dug lump of coal. It's got silver side mirrors and rhinestone studs lining the seat. It's got these two little signs hanging on each side of the back fender, so anybody coming up from behind could read them. The one on the left says "PASSIN' SIDE." The one on the right says "SUICIDE." Cute. I stand there looking at the little signs.

I go back to my truck in the dark and find my sawed-off pool cue under the seat. Three feet of heavy, slick polished wood. A carved handle so you can grip it. I go back to where the hogs are parked. I swing my stick and knock the little signs off into the weeds. Then I start in on the first windshield. I swing as hard as I can and the glass is like iron. Then it smudges. Then it shatters some. I keep flailing away. I lose my breath, but I'm banging and chopping. My pool cue splinters in my hand, comes apart, and I fling it into the ditch and go back and get a tire iron from the toolbox behind the cab.

Then I really go to work on them bikes. Glass and metal flies. I move from windshield to windshield, knocking off mirrors, too. I hear someone say, "Hey," from the doorway of the cafe, "Hey, what the...?"

I'm like a maniac. I'm blind with my own sweat. I'm swinging away like crazy and the sound of the tire iron on glass and metal is like explosions in my ears. I can see the glass from the windshield spraying like bits of ice, and for some reason it strikes me as funny, and I start in to laughing. I can't help it, I'm laughing fit to kill, and all of a sudden I'm crying, too, and I don't know if these sounds I'm making, these gulps and sobs and carrying on, are laughing or crying or both or what. I'm flailing away and I must be making one hell of a racket, what with the tire iron on the bikes and these sounds coming out of me, and I can't catch my breath and I have to stop from time to time to heave and struggle and try to inhale. I keep on, my whole body getting numb and cramped.

And all the time I'm laughing and carrying on, howling like a crazy hyena. My arms are heavy under the numbness, but they keep moving, gripping the tire iron with both hands, and I'm ruining the hogs, really trashing them, and I see but never hear the old boys come boiling out of the door, all of them, all on me at the same time.

Walk the Fertile Fields

(First Published in "Region", 1970)

THE children had gotten the name Plastic Woman from an old, worn comic book that somebody had brought to school, and they called her that because she was so tall and thin and she could snatch them up and paddle them. They could really have no idea how apt the title was, since she had been a beauty queen in college and was still being one; they knew only that she was pretty in spite of being mean. And they didn't know that it was her first year to teach, that she was only twenty-three years old; to them, she was a teacher, and teachers existed in one lump of telescoped time, beyond some ageless barrier that not a single one of them had ever considered in some future time he might cross.

It was a small school that had only had a special education class for four years; in fact, the teacher before Amy (for that was Plastic Woman's real name) who had quit to have a baby, had been the first Special Ed teacher assigned there. Amy had only eleven students, but with their special kind of retardation, the room was full enough. There were eight blacks and three whites, that is if you counted Jimmy as only *one* black; she was inclined to count him as three or even four. He was twelve and a half years old and almost six feet tall, and he looked ridiculous sitting in the cramped desk, so the first day she had had a desk sent down from the Junior High division for him, and it sat in the middle of the room, holding him like some maniac African Chieftain surrounded by his pygmy warriors. And three little Albert Schwitzers or Dr. Livingstones.

From the start, she was at a complete loss with him. He raised his hand the very first day and asked if he could tell why he had left his last school. She sweetly acknowledged him, and he announced that he had left because he had gotten caught "screwing" a white girl. She was speechless. The other kids giggled, but she was sure that most of them had no idea what he was talking about.

"Jimmy!" she had said.

"Yessum?" he said, looking at her, all innocence.

"THIS WILL simply never do," she said to the principal in his office later, during her first off period. "I mean, he's much too old and well, worldly for the other students."

The principal, who wore a flat-top crew out and smoked a pipe, looked at her over the curls of gray smoke rising from his freshly lit bowl. "What do you propose we do with him?" he said.

"How should I know," she said, "that's not my job."

"Isn't it, now?" he said. He puffed on the pipe; it made little gurgling sounds when he drew on it.

"No," she said, "he simply doesn't belong in there with those poor children. His mouth is filthy, he's liable to say anything at any time, and I won't have it."

"It sounds as though you have a discipline problem," the principal said, looking at her over his pipe.

So she was furious with him when she went to lunch, and she sat silently, half listening to the other teachers' chatter. She tucked her long, brown hair behind her ears and tried to concentrate on her wieners and kraut. She didn't much like the other teachers, and she tried to shut them out; they seemed a remarkably colorless and a boring bunch. She sat there slicing her wieners, thinking of Robert. They had only been married little over a year, and they were already having problems. Robert was working on his Ph.D. in biochemistry at the University, and she, after they had both graduated, was supporting them; he was home a lot when she was at work, and there was a girl, Becky, who lived with her husband upstairs in their apartment building, and she was fond of sunbathing in her bikini out on the patio behind the building. Robert had mentioned that he thought her rather attractive but somewhat cheap, and she had immediately started to hate her, even though the four of them were always being thrown together for cookouts and movies on weekends. She had just about convinced herself that something was going on. For one thing, Robert was smoking more and more dope, and Chad, Becky's husband, who was an attorney, kept them well and cheaply supplied with very good weed that had been confiscated by a city detective who was a friend of his. Robert had even taken to smoking a joint in the bathroom every morning while shaving. He was stoned most of the time, and Amy thought he was becoming very politically radical, too. And his grades were not the best in the world.

"Jesus, you look tired as hell already," someone said at her elbow. It was Al Lovoy, who taught science in the Junior High division; he was, she had decided, about the only other teacher worth talking to.

"It's Jimmy," she said.

"Jimmy Raymond?" he said. "He's harmless, believe me."

"You should have heard what he said in class this morning, about why he left the last school he attended. He left nothing to the imagination." She sighed.

Al was looking at her. "Jimmy's never been to any other school," he said, "he's been here since he started." She looked up from her plate. "Becoming something of an institution, as a matter of fact," he said.

"Why that little bastard," she blurted, before she thought, and she looked quickly around to see if anyone had heard her. All the others were finishing their meals and talking among themselves. "But he told me..." she said.

"Believe very little of what Jimmy says," Al said, after a moment, "that's the only way to deal with him. But anyways, you got his category right."

"What?"

"Yeah. Bastard. Nobody knows where he came from. He lives

with an old woman he calls his aunt, but nobody seems to know how he got up with her."

"Are you kidding?" she asked.

"Of course not," he said, "Jimmy is a most interesting young man."

She didn't answer. She was thinking that, interesting or not, he was the first real pain-in-the-ass of her teaching career. But she didn't say it out loud.

SHE WOULD be doing reading lessons, the painstaking, word by word coaxing (she: "He...," student: "He...," she: "took...," student: "took...," etc.) when suddenly Jimmy would start to sing. He was particularly fond of that song then popular, one she had heard on the car radio on the way to school, that went something like "Gotcha now, uh-huh, uh-huh, gotcha now," and he would snap his fingers and suddenly launch into it, just as though he were all alone a thousand miles away.

"Jimmy!" she would say, glaring at him, and he would look sullenly at her, his lip poking out.

"Do you want to go in the cloak room?"

"Nome. I ain't done nothin'."

She would sigh. "Just be quiet, okay?"

"When you gone let me read?" he said, sulking. She had tried. He couldn't tell one letter from another, much less read words, so he simply made up what he was supposed to be reading, and she could never be sure of what he might come up with. Even the smallest children could tell that he wasn't really reading, and they giggled, but he seemed oblivious to their amusement and continued to insist on reading.

So, playing strictly by the book, she had, early in the year, called his aunt in for a conference. She and Robert had a tremendous fight the night before and she had slept badly, in spite of having smoked three joints of what was supposed to be very good stuff. (Robert had gotten very high and ended up giggling like mad at Don Rickles on the Tonight Show; she could see nothing funny about Don Rickles, and she drifted into a restless, irritated, sleep.) The woman turned out to be quite old, with wooly gray hair, and she had on what must have been her best dress, an old, worn black gabardine, and she had put on a hat, which depressed Amy the moment she saw her, though she didn't realize immediately exactly why.

"What he done?" the old woman said, sitting down beside the desk. She was twisting a white handkerchief between her fingers and she seemed very nervous. "What that boy done? I'll whup the tar out of 'im when I gits 'im home!"

"No," Amy said quickly. "I..." She stopped. She found herself intimidated by the old woman. "I don't know about whipping," she said. "It's... it's more Jimmy's attitude."

"I'll warm his attitude wit a razor strop," the old woman said. Then she chuckled, and Amy smiled nervously.

After a moment, Amy said: "I mean, Jimmy doesn't seem to care anything much about school."

The old woman peered at her, cocking her head; Amy could see that one of her eyes was covered with a grayish glaze, as though she were blind or had a huge cataract or something. The old woman stared at her with her one good eye for a moment. Then she said.

"He ain't bright."

"What?" Amy said, startled.

"Jimmy ain't bright," the old woman said, "he can't learn nothin', outta no books anyhow. He ain't bright."

"Jimmy..." Amy said, looking at the old woman, "Jimmy's retarded! He's in a class for retarded children!"

"That's what I say," the old woman said.

"Well," Amy said, after a moment of silence, picking up her glasses and putting them on, "the child can learn *something*, his tests show that. But not without the proper attitude." The old woman continued to look at her, and she nervously cleared her throat. "I mean, why is he staying in school then? Surely there's something he could do, work in a filling station or something, or..." She paused. The old woman cocked her head, then shook it slowly back and forth.

"He be in reform school inside a year," she said.

Amy took off her glasses and slowly laid them on top of a pile of papers. She didn't know what to say, and she shook her head as though to clear it. The old woman was staring at her, her good eye watery and weak.

"Jimmy a good boy," she said, after a moment. "He ain't bright, but he a good boy."

The girl and the old woman sat looking at each other for a moment. "Yes," Amy said, after silence, "I suppose so."

"GOD, IT was depressing," Amy said to Robert that night, "I mean, I couldn't even *communicate* with her!"

"I'd think the whole thing would be depressing," he said. "I can't think of anything more depressing than walking into a classroom full of blithering idiots every day."

"They're not blithering idiots," she said hotly. "They're really very loveable human beings who just happen to be dumb."

"All except Jimmy," Robert said.

"Not dumb?"

"No," he said, drawing on a joint. "not a loveable human being."

"Oh," she said, standing there idly patting out the hamburgers. And that was the germ of the idea, that only later began to grow. That night, lying awake in bed, Robert snoring gently beside her, the idea grew and took form... maybe he really *wasn't* retarded? Maybe he was only pretending! She had almost convinced herself of it by the time she drifted off to sleep.

SHE WAS sitting in the principal's office the next morning when he came in, poring over Jimmy's file.

"Not Jimmy Raymond again," he said, knocking his pipe out in his clear glass ashtray.

She looked up. "I see Jimmy hasn't been given those new tests they've worked up at Cornell," she said.

"There's nothing new there," he said, sitting down beside his desk, his chair squeaking under him. "I read them carefully, and they're not as good as the standard ones."

"Really?" she said. "I should think you'd want to give them a try, anyway."

He looked at her, then picked up his pipe and slowly began to stuff it. "What good would it do to give Jimmy more tests?" he said.

"It might be very revealing," she said with a crooked grin. "I mean, maybe he doesn't belong in a special ed class at all."

He was lighting his pipe, and he peered at her through the gray smoke; she thought of herself as constantly looking at people through some thick smoke-screen. "Now," he said, "if you'll excuse me, I have the week's lunch money to tote up."

Her hands shook slightly as she put the file back in the cabinet and went quickly down the hall toward her room. And Jimmy.

SO HE continued to plague her. Once, when he had been particularly insolent in refusing to sit down when she told him to, she took him into the hall and threatened him with a trip to the principal's office. He drew himself to his full height and looked levelly at her.

"You don't like me cause I'm black," he said.

"That's ridiculous," she said, "maybe you don't like me because I'm white."

"Maybe dat's right," he said, glaring at her. They stood there in the hallway staring at one another for a few moments.

"Jimmy," she said, sighing, "Jimmy, tell me, are you sure you can't read?"

"I can read," he said, swelling himself up. "Who say I can't read?"

"But..." she said, and stopped.

"You done heard me read, MuhHollis," he said, "an' if you don't believe it, ask MuhJohnson." Mrs. Johnson was the name of the teacher who had preceded Amy.

"You," she said, "you call what you do reading?"

"What you call it?"

"Well, I'm inclined to call it very creative playacting," she said, looking shrewdly at him.

"Call it what you wants to," he said, then he looked away from her and snapped his fingers. "Gotcha now, uh-huh, uh-huh, Gotcha now," he chanted.

She felt the redness creeping up her throat, and she turned on her heel toward the door of the room. "When you get yourself together and calm down and decide to be nice, you may come back in," she said over her shoulder, going into the room and slamming the door, much harder than she had intended, behind her.

SHE BEGAN to be uneasy about the way he would sit and look at her. And sometimes, when he would be up at her desk while she corrected his spelling, a list which bore no correlation at all to the words she had called out, she would be aware of his arm pressing hers. Once he had even put his hand on her shoulder as he leaned close to look at his paper.

"Jimmy!" She had said shortly, "you can keep your hands to yourself, if you please," and he had looked at her with such a look of hurt and innocence that she had been momentarily confused and speechless. She shook the wrinkled, smudged paper. "Now, what is this word," she said, pointing to something that looked like JIMOBUEGN.

"Dat's James Brown," he said.

She looked at him. "I didn't call out James Brown," she said.

"Sounds lak you did to me," he said, "I can hear, can't I?"

She marked a big zero on the paper and handed it to him, and he took it and held it in front of his eyes.

"Take your seat," she said.

"But..." he sputtered, "but you give Carl a eighty."

"Carl *made* an eighty. I didn't *give* him anything."

He stood there, his lip poked out. "Sem lak if Carl get a eighty, I ought to," he said.

"Take your seat."

He slouched back to his desk, grumbling under his breath. His friend Carl, who was not much better than he was, but who could spell, was frowning and murmuring, too.

"*What* was that you said?" she said, suddenly and sharply, and he looked at her, scowling. "What did you call me, Jimmy Raymond?"

He looked at Carl, then back up at her. "I only said you was rich," he said. "You know you always loanin' us a dime a recess." Both boys sat there looking at her with their big eyes, and she sat down wearily behind her desk. She looked at her watch.

"All right, go on out to the playground," she said, and the room erupted as they raced to the door, desks scraping on the floor and much pushing and giggling. Jimmy, as always, won the race.

SHE WAS crying when Robert came in late from a lab that afternoon. He glanced at her and threw his bookbag into a corner.

"What's the matter now?" he said.

She sniffed. "He called me a bitch today," she said.

"Who?" he said, matter-of-factly, getting his dope and papers out of a drawer.

"Jimmy Raymond, you know," she said.

"Oh, for Christ's sake, Amy," he said. "Look, I'm tired, and I get damn tireder with you coming home bitching about your job every afternoon."

She wiped her eyes and blew her nose. She sat for a moment, watching him roll the joint.

"I saw her car in the parking lot at the hospital," she said suddenly.

"Who?" he said, looking up.

"Becky," she said.

He looked away; then he carefully licked the cigarette and sealed it and sat shaping it, watching his fingers move on the brown paper. "So?" he said, after a minute.

"Was she in the lab with you?" she said.

He held a match to the joint and puffed, then inspected the ash. He took a deep drag, and sat back in the chair. When he let the smoke out, he looked at her. "I don't think I should even answer that question," he said. "Of course she wasn't. I told you, *I was working!*"

"Then what was her car doing there?"

"How in the hell should *I* know? Maybe she was seeing the doctor, how should I know?"

She sat there quietly, slowly pulling herself together. "Sure," she said, when she felt a little better. "Sure."

He sprawled in the chair, his head back, watching the smoke curl toward the ceiling. "Say," he said, breaking the silence, "there's a rally tonight, to raise money for the Berrigans. Wanna go?"

"No," she said. "I'm too tired, but you go ahead."

THE NEXT morning Becky and Chad had interrupted their breakfast by bringing in the morning paper. Their picture was on the front page, and they were very excited. The article claimed that the University had given permission to the authorities to photograph the crowd, secretly, and the editors maintained that this was one of the photographs. And there they were, the three of them, with Becky in the middle, a portion of the group at the rally.

"The bastards," Robert said, "the bastards."

"Yeah," Chad agreed, but they were both clearly proud and excited.

"They can't win with gestapo tactics like that," Robert said, "we'll get em yet!"

"I'd better go, I'll be late for work," Amy said, and she left them in the kitchen, Chad and Becky reading the article over Robert's shoulder. The only thing she had really noticed was that Becky, in the picture, seemed to be sitting closer to Robert than to Chad.

She found herself growing tired very easily. And she grew increasingly more impatient with the children; they seemed to get on her nerves more than ever. She slept fitfully, and sometimes, in the quiet early morning hours, she would awake with a start, aware that she had been dreaming of Jimmy Raymond; he was usually just standing, looking at her, wearing this pale blue, ridiculous looking hat that he had bought at some carnival, holding a long switchblade knife. (He was forever talking of "cuttin'" somebody.) Even the principal, who most of the time, seemed oblivious to what was going on around him, noticed her state of mind.

"Mizz Hollis," he said one day, stopping her in the hallway. "Is something wrong?"

"Why no," she said, "why do you ask?" He seemed to be staring at the part in her hair, and she was very much aware that her roots were showing, that she had been shamefully negligent of her hair, but she couldn't seem to remember to pick up the Nice 'n Easy at the drugstore.

"You seem, well, not entirely yourself," he said, after a minute.

How in hell would you know? she almost said, but she straightened up and looked him in the eye. "Well," she said, "I'm not." And she turned and continued down the hall, aware that he was probably looking at her hips under the tight skirt she was wearing, hearing her high heels echoing loudly in the hallway. She found herself swinging more, in spite of the fact that she hated his guts and couldn't care less if he were looking at her.

"MuhHollis, MuhHollis," Jimmy was shouting when she came into the room, "MuhHollis!"

"What now, Jimmy," she said wearily.

"MuhJohnson's comin' to see us, she brangin' her baby," he said. He seemed almost delirious with excitement.

"Where did you get such an idea as that?" she said.

"She sent word, I know," he said, his face turning hostile. "*She* wouldn't say she was comin' if she wasn't."

"What do you mean by that?" she said. She had found herself, in the last few weeks, slipping into arguments with him, allowing herself even to sink to his level as though they were two adults. When it happened, she felt ashamed, almost unclean. "Never mind," she snapped, "take your seat." She watched him slouch to his desk, the blue floppy hat on his head; she had become convinced that the way he dressed was a deliberate way of showing his contempt for her. "And take that ridiculous hat off when you're inside," she said. He glared at her. Then he snatched the hat from his head and sat down, grumbling. She wondered if someone with the I.Q. he was supposed to possess could possibly have such open hatred and hostility for someone; he almost was like some wild, untrainable animal.

"Get out your reading books," she said, and Jimmy's hand was the first one in the air, waving frantically in front of her face.

Robert's grandfather died and he went to the funeral on the bus; she was to stay at home so as not to miss work, since your husband's grandfather was not counted as immediate family and the school system would have docked her pay. He left in the afternoon, an all night trip; he was to call her the next morning when he arrived, and when he didn't, she went to work puzzled. When she got home that afternoon, she placed a call.

"Why, Robert's not here yet," his mother said. "But then the funeral's not till tomorrow. Is anything wrong, Amy?"

"No, that's okay," she said. "I guess I just miss him."

After some small talk, they hung up and she found herself automatically dialing Becky and Chad's apartment. Becky answered.

"Becky," Amy said, "Robert's not there, is he?"

"Robert?" Becky said. "I thought he was gone to a funeral."

"Yes, I..." she said, faltering. The line was silent for a moment.

"Amy?" Becky said, "are you stoned, or what?"

"Maybe," she said. "I'm sorry I bothered you." Her voice was cold.

"No bother," Becky said, "but you did catch me doing my nails, so I better hang up."

"Bye," Amy said. She sat staring at the phone for a long time, in the empty apartment.

He got home on Thursday night. He put his bag in the bedroom and then sat down and looked at her. She looked away.

"Okay," he said. "I didn't call, so what?"

"Who was she?"

He yawned and stretched. "A girl I met on the bus," he said, "we smoked some dope, and one thing led to another." She was just looking at him, her eyes wide. "We stopped off at a hotel in Richmond; it was just a spur of the moment thing."

They sat looking at one another. Slowly, one large tear left Amy's eye and slid down her cheek.

"Oh, for Christ's sake," he said. "It was nothing. I didn't even know her name, nothing more than shaking hands, for Christ's sake."

"How could you do something like that?" she said, softly, her voice cracking. "To me?"

"Oh grow up, Amy, will you?" he said. "It was nothing."

She just sat there, her head down.

"Say, what's for dinner," he said, "I'm starved."

HER HANDS were shaking as she drove to work the next morning. Robert had stayed up quite late studying, and since he had no Friday classes, he always slept in. And she had hurried, not fixing herself up very well, wanting desperately to get out of the apartment as quickly as possible. She took a quick glance at herself in the mirror of the teachers' lounge and was surprised once again at how haggard she looked. Then she hurried to her room.

And Mrs. Johnson was there. She was a plain woman who wore her hair in unattractive braids at the back of her head, and she was slightly dumpy, but her smile was open and friendly. She had brought little gifts for all the children, and Amy had never seen such excitement, not even at the Christmas party.

"MuhHollis, MuhHollis," Jimmy was shouting. "I tole you she'd come, I tole you, didn't it? An' look at her baby, ain't he fine?" A little baby was sleeping in the corner, in a portable bassinet.

"Mrs. Hollis," Mrs. Johnson said, coming up to her, "I hope you don't mind my taking the liberty of dropping in. I knew it might be a little disruptive, but," and she leaned closer to her, "I do love them so. And I miss them." She looked around the room, smiling, and all the children were watching her.

"Of... of course not," Amy said. She had never seen them look so happy. Jimmy came up to them, and Amy watched as Mrs. Johnson put her arms around him and hugged him, Jimmy resting his head on her ample shoulder.

"And how's this big old angel coming along?" she said.

"Well..." Amy said, looking at them, "fine, I suppose."

"Well, you just go sit down," Mrs. Johnson said, "Mrs. Hollis and I want to talk." But Jimmy kept clinging to her. His arms were locked steadily around her. Mrs. Johnson patted him on the back, and looked over his shoulder at Amy, the warm smile on her face. After a minute, Jimmy stepped back. He looked at Amy.

"I do love MuhJohnson," he said.

The two women talked about the special problems of some of the children. And then Mrs. Johnson had to hug them all again as she packed up all the baby paraphernalia, and they all gathered around her, unable to stand still as she was leaving, promising to come back and see them again soon. And not long after she had gone, Amy missed Jimmy; she had no idea where he might be. After almost an hour, she found him in a remote corner of the playground, sitting on the grass.

"Jimmy, what are you doing out here?" she said. And he looked at her. His eyes were red-rimmed, and huge streams of tears ran down each ruddy cheek. He said nothing, starting to sob again.

"Jimmy, what's the matter?" But he didn't answer her. He just sat there, sobbing uncontrollably, this giant of a boy crying openly like a tiny baby, the oversized, pale blue carnival hat on his head. She stood watching him for a long time, her own eyes suddenly stung with tears, the two of them there like some tableau against the fresh, new-mown green of the playground.

After a while, when his sobs had subsided some, and he sat with his face turned from her, sniffling, she said softly:

"Come in our room when you want to, Jimmy, okay?"

"Yessum," he said.

The Flowers of Her Summer Garden

(First Published in "Somewhere In All This Green and Other Stories", 1999)

MARGARET Bielkowicz Simmons no longer spoke with an accent; she grew roses. She looked forward every year to the Brownie Scouts who came to her door selling cookies, and she would have been fine if her daughter and her son-in-law, both of whom were professors of history at the nearby university, had not engaged the girl, the "graduate" student, to house sit for them while they were in Europe. They went to Europe now every summer, and Margaret knew that the girl was not really to watch the house but to watch her. Or she suspected it. And she could tell that the girl thought she spoke with an accent, something that Margaret knew that she no longer did, but people persisted in pretending that she did, just as those young men in her church kept getting in her way so she would bump into them when she was walking through the Parish Hall. They looked at her as though they expected her to say "excuse me, please."

"Did you know that most priests in the Episcopal Church are queers?" she said to the graduate student across the back fence that separated her back yard from her son-in-law's and daughter's yard. The girl had on a bikini bathing suit, heading for the pool. She used their pool every day as though she owned it.

"You mean *gay*," the girl said. She looked like a beatnik even in a bikini bathing suit. She loped on down toward the pool.

"I mean what I say," Margaret said. "Hey. You, girl!" The girl kept walking. "When I say somethin', I mean what I say." Margaret watched her go beyond the willow bush. "Ungrateful hippie," she mumbled. Just that morning the girl had gotten angry at her because she insisted on being driven all the way to Food World, and when they got there, Margaret had dabbled and looked and finally bought a package of Gouda cheese and a small tin of anchovies.

"You could of got that at the Piggly Wiggly," the girl said. She complained all the time.

"I like to shop at Food World," Margaret said. "You got to take me anywhere I want to go, that was the deal."

"Some fuckin' deal," the girl said, driving too fast on the expressway, and Margaret said:

"You hush your mouth. Don't you speak thatta way in front of me. Do you hear me? Don't you dare!"

"Yes mam," the girl said.

"People in this world might talk thatta way, but not in front of me."

"I said yes mam," the girl had said under her breath, and they had driven home in silence. Margaret had sat there, knowing the girl probably wanted to listen to that KICKS 106 rock and roll trash on the car radio. She had smiled to herself in the silence.

She couldn't see the girl at the pool, so she turned to her roses. She wondered when the Brownies would come to sell her cookies. She couldn't remember if it was in summer or winter when they came. At least they *had* winter, or something like it, here in Alabama. All those years in Fort Lauderdale, when Mr. Simmons was still alive, they'd had no winters at all. But further back, in Chicago, Ahhh, then they'd had winters. She enjoyed telling her grandson about the winters in Chicago in the old days. When she was a girl. All she could remember really was the snow, but her grandson had seen that on television, and once it had even snowed a few inches in Alabama, but nothing like Chicago when she was a little girl. People didn't want to hear about that any more, all the snow. Chicago was a cloudy dream now to her, though she didn't really think that was so; she remembered Berwyn, and the old house where she'd grown up, and then Czermak Road with Alan (Mr. Simmons), then Oak Park. The place names were real. The rest was pale memory, but her memory was as good as anybody's she was quick to tell anyone.

She saw the troop of Brownie scouts going by in front of her house. They walked silently, with the air of an urgent mission. She wondered if they were on their way to make the cookies, like the elves in the television commercial. The thought amused her, and she smiled. She wondered, for a moment, if the girl, now splashing in the pool, probably naked, had been a Brownie Scout; Margaret, of course, had not, and neither had her daughter. Her grandson was a Boy Scout. She thought of the naked girl in the pool; later she might walk down and catch her. She had done it before, walking up to the girl lying buck naked in the morning sunlight.

"Have you no shame?" she'd said, and the girl just looked at her, making no effort to cover herself. Margaret could see her large bush of black hair that seemed to come almost to her navel, and her small breasts jutted out in a harsh, impertinent way. "Do you think this is *Playboy* magazine?"

"God, there's nobody within twenty miles," the girl said, and Margaret said, indignantly:

"*I'm* within twenty *feet!*" and the girl just lay there, whispering to herself, something that sounded like "Piss off," which made no sense to Margaret in that context.

THE TROOP of Brownie Scouts usually carried signs, which they turned toward Margaret when they went by, but she could not read what was written there, if anything were. Her eyes were not at all what they used to be, but she could see well enough. She could see mites on her rosebushes, for example, and she could see dust in the house. She thought of the girl again; later, when Margaret had seen her drive away in her son-in-law's station wagon, she would go down and unlock the house, knowing that the girl couldn't put on the chain when she was out. When she went out, Margaret could go in and look around to her heart's content. She enjoyed poking in the girl's drawers and reading her mail, though the girl never got anything very interesting. And Margaret checked for dust and dirty dishes that would attract the roaches, and once she found a pile of damp towels on the floor of the basement play room and left the girl a note: WE DO NOT LIVE LIKE ANIMALS HERE AND IF THE DINING ROOM FLOOR GETS WET IT WILL WARP AND LEAK TO THE PLAYROOM SO WATCH OUT. One day, a week or so later, the girl came home and caught her in the house.

"You will be responsible for every penny's damage you do, I hope you remember that," Margaret said, and the girl just stood there, her hand on her hip, her backpack slung over her shoulder, looking at her with this smirk on her face. "Well," Margaret said, after a full minute of silence, "what do you have to say for yourself?"

The girl laughed. She shook her head. She turned and walked out of the room and left Margaret standing there, without so much as an *excuse me*.

"What?" Margaret said. "What did you say?"

"I said," the girl said, her voice coming from the next room, the sound of her heavy backpack hitting the floor with a thud, "that your manners are as ugly as your face."

Margaret grinned. It was certainly to be expected. It was just like her. That she could stand there smirking after Margaret had seen her naked as the day she was born; Margaret had always wondered how those women in those magazines could show their faces in public after letting somebody put a naked picture of them in there for everybody to see. Margaret always said that she thought the ugliest thing God ever created was the naked human body. One day, Mr. Simmons said to her, after she'd said that for the umpteenth time, "Margaret, even a buzzard was born to fly," and her son-in-law and Mr. Simmons laughed, both of them drinking their shot-and-a-beers and watching Thanksgiving Day football, and her daughter just looked at her with this half-grin, half-smile on her face, sometimes dumb-as-a-post acting, Ph.D. or not. It was the same look her daughter had looked at her with, later on, after Mr. Simmons died and she told them she was selling the house in Fort

Lauderdale and taking the money from that and the insurance and building a small house next to theirs up in Alabama, on a corner of all that land her son-in-law had bought, so she could be near them and her grandson. "That nice corner toward town," she said.

"We were gonna fence that off for Alan the third's pony," her daughter said, smiling at her, and Margaret said:

"Alan the third ain't got a pony."

MARGARET piddled at her roses, listening for noises from the pool. The sun was high, and the day was hot, and she couldn't remember exactly what time Father Troup was supposed to drop by to see her. She considered taking Father Troup down to the pool to expose the naked jezebel to him, and she got tickled to herself, thinking of what he might say and how he would look, standing there sputtering away in his little white collar. She was almost sure he wasn't a queer, but you could never be sure; he liked to get drunk with her daughter and son-in-law, and sometimes on Sunday mornings his hand trembled when he placed the wafer. Margaret would sometimes move her hands just a little bit, for meanness, and even let the chalice clink on her teeth. Father Troup never let on if he noticed. Margaret was on the Altar Guild, and once, all alone in the Parish Hall on a quiet Saturday morning, just for devilment, she had left the silver wine cruet at the back of the church empty, so that when the elements were carried down in that new way she thought was silly, there was a quiet panic down in front of the altar, and Father Troup had to send one of the little Altar Boys out to find the wine and fill up the time with this little ad-lib homily about the meaning of wine in the service, and Margaret was grinning all the time and Father Troup wouldn't look at her.

Father Troup was old fashioned, he said, though he was a young man; he was from Brookhaven, Mississippi, and he told funny darky stories to selected members of his parish. Sometimes he acted queer. This whole religion business now sometimes seemed crazy to her; she'd heard that over at the Catholic church in town they had a young priest with a beard who wore blue jeans and sang mass with an electric guitar. In Fort Lauderdale, she and Mr. Simmons had gone to a huge church where you didn't even have to speak to anybody if you didn't want to, but here the church was small and the college students came in in their blue jeans and open collar shirts and were always sticking out their hands at her and saying: "PEACE!" Like they'd just discovered a new word. She wasn't too keen on being touched by most of those hands, considering where she figured they'd been on Saturday night. So she'd walk without looking people in the eye, and she bumped into people a lot. The church was called The Church of The Holy Comforter, which privately tickled Margaret, since when she heard the name she thought of an image of prissy Father Troup blessing a nine-diamond quilt.

When she walked around to the front of the house, the Brownie Troop was just passing by on the way back from wherever they'd been and she stood there watching them. She wondered why they never seemed to be having any fun; they didn't laugh very much. Just as they went around the corner, the last little girl, a little blonde, help up a sign toward Margaret, and Margaret strained to read it without her glasses. As near as she could tell, it was blank. The little girl just stood there, holding it. "What does it say?" Margaret called out.

The little girl didn't answer her. Margaret clucked her tongue as the girl ran around a corner. She shook her head. Just last Sunday, a little girl from one of the Sunday School classes had come up to her and said: "Why do you put mustard in your hair?"

FATHER TROUP arrived smelling of Scotch and tobacco, and Margaret was annoyed because he had timed his visit perfectly to interfere with *The People's Court,* which was the only show that Margaret liked to watch with any regularity. She was intrigued that they were *real* people, crying real tears when they wound up having to pay for the bent fenders and all. That was something to cry about. Not like all that sex and queers she heard people on *The Donahue Show* talking about; that was X-rated filth. Men who liked to dress up like women. What could you expect? Father Troup was lighting his pipe in the living room while Margaret searched for the cream sherry, and when she found it the cork had gotten so dry and brittle that it disintegrated and crumbled in her fingers. She poured the sherry and held it up to the light. There were only a few specks of cork in the pale liquid, and she sipped, winced, sipped again. A bit tart, but it was what she had. Her daughter and son-in-law bought scotch and bourbon and gin in those large jugs from the state liquor store, but she was be-damned if she would, not for Father Troup, anyway. He accepted the glass and sipped it and smiled at her.

"And how are we getting along?" he said.

"Just close your eyes and pretend it's Scotch," she said.

"What?"

"Never mind."

He just sat looking at her, his pipe poised halfway to his mouth. He had large, sad, liquid eyes. Very dark. But his mouth was a half-smile, and his right leg, crossed over his left, jiggled up and down. Margaret grinned at him. "Ehhh?" he said. "Well?"

She continued to grin at him and after a few moments she said: "I notice that you're looking at my hair."

"Beg your pardon?"

"My hair. You keep staring at my hair."

"No, you're mistaken," he said. "I wasn't looking at your hair, nothing of the sort."

"You find it so ugly, then? That you can't even look at it?"

He chuckled and sipped the sherry. "Ahhhh, the games you play, Margaret," he said. He chuckled again, and sucked on his pipe; it made a little wheezing noise when he sucked on it. He sighed. "It's so peaceful out here," he said.

She sat, wondering what to tell him about. He was like all the rest: ignorant as the day he was born. Maybe he was even ignorant of the fact that he was an agent of the devil. There had been times when she was sure that he was the devil himself, and equally sure that he knew it. He flirted with her. He was so charming that butter wouldn't melt in his mouth. He loved his mother.

"How's your mother?" she said.

"Fine, she's just fine," he nodded, smiling.

He was lying. He had no mother.

"The coon niggers have taken over the public schools," she said.

"You may be right there," he said.

She just grinned at him. What did *he* know? The station wagon came up the road and turned into the driveway next door with a great squealing of brakes. Doors slammed and she heard laughter, female and male laughter. She would go down there later and unlock the door, but the girl would have the chain on, and Margaret would stand there and hear them laughing at her from back in the house. They would make the bed rattle loud and giggle at her. They would cook up something that smelled rancid and charred. Sometimes at night Margaret heard splashing in the pool.

Father Troup had finished his sherry. He would probably ask her if she wanted to pray for the "Travellers." She did not want to pray for anybody, especially with the devil. They were showing Alan the Third all the major battlefields of Europe. She wondered how they could get a Ph.D. each and still not know any more history than that. Alan the Third had a large picture of George S. Patton on his bedroom wall. Actually, and she had never mentioned this to them, it was actually a picture of George C. Scott *as* George S. Patton. On one of her explorations of the house, after the "graduate" student moved in, she had found three darts sticking on the large picture, right on George C. Scott's tallywhacker.

SHE STOOD out front, by the yellow roses, watching Father Troup drive off in his shiny black Buick. She had patiently let him say a prayer "for those of our own in distant lands. Protect them, Oh Lord, in thy tender mercy, and keep them in thy care. Amen." "Amen," she said. Once, when she'd been sick with the flu, he'd come out and given her the Reserved Sacrament, and the wafer tasted stale, lying on her tongue like old paper. She'd had to fight the temptation to spit it out. She wondered what he would have said if she had. She wondered why they called it bread. She had to laugh out loud, thinking of Jesus daintily buttering little thin wafers and passing them out at the last supper. One for you, and you, and you. A baker's dozen.

Margaret chuckled to herself, walking about in her front yard. The sun was getting lower in the sky. She wondered if the two little urchins from down the street would come and beg her to let them mow her lawn. They came every other day. She saw them coming down the street, so she hurried into the house and locked the door behind her. She put the chain on the door and peered through the door panes at them. She watched them coming down the walk, talking between themselves, plotting, she knew, some new strategy to take advantage of her. They took her for a fool.

"Can't you see my yard don'ta need mowin'?" she said through the door at them, just as the slightly larger one was poised to knock. They smiled. She hated their triangular, fox-like faces, their yellow eyes. Their hair was too long, and it hadn't been washed in a month.

"Come on, lady, let us cut it, please, come on," the smaller one said, as though they hadn't at all heard what she'd said. They lived down the road in a "mobile home." That's what everybody called them now. Margaret associated trailers with gypsies.

"Get outta here, you both belong in reform school is what I think," she said to them.

"Aww, lady," the older looking one said. They smiled at her. "You better let us cut it," he said.

"It don'ta need mowin'," she said. What could they do to her? Come back at night, when she was asleep, and do something to her house, stomp her flowers maybe. "Roses got thorns, you better remember that," she said to them, and they only looked at her. "Get outta here, now, or I call the police, you hear me?"

She watched them go down the walk. She would not be intimidated. She had seen their kind on television, and she knew them well. She watched them go out of sight, then eased the chain and opened the door. She went back into the yard, looking after them, watching them disappear over a hill down the road. They were close to Alan the Third's age, but she knew her daughter would not let him play with them. Alan the Third went to a private academy, where there were no trash and coon niggers. She snorted, thinking of them showing Alan the Third all the major battlefields of Europe. She knew that her daughter and son-in-law were walking around Europe like they *owned* all of what they were showing him. They always acted like they owned wherever they happened to be. She thought her son-in-law's smile said that whatever he didn't own now, he was planning on taking back.

She moved slowly into the side yard, glancing over the fence at her son-in-law's house. She stopped, startled; the door on the driver's side of the station wagon was standing open. She shook her head. Animals. In such a hurry they couldn't even remember to shut the door. Hippies and scum. And the devil himself, prowling around in a black Buick.

Out of the corner of her eye, she saw the Brownie Troop passing by again, and she smiled and went toward the front, moving through the flowers of her summer garden. She would not listen for the splashing in the pool. She looked all around, at the whitewashed picket fence that surrounded and defined her small place. To hell with the famous battlefields of Europe, she thought to herself, chuckling, smiling, going toward the Brownies, who went by single file, staring straight ahead.

Walking Strawberry

(First Published in "The Southern Humanities Review", 2005)

HARRY's BRUSHSTROKE IS strong, the paint clotting and thick, much bolder than it had been when he was a young man. His model's name is Annie. She is twenty five years old, and her face is as cold and precise as a stone angel's, and as enchanting. Her eyes, pale blue, are expressionless. Her naked body is like a burnished statue. He sees her exposed curves and angles and pores and flesh and hair and he sees through the parts, too, beyond them, and he lets his eyes caress her. He squints at her. He feels her in his fingers as he paints, warm and alive.

***

"IT WAS a terrible series," Harry says. He sits at the bar in the Grayton Beach Saloon, his gnarled fingers curled around his beer glass. The afternoon sun is muted by the dusty windows. The old wood of the bar, in the soft light from the frosted globes behind it, glows as though lit from within. Duane, the young man keeping the bar, nods in agreement. He has a pony tail. He is heavyset, in his twenties. It's just after three o'clock on an October afternoon, still hot, and Duane wears a short sleeved white shirt. Harry is the only customer in the place.

"Not worth watchin'," Duane says.

"You know when it completely turned? When it went down the tubes? When Maddox walked Strawberry, in the second inning of the second game. That was the end. After that, there was no way."

"Naw," Duane says.

"No, really. I was sittin' there watchin', and when it happened I told Helen, 'that's it.'" There is green oil paint under Harry's fingernails. His fingers are long, his knuckles swollen and bony. Arthritis has changed the shape of his hands over the last few years. His hair is completely white, his beard still rust red and sprinkled with gray. His hair looks sleep matted, off center and mussed. He wears faded jeans and a dark blue Duck's Head work shirt, both speckled with paint, and he stares at his glass of beer for a long, silent moment. A bubble escapes the bottom and rises slowly to the top as he watches it, curious and concentrating, his brow furrowed. "'That's it,' is what I said," he says softly.

"Naw," Duane says again. "They coulda come back."

It is as though Harry does not hear him. Then he looks up. He blinks. He smiles. "The die was cast, so to speak," Harry says. "There is a moment when what you do – and maybe even more important what you don't do – when it changes everything. Just one little tiny moment. It changes everything that follows. You know it when it happens, and you know that nothing will ever be the same after that. Greg Maddox knew it. Did you see him slap his glove on his thigh and whirl around and look into the outfield? He knew, in that one crystallized moment, that the Braves had lost the series, and it was forever, and the chance to change it would never come again."

"Naw," Duane says, "it ain't over till it's over."

The air in the bar is full of decades of cigarette smoke, exactly the way the imprisoned and suspended air in an old stone church cleaves to its ancient incense.

"I TOLD HER I hadn't seen my nipples in twenty years," he hears Helen say. She is talking on the phone to her best friend Mylene. They are talking about a mutual friend who has had a breast reduction and lift. Mylene is a novelist, now married to a fourth husband, this one seventeen years her junior. Years ago Mylene and

Helen and Harry had lived together for several years. In their own minds they had all been married. Helen refers to Mylene as "my ex-wife." They had all shared a bed and they had been young and uncomplicated. Mylene and Helen are both as dark and lean as gypsies. And as mysterious and elusive. He has been married to Helen for forty years. He knows everything about her. And he knows nothing about her.

Harry shuffles on through the house, out to his studio. Annie sits on a folding chair, looking out to the gulf.

"There were dolphins this morning," he says. She shrugs. She stands and begins to undress. She wears tight jeans and an Octowanna Junior College sweatshirt. She wears no bra and her small breasts swing free. He looks at her nipples. They are pink, the size of dimes. Her pubis is golden. She lives in Grayton Beach with her divorced mother. Her father is a shrimp boat captain in Destin.

"Turn a little sideways," he says when she is seated, stretched out. She is as pliable as clay. "Right," he says, "just like that." She knows what he wants, immediately and exactly. She picks up an orange on the low table in front of her, looks at it, replaces it. Her face settles into her familiar remoteness, and then she is still. He imagines that she daydreams when he paints. That she fantasizes. But he does not ask her.

He uses a big brush, its handle thick and comfortable in his hand. He uses a trowel as his palette knife. His canvas is large. It is heavy with paint.

HARRY WALKS ALONG the beach. The sand is blindingly white, even in the setting sun. The tide is coming in now, so Harry's bare feet are occasionally dashed with foam. His jeans are wet below the knees. The sound of the waves will be its loudest when the tide is high. They can hear it all night from their bedroom, through the screens, crashing and roiling and receding. "I couldn't sleep without that," Helen says. Seven years now they have lived here. Harry never wants to leave. The light is pure, as pure as in Provence. He has never seen colors quite like these.

He stands looking out over the water, at its changing shades of green and azure; it is emerald and pale lime. It is a blue so deep he cannot tell where the underlying black begins. Streaks of orange and yellow erupt from behind a low ridge of gray clouds near the horizon, and he can see the red sun behind them, pasted there like a hot wax seal against the bleached sky.

He stands for a long time gazing at the sunset. He is having a hard time finishing the painting. He has been sketching with charcoal. He has done at least fifty sketches, and Annie does not notice when he begins sketching instead of painting. She is absorbed in being what she is, the figure in the painting. She had said one morning, suddenly and with no preamble at all, no warning to Harry: "If I think on it hard enough, I can feel like what it would be like to be the girl in the picture, hanging on the wall. In the museum or the gallery or whatever. With people looking at her. At me. I mean...I become her. I am her." She had smiled. One of her front teeth was slightly crooked. Her voice was clear and startling in the quiet of the studio. He stopped painting. He stood there motionless, his brush poised in midair. She resumed her pose, now oblivious to him again.

Something had changed. Something vague and unsettling, but as palpable as a sudden change in the temperature of the air. Since then he had been sketching in charcoal.

He could not finish the painting.

HELEN PREPARES HAMBURGERS with thick slices of Vermont cheddar. It makes him think of their early Vermont years, their house outside Bennington. He had known Pollock in the early years; he remembers the day of his death. Harry was a young teacher then, his studio on the edge of campus, near the sheer drop off the students called "The End of The World." He and Helen had known Frost and Kay Morrison in the early years. Later the Berrigans had sat around their fireplace with them and their friends, drinking their wine and smoking their dope, the heat of all their excited voices jumping and dancing like the flames on the logs. He recalls long Vermont August days that were cooler than Northern Florida October days like these.

Helen sits across from him. He watches her chew and swallow, her eyes focused on the blue tile wall across from her. He can see that her mind is distant and he wonders what she is thinking of. She had designed the house herself and their kitchen is modeled on the kitchen in Monet's house in Giverny, full of sunlight and shades of blue and stark, clean white, with an antique wood stove rebuilt for gas. She likes the bright kitchen, though she does not cook much anymore. She sits in there and reads much of the day. Her face is like an abstract refinement of what it had been as a girl, when he had first known her. There are fine lines around the corners of her mouth and eyes, like the tiny cracks in good marble, and she still wears her hair long and parted in the middle though it is not dusted with gray.

Mylene had told her that the style was too "kittenish" for her. For a woman her age.

"I don't care," she had said. "It's me. Besides, 'kittenish?' I'm not married to a child."

Mylene had laughed. Even the sound of her laughter was coarsened, like her voice, by years of cigarettes and whiskey.

Helen's eyes are dark, olive brown. They are sharp and alive, not at all the eyes of a woman approaching seventy. Her body is still slim. She has gained only a little weight, in the hips and breasts. He had observed her earlier that morning as she stepped from the shower. She had been his model once, long ago. Her breasts now sag just slightly, barely discernable bulges on the undersides. Her nipples are almost black, large and still ripe. She exaggerates to Mylene and to the woman who has had her breasts reduced. It is like Helen to be that self-deprecating.

She had come in response to his ad in The Village Voice, in New York. Almost a half century ago and he could still see her as clearly as now, bathed in sunlight, standing in the doorway of his walk-up on Bank Street, just off Hudson. She had worn a black turtle neck sweater, a long, wrinkled khaki shirt. She had been barefoot, a bracelet of colored beads around one ankle. Her hair was dirty. She had bathed in his old claw foot tub before posing, as lovely and innocent as a new flower.

Her body has mellowed, has grown worn and smooth with age. Their lovemaking is less frequent now, but is still fiery and lustful. It is intense. It is open and free. Even more so, he thinks, than it has always been. There are just the two of them, together in the weathered house in the dunes. And Annie, the girl in the painting.

"How's the painting coming?" she asks him suddenly. "The big canvas of the girl?"

He looks up from his plate.

"Fine," he says, "great."

***

"TELL EM YOUR theory," Duane says. "Tell em why the Braves lost the series."

A couple, Ann and Nathan Palmer, sit at the bar. They are in their thirties and both teach English at the junior college. They are drinking gin and tonics.

"It was Maddox walking Strawberry in the second inning of game two," Harry says. Ann and Nathan look at him as though he has made some divine pronouncement, but Sam Mike Sullivan, the fourth person in the group of afternoon drinkers, says,

"Bullshit." He grins. The high sun is brilliant against the broad, freshly washed plate glass window at the front. Inside, the bar is dark and cool. The air feels damp to the skin.

Harry knows that both reactions have more to do with who he is than with what he has said. Everyone knows Harry Whitaker, the famous artist, on sight. Tourists point him out on the street. His paintings hang in museums and galleries all over the world. They hang everywhere, even in the White House. The Palmers are in awe of him, and so is Sullivan, but his way of responding is to challenge Harry, all the while winking and smiling. He pushes his light green golfing cap to the back of his head and tosses back a shot of Jack Daniels, then sips his beer. "Ahhhhhh," he says. He pushes the empty shot glass toward Duane and nods.

"No, really," Duane says," it makes sense."

"Come on," Sam Mike says. "You sayin' that just one walk... come on."

"Yep," Harry says. "That walk was the sound of the fat lady singing." They all laugh. He sips his beer, his mind wandering to

Annie, her thighs like butter. Her bare skin is warm to his touch. He wants the heat to enter his hand, wants it to be transferred to his brush. She sighs and her breathing quickens. "Maddox was trying to be too fine, and he knew it," he says to them. "He knew he should have grooved it. Of course Strawberry could have launched it into the seats. Or he could have flied out, popped up. Or struck out. Or hit into a double play. There were all those possibilities. Figure the odds. But ball four. That is irrevocable. No defense against that. Final. Kaput. Done."

"A lot of other things happened in that game," Sam Mike says. He is a retired stock broker. His face is red, and he is still sweating from being outside. He is still sweating from his morning golf game. He frowns.

"Of course," Harry says. "You are correct. But that was the defining moment. Maybe there were others. I don't think so, though." He slides his empty pilsner glass toward Duane, who deposits it into the sink behind the bar. He takes another glass from the freezer, frosty with a thin screen of ice, and fills it slowly and carefully from the tap.

"I think you're right," Ann Palmer says, nodding. She turns to her husband. "I think he's right," she says.

"Thank you, mam," Harry says. He grins. His teeth, in his beard, are very white in the dimness of the saloon. "Think about it for a moment," he says. They all lean forward. "During that one split second, when ball four drifted outside, just think how many lives were changed. How many would never, ever, be the same again."

There is a long silence. There is the muffled sound of a car passing on the street. Harry says, his voice low and modulated, "You only have one chance in those moments." Harry sips his beer. The others sit quietly, staring at him.

"Well..." Sam Mike says. He scratches his gray widow's peak with his middle finger. He tries to laugh. He tries to smile, but what Harry has said forces his face down into a frown.

"That's the way it is. For all of us," Harry says.

Ann and Nathan Palmer nod in unison. Sam Mike Sullivan squints at his empty shot glass. Harry can see the tension in the man's neck, the rigid way his head is locked. He is angry. He will not look up, will not look at anybody. It is as though Harry has pronounced a death sentence over him.

SHE HAS A SMELL. A scent. It is there among the oils, the turpentine. The only sounds in the cluttered studio are the scratching of the charcoal on the rough paper and the distant murmur of the surf. She moves her legs. She looks up at the skylight. He sees her eyes swing upward, as though in some mysterious yearning. That's it, he thinks, that is the right expression. That is what I want. The light is wrong: the day is cloudy and gray, and there are stray drops of fine rain scattered on the glass in the skylight.

He smells her. He can taste her. He feels a youthful prickling, the beginning of an erection. He puts down the sketch pad and picks up a brush. He squeezes several large tubes, one by one, then mixes on the palette using the brush. She stares off into the space beyond the skylight. She is gone. She is already the woman in his painting.

**

HELEN LOOKS UP from her book. He stands in the doorway, saying nothing. Helen stares at him. He sees a soft accusation in her eyes, a question. Then he sees an acknowledgment, an acquiescence. Her eyes glow warmly, ignited and full. She nods. The novel is closed on her finger. The room is empty of sound. The surf is too far away to be heard back here.

"Did you finish it?" she asks. She smiles. She pulls her hand away and lets the book close. She rises.

He stands there for a long time looking at her. She wears a black T shirt and wrinkled khaki shorts.

"Yes," he answers. "Yes. I did."

The Queen of the Silver Dollar

(First Published in "Amaryllis", 1988)

For J. L.

I

I didn't know why in God's name Cyrinthia can't just admit that that *was* Emmylou Harris that come in here the other night and ordered a steak. Ever since Cyrinthia finally brought me home from Valleydale Village and let me live in that room behind the café she's treated me like a child, and me, come Christmas Eve, will be fifty years old. She acts like I would just *make it up* that Emmylou came in here, but I wouldn't. Now some of those people at Valleydale *would* have, no doubt about it. Talking about getting on somebody's nerves! There was some crazy folks at Valleydale, and they wasn't all the "Villagers," as they called us, but some of the counselors, too. And even the doctors. They would look at me with their eyebrows raised up to their foreheads like little McDonald arches. Like the time I told em I was thinkin' of buying Delta

Airlines. I had come home for a visit with Cyrinthia, and she let me fly back over there, and the fight attendant took me up in the cabin and let me visit with the pilots, and one of 'em said to me, "You like this plane? You ought to buy it."

"Maybe I will," I said. They laughed like I didn't know they was funnin' me, so I said real serious, "I might just buy the whole airline." They laughed some more, and the flight attendant, too. I was thinkin' that I would fire all three of 'em if I did. So it was just on my mind when I got back to Valleydale. The doctors there don't know what to make of me because in a lot of ways I'm smarter than them. I told 'em one time I worked for the FBI, that I was a plant, and I could tell it put 'em in a stew because they halfway believed it. I'm sure they went quick as they could and checked it out.

But Valleydale was better than that place over in Mississippi where I stayed I don't know how many years, playin' softball and makin' key rings in their little shop. At least after a couple of years the folks at Valleydale let me work outside at Shoney's, moppin' and bussin' tables, and I made some money and watched them set up a little account for me to buy chewing gum and shaving cream out of that they would show to Cyrinthia when she'd come to visit, and Cyrinthia'd tell me how proud she was of me.

"If you so proud of me, how come you don't let me come on over there and work at The Pit?" I'd say. "I can mop and bus tables there just as good as Shoney's."

"Don't start that, Moon," she'd say, and make like she was gonna get right up and leave right there. Cyrinthia is my older sister, and I just feel like I ought to live with family. That's the way it's supposed to be. A person is supposed to live with his family. It makes a person lonely, specially if you live around folks that ain't got any imagination or vision. If you're around family, they see things like you do, and you don't have to explain yourself to 'em all the time. But I don't reckon that's true with Cyrinthia, now that I think on it. She thinks I make up half what I tell her, like that business about Emmylou Harris stoppin' in here to eat on her way to sing down here at the Central Alabama Music Park.

I finally convinced Cyrinthia to let me come over here and live. She runs this restaurant called The Pit, right here along the

Interstate in Alabama. She's got a room with a bathroom tacked onto the back of the place, and I talked her into lettin' me live back there. On a trial basis, she says. I've heard that before. Years ago, right after Mama died, mine and Cyrinthia's uncle, Cyrus Crenshaw, lives up near Guntersville on Sand Mountain, took me in and even built a room on his house for me. I get a check from the government, enough to take care of me, enough to pay Uncle Cyrus or Waynesboro or Valleydale to keep me, ever since they drafted me during Vietnam and took me out to Fort Sam Houston, Texas. They kept me three weeks and then discharged me with a full disability. Cyrinthia's husband Robert got drafted about the same time and he wound up over there across the water in Vietnam, and he never came home. He got killed. His name is on that monument up there in Washington, but I've never seen it. I want to go, but nobody'll take me. I'll get up there someday. Anyhow, Uncle Cyrus's wife, Aunt Bertha, was real nervous. They hadn't ever had any children of their own, just this little scrawny dog that looked more like a rat than a dog — they called him "Yip" — and the dog was just about as fidgety as Aunt Bertha. Anyway, finally Uncle Cyrus told Cyrinthia that it just wasn't gonna work out, since Aunt Bertha was too nervous and I was drivin' her crazy because I wouldn't eat what she cooked and I talked all the time while they was trying to watch television, but it was a lie. Sometimes I'd notice things on television that they didn't seem to see, is all. Like one time we was watchin' and I saw this woman named Martha Polk, ran the Seven-Eleven out at Moore's Crossroads, on that show will Bill Cosby, *You Bet Your Life* they called it, and Uncle Cyrus and Aunt Bertha swore up and down that it wasn't, that it *couldn't* be Martha Polk, and it turned out that it *was*. It got off with 'em somethin' terrible. Stuff like that. They finally made Cyrinthia come and get me. Cyrinthia said, "Well, at least they got 'em a room built on their house out of it," and she found this place over in Mississippi. Called Waynesboro. It looked like one of those plantations in *Gone With The Wind*. They like to drove me crazy with their softball and makin' their key chains and these little molded plastic prayin' hands. Most of the folks there was younger than me. Downright dumb people. I kept callin' Cyrinthia up on the phone and tellin' her how much I hated the place, and she finally moved me to Valleydale Village.

"Now this place is the best in the Southeast," she said, "everybody says so. There's people of all ages here."

"How come I can't just come live with you?" I said.

"Because you get on my nerves, Moon. I got a life of my own to live, remember?"

Some life. She lives by herself in that little house her and Robert built. She's fifty-three years old and she goes to these clubs in Birmingham and drinks whiskey and kicks up her heels. She wears cowboy boots and goes out with this lawyer named Alston Rawls. Alston sits in The Pit all day and drinks coffee. "This is my office annex," he says.

"I tell you," I say to Alston, "I'll just tell you. If I was gonna get married, it'd be to a woman like Emmylou Harris."

"You too mean to get married," Alston says. "How come you didn't ever get married?" He talks to me like I'm regular people. and I appreciate that. I've had girl friends. Both at Waynesboro and Valleydale. Cyrinthia wouldn't never think to ask.

"Cyrinthia's enough woman to have to put up with," I say.

"A woman ain't *but* a woman," he says.

I don't know what he means. We talk all the time since I came over here and moved into the back of the cafe, but he's full of lawyer talk and half the time I can't understand him. I asked him the other day if you had to be a crook to be a lawyer and he sat there thinkin' for a minute, then he looked up at me and said, "No, but it helps."

The night Emmylou came in I didn't recognize her at first. Cyrinthia lets me wait tables after Luanne, her regular waitress, has gone home, and it was late. She looked like just a regular girl, and I didn't notice her at first, but I recognized the man with her right off. I knew him from somewhere. I said to myself, "I know that man." They looked at the menu. I looked at the man sittin' with her. He's one of these little short, bald fellows with a real big head, that if you've seen him somewhere before you don't forget him. He is her guitar player. One of 'em. He stands kind of cocked over to the side from the waist with his ass stickin' out when he plays. You can't forget that. I saw em on *Austin City Limits* just Sunday night. I have color television in my room in the back and I get cable. He rolls his eyes around in his head and asks me if we cook good steaks. I say, "Does a bear shit in the woods?" They both laugh, and I see her face then, I see how her eyes glitter, and I know who she is. Like I'd been knowin' all along but I didn't *really* know till I saw those eyes. My stomach feels cold and then hot, and I want to run. But I don't. I just grin. They both order T-bones. Medium rare for her. He says, "Rare." Then he smacks his lips. They're big, thick lips, 'bout the biggest I've ever seen on a man. "Very rare." He shakes his head up and down. "I mean, sho nuff rare," he says.

I say, "You want me to just run the cow through and let you cut yours off?" They both fall out.

Cyrinthia has run down to the night deposit in her pickup, and there's nobody there but Charlene, the cook, and I turn the order in back in the kitchen and she starts makin' their salads, slappin' two thick T-bones on the grill, and I say, "You know who that is out there?" and she doesn't even look at me. She's sweatin'. I can tell she doesn't like me much. I heard her telling Cyrinthia that she wished she wouldn't go off and leave her here alone with me, and Cyrinthia laughed out loud.

"No, who *is* out there?" she says still not lookin' at me.

"Emmylou Harris," I say.

"Emmy*who?*" she says, real sarcastic.

I know better than to go on talkin' to her. She's so fat her eyes sit back in her face like agate marbles that somebody has taken their finger and pushed down into biscuit dough. I know why she's scared of me. She thinks I want to jump on her and do it to her. She's got no cause to worry. They wouldn't take me at Waynesboro without Cyrinthia signing the paper for an operation that makes me not likely to do anything to her, even if I wanted to. But I don't tell her that. The doctors told me I'm not supposed to have these feelings any more after that operation, but I do sometimes, like late at night or when I see the light glintin' in Emmylou's eyes. I don't have these feelings when I look at Charlene.

They've finished their salads and I've brought 'em their steaks, and I run the mop by while they're eatin' and they stop talkin' and look up at me. "Anything I can hep you with?" he says, and I say:

"Nope, just doin' my job." I keep pushin' the mop, and they go on eatin'.

He pays their bill with a twenty dollar bill, and I have to call Charlene from the kitchen because Cyrinthia won't let me open the cash register, and after they've gone Charlene says, "Shit, if that was Emmylou Harris, then I'm Hillary Clinton!"

Cyrinthia misses em by five minutes. She just stands there listenin' to me while I tell her about it, just listenin' without saying anything. Finally I say, "We ought to put up a sign."

"What kinda sign?"

"You know, one that says Emmylou Harris ate here."

She don't say a word, just walks around behind the counter.

"Can we?" I say.

"Can we what?" Cyrinthia says.

"Put up a sign?"

"Yeah," she says, "right after hell freezes over and the Pope becomes a Baptist."

The trouble with my sister is she ain't got any vision.

II

DOROTHY Whisenant, Cyrinthia's best friend, is over here helping Cyrinthia put up Christmas decorations. It's Sunday afternoon, a real slow time, and I'm watchin' 'em work and I can tell it's gettin' on their nerves, because they don't want me listenin' to whatever it is they want to talk about. I know they're goin' on about this woman over in Eastaboga who got wrote up in the paper because she kept seein' the face of The Virgin Mary in a pan of scrambled eggs. Folks come from all over, and no matter how much she washed that skillet nor how many eggs she cracked into it, that face would still come up there. I hear Dorothy say they'll have a shrine put up in her front yard fore you know it. I asked Alston if he would take me over there to see that, and he said maybe. He told me Eastaboga had to hire two new policemen just to control the traffic. I'd like to meet that woman and look at that fryin' pan. I wonder if it's cast iron or aluminum with Teflon.

Then Cyrinthia and Dorothy're talkin' about somethin' they seen on Sally Jesse Raphael this mornin'. I don't really listen to *what* they say, I just like to hear people talking. That's one of the things I miss about Valleydale Village. There was always a racket goin' on.

"Ain't there somethin' on television you want to watch?" Cyrinthia says.

"Ain't nothin' but car races," I say. "That's how come folks have so many wrecks up here on the highway. Folks tryin' to make their cars do like them cars on the television."

Neither one of em has an answer to that. They've got these strings of lights all over the tables in the cafe. Looks to me like they'll never get em untangled. I offer to help but they don't want me to. Dorothy smiles at me. She's been eatin' banana cream pie, and she's got a little patch of it on her upper lip. "It just needs a woman's touch, Moon," she says.

I go over and stand in front of the jukebox. I hold my quarter in my hand, lookin' at the labels. I can't read 'em, but I know what they say. Cyrinthia has got a lot of old songs on there, because that's what people that come in The Pit want to hear. There's even some Elvis songs on there. I drop my quarter in the slot and listen to the deep beep, and I punch C-9. That's Emmylou's song "The Queen of the Silver Dollar." Alston found it for me and told me the number, and I never forget that. Cyrinthia hears the jukebox warmin' up and she says:

"You ought to save your quarter, Moon. Go listen to the radio. That's free."

"They don't play enough Emmylou," I say, and Cyrinthia says:

"Oh Lord!"

"Call you in a request, Moon," Dorothy says. "They'll play it."

I don't answer. I know better than that. I know they wouldn't play it. They would *say* they would, but then they wouldn't. I listen to the beat of the song. I listen to her voice, then, like an angel's. It makes me see high clouds and tall green trees like they have out there in California. I see the queen, then, so close I can smell her. She's got on a red dress. And she's smilin' at me. "*A wine glass is her scepter,*" Emmylou sings. Alston told me what a "scepter" is. "*And a bar stool is her throne...*" I've never heard anything sweeter in my life than her voice. Unless it was Mama, singin "Comin Home." I remember that. I can't really remember what Mama looked like, but I can remember her voice, singing "Comin Home." "Never more to roam..."

When the song's over I say, "We ought to get us a beer license and change the name of this place to The Silver Dollar Saloon."

Dorothy laughs and Cyrinthia says, "Lordjesus!"

She's puttin' up a big plastic Santa Claus on the wall. Santa is holding up a sign, and I say, "What's that say?"

"Roll Tide, Moon," Dorothy says, "it says Roll Tide. Why in the world would you want Cyrinthia to change the name to The Silver Dollar Saloon?"

"Cause everybody calls it The *Pits*. You ain't gonna ever get rich less you have a beer license."

"Who says I want to get rich?" Cyrinthia says.

"A person would have to be dumb not to want to get rich," I say. They go right on working with the Christmas lights, not answerin' me. The trouble with people is they not only don't *hear* me, they don't *see* me neither. It's like somebody, God maybe, took one of those big wedged-shaped erasers the color of bubble gum, like they had in the drawin' shop at Valleydale, and just erased *me* with it. It's been like that ever since Mama died and there hasn't been somebody there to want me. Cyrinthia *wants* me, I don't mean that, but it's just not like Mama. It's funny I can't even remember what Mama looked like. Cyrinthia says I'm bound to, that I was grown and come back from Fort Sam Houston, Texas, by the time she died, but I don't even remember goin' out there to Texas, to tell you the truth. "Of course you do," Cyrinthia says. "you was there." I think to myself that I was born in a hospital in Anniston, too, and I was *there*, but I sure as hell don't remember it. Cyrinthia just *told* me about it. How the hell do I know that's what really happened? "Well, you know you were born, because you're here," Cyrinthia says. "And how come we're plannin' a fiftieth birthday party for you Christmas Eve if you wasn't born fifty years ago then?" I guess she's got me there.

Cyrinthia says I used to get twice as many presents as anybody else because my birthday fell on Christmas. I like for her to tell me about my family because I can't recall much about 'em. She says I wouldn't go to bed on my birthday, because I wanted to set up all night waitin' on Santa Claus to come. I'd go to sleep on the floor in front of the fireplace, and Daddy would say he was just gonna hang me on a nail by my overall straps. I remember that. I remember bein' scared he would do it. He told me all the time that I wasn't bright and that if we run out of beds he was just gonna let me sleep like that, hanging on a nail drove in the wall by my overall straps. That scared me. I sometimes still dream about that.

III

I DREAM about it the night before my birthday party. I'm hangin' there, and I can't do nothin' but kick my legs and wave my arms. I'm tired and I want to cry, and there's this woman in my dream. She's soft and glowing and she's got a long pale scarf around her head, drapin' down over her front, and I know I've seen her somewhere before but I can't place her because I can't see her face. Then I know she's my Mama, and she takes me down off the wall, just rips me right down and puts me in a bed and tucks the covers up under my chin. Then I see her eyes, and she's smiling, and it's Emmylou, with her long dark hair framing her face under her scarf, and her hands are soft and like ice on my forehead. I say, "Who are you?" and she says, "Don't you know me? I'm your Mama."

IV

DOROTHY Whisenant and Alston come to my birthday party. Patrice Vaughn is there with her little daughter Courteny. Patrice teaches aerobic dancing to women over at the high school gym, and she eats lunch in here most days. She fixes Courteny's hair up in these two pigtails that look like muskrat's ears. And old Mr. Byrd who used to own the hardware store till he retired is there. Charlene comes out of the kitchen, and Luanne is there. Luanne just got out of high school, and she's always saying, "Moon, you're a mess," or "Moon, you won't do!" She had her uniform skirts hemmed up so short that Cyrinthia made her let em out again.

"This ain't the Playboy Club," Cyrinthia said.

"You can say that again," Luanne said.

Charlene has baked this cake that has HAPPY BIRTHDAY, MOON wrote on top of it in pink icing. Everywhere you look there's Christmas decorations, little red and green lights blinkin' on and off and holly and sprigs of pine and cedar stuck up here and there and the Roll Tide Santa Claus. Everybody sings "Happy Birthday," to me, and Dorothy Whisenant says "Tomorrow we'll be singin' happy birthday to Jesus!" Everybody is happy, includin' me, and there are five candles on the cake, "one for every decade," Charlene says, and I'm not sure what she means, but they're burning away and I haul off and blow 'em out and they sputter and come right back on. I blow 'em again and the flames just pop right back up. Everybody is laughin' now but me. I don't know what the hell. I just stand there. I try to blow 'em out again and the same thing happens.

"They're those trick candles, Moon," Cyrinthia says. "Ain't you ever seen those before?"

They're all lookin' at me, gigglin' away. Then I say, "No."

They all stop laughin' and just stand there. They don't say nothin' for the longest time, the candle just sputterin' away and gettin' wax all over the top of the cake. They all just stare at me like I've forgot to put my britches on or somethin'. Cyrinthia clears her throat and says, "Well."

"Oh Moon, we didn't mean to —" Dorothy Whisenant starts to say somethin' but Cyrinthia shakes her head at her. They all just look at me for what seems like another full minute.

Finally, Cyrinthia says, in this fake cheery voice, "Well, who wants some cake?"

"I do, but the birthday boy gets the first piece," Alston says.

They're all watchin' Cyrinthia cut the cake when I see 'em come in the door. When Emmylou sees me see her she puts her finger to her lips, shush, and smiles at me. The woman that was in my dream is with her. She's got on a long dress, a robe-like thing, and she's got that long gray scarf around her head, and then I know who she is. I don't have to be told. They stand there for a minute.

"We came for your birthday party," Emmylou says. "Happy Birthday, Moon."

Everybody looks up then, at the sound of her voice, and I swear they all look like they have seen a pure-o-dee ghost. Their mouths fall open all at the same time, like some of these puppets I'm always seein' on the *Sesame Street Show*. Alston is standin' there holdin' a can of Budweiser with his eyes as big as pie plates.

"Y'all, this here is Emmylou Harris," I say. "She stopped in here one night and I told her I had a birthday comin' up. And look here, she has come to wish me well."

Nobody says anything for the longest time. All you can hear is little Courteny Vaughn hummin' "Here Comes Santa Claus." She ain't payin' any never mind. Finally Patrice Vaughn says, "Emmylou *Harris?!?*"

"Yes," Emmylou says. "How do you do?"

"*The* Emmylou Harris?"

"Well, *one* of 'em, I reckon," Emmylou says.

"The singer?" Patrice says, and Dorothy says, "Of course the singer, you ninny. Don't you recognize her?"

"People always look heavier on television," Patrice says, but nobody's paying her any mind now, everybody's going over in front of the two women. They all want to shake Emmylou's hand.

"And who is this?" Cyrinthia says, all smiles and courtesy — maybe she'll think about that sign now — looking at the other woman, and Emmylou says,

"This is my mother. She's travelin' with me." And she does look just like Emmylou, like in my dream, and I hear Luanne gushin' and carryin' on, sayin', "Why she don't look any older than you!"

"She don't! By God she don't," old man Mr. Byrd is sayin'. "*Younger* than you, by God!" and they're all cluckin' away like a bunch of hens at feedin' time.

And she just smiles, and I can see her black eyes glintin' like coal, just like Emmylou's. I never felt so proud in my life. I had forgot I'd even mentioned my birthday to them that night. I had had on my Braves cap, I remember, and an old Shelby County High School sweat shirt that I'd bought at a garage sale for 39 cents, and her guitar player had kept starin' at me while I was moppin', and he had finally said, "How old are you?"

"Be fifty on Christmas Eve," I'd said, pushin' the mop, "I'm havin' a party. Y'all ought to come."

And here she is. And it's like she's family, and I know it wouldn't do one lick of good to try to explain that to the other folks here, so I just watch em flappin' around and carryin' on, gettin' Emmylou and her mother some birthday cake, and I watch Cyrinthia to see if she knows who the woman with Emmylou *really* is, because I know she's *my* Mama, too, *our* Mama, but Cyrinthia ain't got any idea. And it don't matter. I reckon she's got strong enough memories of her own, of Mama's hands on her brow, of Mama's voice singin' "Comin' Home."

So everybody's about as excited as they can be, and I set there at the table with 'em and eat another piece of cake and Charlene gives me a Dr. Pepper. Then Emmylou says, "Well," and she stands up and her mama does, too. So I stand up. I look at both of em, and they're lookin' back at me. I can tell they know what I'm thinkin', so I say,

"Cyrinthia, I reckon I'll go with 'em."

"What?" Cyrinthia says. She laughs. She looks at them. "Y'all just gonna hafta excuse Moon. He's forgot his manners," and I see some of the others whispering at one another tellin' one another what I said, and they're grinnin' all over themselves.

"That's all right," Emmylou's mama says. "We *want* him to come with us," and I can tell Cyrinthia don't know what the hell to say to that. Her mouth is workin', but no sound is comin' out. Finally she says, "Miss Harris, you need to get on down to the music park, I know you got to sing and all that —"

"No, really," Emmylou says, "he can ride with us." And Cyrinthia is lookin' at her face and I can't see it, but I see Cyrinthia's reaction and I know that Emmylou has winked at her. Cyrinthia thinks they're just gonna let me *ride* with em a few miles down the road. The only thing that Cyrinthia don't know is I'm in on the trick. I ain't comin' back.

Cyrinthia smiles. "All right then," she says. "Moon, you can go ride with 'em" and I nod. She's noddin' too, like I'm a child. And the funny thing is, I *feel* like a child, like a silver child borne on the golden clouds, and I think about fresh rain and the smell of Alston's beer and the Queen of the Silver Dollar's eyes in the dimness. And birds and sunlight all at the same time. And soft hands. The three of us are movin' toward the door. We go out into the bright, cold afternoon.

We all three crawl into the back of this long, white limousine, with a driver and everything, and all the rest of 'em are standing in the parkin' lot, their eyes as big around as tractor tires. I hear the motor purr, and we ease on out toward the interstate. It's Christmas Eve and it's my birthday, and I'm with family, and I know I'm gonna ask Mama about that woman's skillet over in Eastaboga. And as much as her and Emmylou travel, we're bound to pass through Washington and I can finally see that Vietnam monument and touch it. But if we don't, then that's all right, too, because I've already seen it in my mind as crystal clear as truth. And I've already touched it with the fire of my eyes.

Brother Bobby's Eye

(First Published in "Shenandoah", 2008)

THE EYE, as blue as a clear spring sky, was knocked completely out of his head at a construction site down near Causeyville and then buried in a canning jar in the cemetery behind the Shortleaf Church of God. Brother Bobby Loomis — whose eye it was — was the pastor at the church on Wednesday nights and all day Sundays, and during the week he drove nails for Davis Wayne Construction Company, which was building the Causeyville house. He was a master carpenter who could have worked for any home builder in the area, so good he was. And he was handsome, with long blond hair that curled around his ears and flirted with the collar of the blue serge suit he wore to preach in, hair just busy and unruly and long enough to give him not just a youthful appearance but a sly hint of decadence.

The people in the congregation did not doubt that he had the Holy Ghost in him. Since he had accepted the call to preach there four years ago, their numbers had more than tripled. Brother Bobby had a high pitched, pinched voice that was more of a shriek, and he and his wife Bonnie often sang duets during the service. He had hired a young crippled fellow from over at the Junior College to paint a mural across the back wall of the church, around the window to the Baptismal pool, that showed in bright primary colors Jesus and John the Baptist standing knee deep in the Jordan River, surrounded by a heavenly choir and rolling green hills into the distance. Jesus, in the mural, looked a lot like Brother Bobby.

But it was his sermons that drew them. He screamed at them about what sinners they were, cajoled them about their behavior and damned them for it. The more he ranted, the more they came. He Baptized people every Sunday. The church got so big they had to put up a new one, an aluminum butler building right next to the old white frame one, with an exact replica of the original mural. Brother Bobby himself framed it and built the steeple on the metal roof that distinguished the church from the warehouses that lined the road less than half a mile away. Things were going very well.

Until the accident with his eye and all that seemed — with some kind of unaccountable inevitability — to follow. The cause of the accident was the sharp jagged corner of a poorly sawn two by four, slid through the window by one of the other carpenters, that caught him just as he was turning that way, and it neatly gouged his right eye out and flung it across the unfinished boards of the floor, through sawdust and mud from his boots, and Brother Bobby felt the most searing pain he had ever felt in his life. He did not know at first that his eye was out, only that he had been hit and his head jarred so that his neck and his shoulders spasmed and caused him to buck back against the unpainted wall board. He was momentarily blinded and he bit his tongue so hard that blood flowed from both corners of his mouth and mingled with the blood from his empty eye socket, which looked, to the men who got to him first, deep and empty and black. As though there was nothing in there but darkness and pooling blood.

By then he had passed out and slid to the floor, and they managed to find his eye and put it in an empty ziplock baggie that somebody had brought a sandwich in (they had to rinse off streaks of mayonnaise), so that when Bobby went to the hospital emergency room in Alabaster, his eye went with him. The damage to the socket and to the eye itself, the doctors said, was too severe to try and reattach it.

Brother Bobby's first appearance in the pulpit after the accident was marked by an eye patch, royal blue to match his suit, and it gave him a rakish, foreign look. His good eye was so fierce it glowed. He brought the eye that had been knocked out with him in a mason jar full of formaldehyde. He sat it on the lectern so that the blue iris was visible to the back of the church, and everybody there, wall to wall, some folks standing in the back, felt that both blue eyes — the one in the jar and the one still in Brother Bobby's head — were together focused directly on them. They shifted uneasily in their seats and shuffled their feet.

"His eye is on the least of these," Brother Bobby said, in his voice like a sawmill blade, and there was not a sound in the church, not even a cough or a clearing of a throat. Even the children seemed to know that something important was happening. Word had raced through Shortleaf about the accident and Brother Bobby's eye. Everybody all over town whispered that the carpenters and nurses in the emergency room had claimed that the eye had been still alive and looking at them. The doctors were going to put it in a red bag and burn it before Bonnie claimed it.

"It's my husband's body," Bonnie had said. "it's the window of a temple."

"It's nothing but tissue now," a doctor, a young man, said. "Nothing but a cluster of cells."

"It's got a shred of his soul in it," Bonnie said.

"Nonsense," said the doctor.

"We're gonna bury it," she said. "Because truth is truth. Bless you."

So they had a grave side service and they buried the eye in the ground behind the church. Brother Bobby preached his own partial burial. The eye sat in its jar on a plank over a freshly dug hole. "Ashes to Ashes," Brother Bobby said, "and dust to dust." He looked around at the gathered crowd. Most of the members of the church had come. It was Saturday and they were in their work clothes, overalls and jumpers, though some had dressed up in Sunday clothes. "Value your toe or your tongue, your knee or your heart," he said, "because you never know what part of you the Lord will call home, what part he needs. You don't know what part of you is so full of sin that it needs reckoning with the Lord!" His blue eye patch was stiff from washing and ironing. His hair was shining in the sun and Sister Bonnie watched him with feverish eyes. It was as though she alone knew what was happening to him.

"My eye itches," he had said to her last night, after supper.

"Scratch it then," she had replied.

"My eye yonder, in the jar," he said, pointing. The eye jar sat on the kitchen table, awaiting its journey to the graveyard.

"You mean your socket," she said. "I've heard about that. About an arm or a finger, keeps on itchin' or hurtin' after it's gone."

"No," he said. His good eye seemed glazed over. "That ain't what I mean. I can see through it, through that very eye over yonder. Cloudy, like through the liquid. Through a glass darkly."

The look in his good eye made her shiver. "Don't be woofin' me, Bobby," she said.

"As Jesus is my witness," Brother Bobby had said. "I put away from me that which is unclean. The Lord meant for it to be that way. The Lord took my eye. The Lord meant for me to put it away from me, to let it go on with Him."

BROTHER BOBBY STOOD beside the grave; he gripped his worn Bible so tightly that his knuckles turned white. "I commend a part of my soul back to the earth," he said. His voice trembled. A cloud was coming up and there was a roll of distant thunder. Everybody in the crowd shivered, at once. He saw Sister Bonnie turn away from the steady level stare of the eye in the jar.

Bonnie had been a majorette at Shortleaf High School ten years ago. She was popular and had been working in the office of the local Piggly Wiggly for several years when Bobby Loomis spotted her for the first time, at a Fourth of July picnic in Orr Park. Somebody, he didn't remember who, had introduced them, and Bobby had held her hand in a warm grip, her hands slightly damp from the heat. Bobby felt his eyes glowing like hot charcoal briquets, and he had said to her, "Praise the Lord!" He had come to town with the construction crew for the new Westinghouse plant over at Calcis.

"Let's break bread together," he had said to her. She had on a WWJD bracelet, and he had on a Promise Keepers T shirt.

"Are you married?" she asked. She pointed to the front of the T-shirt.

"I was married," he said. "My ex-wife ran off with the devil. It was a mistake for me." He squeezed her hand. He could see her going limp. "Thank the good Lord she did it," he said. Two weeks later they were married.

"I ain't like her," she said. "For me it's forever."

"Amen," Brother Bobby said.

Brother Bobby had never been so happy and content. Bonnie was an angel sent to him from Heaven. She was nothing like the first wife who had whored on him. Sometimes Bobby thought that everybody he'd ever loved had betrayed him. His father was but a vague memory who had left home when he was not yet two, and his mother abandoned him to his old grandmother when he was six. The dried up old woman had rarely spoken to him at all, only providing him a cold roof and a sparse table until he was sixteen and able to get away on his own. Bonnie was as pure as spring rain out in the countryside. She was sweeter than the icing on a three day coconut cake. Life with her was bliss.

Until Brother Bobby lost his eye. She changed then. He thought he should never have told her that he could still see out of it, that even after it was there in the ground he could still see out of it and he never knew what it was going to focus on next. He would catch her looking at him sideways, the way she might look at a freak in a show. She wouldn't look him directly in his good eye. She wouldn't talk to him. He thought she had become selfish, self centered. He studied on it, tried to figure her out, and he decided she was not really interested in him as a man anymore, because he was maimed, but only as a preacher who could save her soul. She took to gossiping and backbiting. She spat hurtful things as quick as a cat. He thought that having children might save her, might save them both. He loved her so deeply he could not bear the thought of losing her to sin.

"There's somethin' vile about you," he said to her when she failed to conceive and the doctors told them it would be difficult for her.

He had to go and give them a sperm sample. He had been irate about spilling his seed on the ground. He saw himself doing that, out of his buried eye, like a dirty picture show, and he hated it.

It had turned out to be something wrong with her tubes. They were twisted and kinked. "Somethin' vile that displeases the Lord," he said. He was hurt and disappointed. It was time for him to have a child. A son. He believed that that might set things back right.

"How you know there ain't somethin' vile about you?"

"Because the doctor said so. Because I asked the Lord."

"And what did He say?"

"Don't be cheeky with me, woman!" His voice squeaked like an old man. He lost his temper. He slapped her across the face.

"Forgive me, Lord," he said on his knees, tears running down his face.

Brother Bobby tried to get accustomed to not being able to close his other eye, the one in the ground in the cemetery. He prayed for the strength to live with it. Light filled his head day and night. He saw little children turned into pink angels before they had a chance to become people. He saw Jesus often, and heavenly choirs, streams of people moving toward the bright light of heaven. He saw crowds of the lame and the blind, the afflicted, moving lost in desert places. He saw the seven angels carrying the seven bowls full of the seven last plagues, and he heard a voice say, "Behold, I make all things new."

People came from far and wide to see the preacher who had buried his eye. The inside of the church would be stifling with so many people, and Brother Bobby's hair would mat to his head with sweat. Sister Bonnie would sit in the second row. Sometimes she had marks on her face, as though she had been struck by something, and her eyes were red from crying. "I see a sinful world," Brother Bobby squealed, his good eye closed tight. "I see —" And he stopped. The church was quiet, only the rustle of fans. He could not go on. Because what he saw clearly through the eye in the ground was Bonnie, naked in the arms of another man, and he squinted hard enough to see that it was Brent Eversol, one of the other workers on the Wayne construction crew, naked, too, and on top of her. Her face was thrown back, a look of ecstasy in her eyes that were focused right on him.

He opened his good eye and stared at her, there in the second row. She was wearing a white cotton dress. As virginal as Mary. Her face was full of a mute innocence. He could tell by her eyes that her mind was far away, that she was thinking or dreaming of something else, and he knew what it was. And he knew in that moment why she was barren. His heart sank to the bottom of his chest, like a deflated balloon. He raised his arm and pointed to her. "You are a harlot," he said, "as crimson as blood on the snow!" His voice trembled. The fans shushed. "Get thee from me, woman, until you are washed of your sin!"

Bonnie stood up. She walked slowly to the back of the church, looking back at him once, and then went out the door, her shoulders stooped. Nobody moved or said a word. Brother Bobby's body began to shake. He could still see her, now kneeling in front of Brent Eversol, in bright color. His eye socket burned like acid, and now, with his good eye squint shut, he could see them all, the people in his congregation, some of them sitting bone thin on toilets and others doing the most depraved things he had ever seen. He had known they were dirty and sinners, but this was beyond his wildest suspicions. It was an orgy of depravity. Their faces were twisted grotesquely and their naked bodies were pale, some fleshy, some little more than skeletons. It was so awful that not even he could bear it. Without a word he walked down from the pulpit and slowly followed his wife's path up the aisle and out the front door of the church. The people watched him in silence.

Outside the sun split his head in two. He spat on the ground, almost wretching. He shaded his eye and searched the parking lot, but Bonnie was nowhere to be seen. He closed his eye and saw her sitting at home, at the kitchen table, crying.

She began to fade away, to disappear, before his sight. She lost a third of her weight and was so weak she could hardly hold her head up. The doctor gave her all kinds of tests and then sent her to a specialist in Birmingham. Nobody there could identify the condition, and they sent her to the National Institute of Medicine in Bethesda, Maryland, where she stayed two weeks and then came home. Not even the doctors up there could find out what was wrong with her. Brother Bobby knew it was demons. The devil.

When he looked at her his mouth was dry. His heart would ache, and tears would spring into his eye. He had loved her and she was not a whole woman — and he was not a whole man — and she was a whore. And God has sent a plague on her.

"Please," she said to him, her eyes like dark pools.

"It ain't me," he said. "You done it to yourself. You done it, not me."

She just sat quietly in a rocking chair for hours, like an old woman. Soon there would be very little she could do for herself. Her eyes pleaded with him.

He brought her into the church, sat her up on the podium with him. "Look," he said, "come up here one by one and look, and see the presence of the devil on this earth!" And they filed by, one by one, old and young, and they looked at her sitting there are crying, the big tears rolling slowing down her raw cheeks. There was nothing anyone could do for her because the devil was in her. The crowds were bigger now, and Bobby had to schedule four services every Sunday. They came from as far away as Atlanta and New Orleans to see Sister Bonnie. "Look and take Jesus into your heart and go and sin no more," he said. "Throw the devil out of your heart! Look at what sin can do to you! Look and repent! Look with both your eyes, and see!"

Months passed, and Sister Bonnie sat now with a hollow stare in her wasted eyes. She was as thin as a skeleton. Brother Bobby's heart pained him in the hollow of his chest. He cried when he looked at her.

The women of the church took turns bathing her and feeding her and changing her clothes for her. She sat in the living room of their little house, never speaking, looking at the wall. The women walked lightly, treading softly, preparing meals for Brother Bobby, food that he didn't eat. He had lost weight, too. He had quit his job with the construction company and now held revival meetings at the church several nights a week. He baptized hundreds and hundreds.

Brother Bobby could not sleep. He tossed on the clammy sheets all night long. He continued to see clearly out of the eye, maddening things like scenery passing by as though he were driving when he was lying dark still in his bed, listening to the soft weeping of his wife in the other room. Or he would see plants in another season, flowering azaleas in the dead of winter, in the snow, or daffodils in the fall. Or the daytime sky, with high puffy clouds drifting across. Or he would see old Mrs. Shaw, who lived across the street, washing her dentures. Mr. Shaw putting up drapes. The inside of a strange house somewhere bursting into flame that roared and darted at him like fingers, or the mangled inside of a car, bloody steel and plastic, still noisy and hot with the collision, dust and vapor floating everywhere. He would smell the acrid smoke, feel the shocks to his body.

Sometimes it was as though the buried eye were looking into a mirror at his own face, searching the emaciation of his cheeks and the emptiness of his good eye. And he continued to see all the sins of his congregation, like some vast writhing image of hell, exhausted and insane. Night after night and all day Sundays he glared at them, shouted at them. "You are full of the vilest sin," he would yell, waving his arms. "Unwashed, unclean, dirty with the devil's doings! I see you every one! You have no secrets from me! I know! Repent and repent now! Or you will be lost for eternity! You will burn in hell for all of time."

"Please," Sister Bonnie said to him. That's all she said anymore. That one word. Brother Bobby stopped eating altogether now, because he saw himself starving to death along with her. Is that it? He thought. Am I seeing into the future?

"You did it," he said to her, "you did it with him, didn't you? Brent. You did, didn't you? Tell me I'm right, that it's true."

"Please," was all she said.

"Of course you did it. You sinned with him. I know that. God is punishing you, and punishing me." He sobbed aloud, his whole body shuddering.

He saw himself dead, in the rain, mud streaked on his face. He saw his dead grandmother sitting looking at him, the rain splattering on her thin gray hair. He went into the bathroom and pulled up the eye patch and looked as deeply as he could into the socket. The skin was stretched, and he could still see the scars left from the stitches, but the socket seemed to go deeply into his head, like the old well behind his grandmother's back porch when he was a child, disappearing down into murky darkness. He had known as a child that that was where hell was. He could see two images. The one in the mirror, and a clear image of himself peering into the mirror, from outside and above, as though his dead eye were not in the grave at all now but drifting about in the corner of the ceiling like a soul before it departs.

APRIL IS A TORNADO MONTH in central Alabama. They form out of vast dark thunderheads that come up out of the west, creeping and spurting eastward, flinging hail sometimes as large as softballs toward the ground, shattering windshields and battering roofs and ripping through trees just leafing out with their incipient springing. The clouds are coal black, as ominous and oppressive as fate itself, and the lightening against the darkness is golden and spectacular. They turn a noon to midnight, a dusk to the dark of the middle earth. When the storms would come, Brother Bobby would never cease to think, "And God shall show forth his handiwork!" The very ground would tremble with the power and majesty of the storms.

It was Palm Sunday morning, and a cluster of thunderstorms formed along a line between Tupelo and Starkville in Mississippi and moved steadily into Alabama, pointed directly toward the center of the state. Tornadoes began to touch down in Fayette County, then in Cullman County, just northwest of Shortleaf. The churches all over were packed, Brother Bobby's Shortleaf Church of God being no exception. They crowded the benches and stood against the walls. The heavens rumbled and the rain began to thunder on the metal roof.

"PRAISE GOD!" Brother Bobby shouted. The PA system crackled with lightening and bounced his voice off the metal walls, which shook against the rain and the hail coming now in almost horizontal sheets. The lights flickered. The windows darkened. Brother Bobby raised his arms to the ceiling. "LORD JESUS!" his voice boomed out. "He will come on the whirlwind! He will come bearing a sword!" The people huddled on the benches, looking around, their eyes beginning to panic. They surged together in groups, as in his vision of them naked and writhing. Miss Willodelle

Summers began to pound on the piano keys and ragged voices began to sing along with Brother Bobby, who held the microphone in front of his face. *"There's a land that is fairer than day,"* they sang against the whirling of the wind and the pounding of the rain. *"And by faith you can see it afar! Where the master waits over the way...to prepare us a dwelling place there!"* The building shook. There was a great roar all around them. *"In the sweet by and by,"* they sang, *"we will meet on that beautiful shore..."*

The tornado touched down on the outskirts of Shortleaf and chewed its way up Middle Street, bending trees flat to the ground and exploding houses and sending mobile homes tumbling about like toys. It made the most God-awful sound anyone there had ever heard. It ripped through the row of warehouses along the road toward the Shortlead Church of God, propelling huge sheets of metal through the air like frisbies, twisting and snapping thick iron beams like matchsticks. It moved itself on north of town, leaving the elementary school a pile of bricks, flattening an area a mile wide and six miles long. Several full churches were totally wiped away, the worshipers — men and women, children and babies — hurled about like bundles of rags. The raging, angry tornado destroyed everything and everyone in its path.

Except the Shortleaf Church of God and all those inside. Just at the end of the hymn the winds began to lessen, the pounding began to cease, and they all looked up in wonder. The storm had passed them over. Brother Bobby stood before them, his arms still extended skyward. Soon outside there was only a spring thunderstorm, rain brushing the roof, the rumbling way in the distance now, and they surged toward the door, crying out, laughing, glancing tentatively at each other in disbelief.

Outside the devastation was total. Everything in every direction was leveled. Except the church. They milled about in the muddy yard, touching each other to make sure, praying and crying because they knew their homes were gone, everything, cars turned over in the parking lot and twisted together like a pile of pretzels. But they were alive. They had been spared. The rain pattered against their upturned faces.

Brother Bobby stood alone on the raised pulpit, his good eye closed tight. His suit sagged on his gaunt body. He saw every house in town, one by one, shaking and imploding as though they had been swept away by a giant hand. He heard the townspeople's cries, felt their pain like sharp shards of glass in his skin. His head pounded. His socket burned like fire. He clearly saw Bonnie, at home, sitting helplessly in her chair, her face cocked to the storm, sitting, waiting, and he saw her dashed against the wall and through it, her body crushed and her head battered into oblivion.

Brother Bobby went out the back door of the church and out to the graveyard. Falling on his knees he began to claw at the ground where his eye was buried. The dirt was still loose and it was soaked and softened, and he pulled away at it until he reached the jar. He pulled it out, letting the rain wash the mud away from the outside. He saw the eye. The eye stared back at him. He shivered. The rain fell steadily on his head.

He looked upward at the roiling clouds overhead, purple now and bruised. He opened the jar and poured the eye out on the ground. Standing, he crushed it beneath the heel of his shoe. A blinding whiteness raged through him, so sudden and powerful that it knocked him to his knees again. He could not see. He was completely blind, and he felt the storm again, heard it raging again. Gradually, then, everything seemed to ebb from his mind and there was only silence around him. He opened his eye.

Bonnie stood before him. She was whole again. She wore the white dress, and she opened her arms out to him, as though to embrace him. She smiled. She turned and walked away from him, moving between the tombstones, almost floating.

Brother Bobby knelt on the wet ground, the rain all around him fading into a fine drizzle. His hands and his suit were smeared with mud, were stained with the dark red earth of his own burying place. He could just barely see Bonnie's white form drifting away, wafting away among the pale monuments. He squinted and strained, leaning forward toward her, trying to follow her with his one good eye. He watched her dissolve and vanish into the gray and gathering.

The Best of It

(First Published in "The Hermit King and Other Stories", 2010)

WHEN MY FATHER calls me at my apartment in New York to tell me my mother has died, I prepare to make the trip again. It's not a surprise to either of us. I had just been down there. She'd been hospitalized: pneumonia. She was bleeding internally as well; in the hospital they discovered she had severe diverticulitis. But she got better. Her lungs cleared and the bleeding stopped, so we moved her to a convalescent home with neatly clipped lawns and tightly trimmed hedges. I flew back to the city on a Tuesday. She died the following Friday morning.

"Gideon," my father's voice on the phone says, "I'm afraid I've got bad news," and of course I know what it is.

"When?" I ask. I can hear breathing, over all those miles. I can hear the faint whistle of his hearing aid.

"This morning. She was eighty-eight years old. She lived a good life."

For a long time, I say nothing at all.

On the flight to Birmingham and the drive down to Hammond in my rental, I keep recalling a similar trip ten years before, when I had come down for my sister Celeste's funeral. I hadn't been back to visit but once since then, only one Christmas. I used as an excuse my extended stay in Cassis, in Provence, where I was working on a new play, but I was back in New York from time to time and it was difficult to keep that secret.

"Tom Whitfield's mother called and said you were back in the country last week," my mother whined by transatlantic wire. Tom and I grew up together in Hammond, and he lived two buildings down on West End in Manhattan. "You didn't even call. Why don't you ever come home?"

"Because I don't want to see him," I said.

"Oh, Gideon," she sighed. "Whatever am I going to do with you two?"

My mother still pretended my father and I were having a silly argument, just something between "the boys." She knew better, of course. In her deepest heart, she knew, just as I did, that my father had murdered my sister, just as certainly as if he himself had wielded the razor Celeste used to slash her wrists. He would not let her live.

My younger sister was mentally deficient, "mildly retarded" it was called back in the late forties when she was diagnosed. I was four years older, eight or nine when we found out, and though my parents whispered a lot between themselves, and though neither of them ever sat me down and explained it to me, I knew. I knew it from the way they acted, knew that our family had somehow been disgraced, that there was now something in our midst of which we should all be ashamed.

My father was a war hero. He was wounded in the South Pacific, at Peleliu. He lost his left hand, blown off at the wrist by a land mine. When he came home he wore on the end of his arm a strange contraption like a hook with pincers. He strutted around town, holding the device across his chest, proud of the sacrifice he had made, and talked about how his great grandfather had lost a leg at the Battle of Franklin up in Tennessee. He made speeches at the patriotic rallies at the Elks' Club. But at night I heard him cursing and crying. I heard their voices in the bedroom, murmuring heatedly, sometimes raging, and I was frightened of him. I heard my mother crying, and I heard what sounded like my father hitting her. Sometimes she had marks on her face that she covered with makeup.

By the time the war was over, my father had developed political aspirations. He never talked to me about them, but I overheard him tell my mother on more than one occasion that he would someday be governor of Alabama. He started with the office of mayor of Hammond, which he won. Easily. The Westlake family had been in Hammond for four generations, counting me and Celeste, and we lived in one of the biggest, whitest houses in town. My father also owned a great many acres of land, practically a whole county, which he and his younger brother — killed in action in Europe during the Battle of the Bulge — had inherited from their father, my grandfather. Though my family claimed that the family had come out of the depression "land poor," by the end of World War II — during which he had sold timber off thousands of acres — he had made quite a bit of money again, though how much I have no idea.

Celeste was a beautiful little girl, with a chubby body and soft brown eyes. She was bald until she was almost two, then her hair came out curly and dark, like our mother's. Her face was like a miniature of Mother's: high cheekbones, a narrow, pointed face, and full, lush lips. But she never ran around like other children, and she played slowly with her dolls, very deliberately, her movements hesitating and calculated. She did not like to be read to, grew bored very quickly. A few years passed and Celeste did not begin to talk.

My mother had three years of college at a state normal school, where she had been studying to be an elementary school teacher when she dropped out to marry my father. She insisted they have Celeste tested.

"She won't be able to learn," she said, "we can't put her in school."

"No, I don't want to hear it," my father said, "there ain't a damn thing wrong with her. She's slow, that's all."

"That's right. Call it what you will. But she —"

"No! Not another word about it."

Finally she convinced him, but my mother had to take Celeste all the way to Atlanta to get her tested. My father would not hear of Tuscaloosa, nor even Birmingham, for fear that someone would find out. "In my position, I can't be havin' folks known I've got a daughter that some fool doctor calls a retardate. All right?"

"For God's sakes, Franklin," my mother pled, "she's your daughter."

"How the hell do I know that for sure? The only thing we know for sure is that she's your daughter!"

"Oh, go to hell," my mother said. The air crackled between them. Never in my young life had I seen such hatred as I saw in my father's eyes, but it wouldn't be the last time I'd see it. I could see how unhappy they were, but it terrified me. I heard his false hand clicking, like scissors snapping. It was a nervous habit, something he did when he was tense or anxious. It became a warning sign to me. Clinka, clinka, clinka.

"Do whatever the hell you want to do," he said to my mother. "Just keep it under wraps and don't bother me with it." He glanced over at me. "What the hell are you lookin' at?" he asked sharply.

"Nothin'." I ran out of the room before he could take a step toward me.

My father was something of a learned man, too, having attended that same state normal school before he dropped out to find a job in that bleak fading depression year of 1937. "I had to have some cash money," he often said in later years, "you can't eat dirt, no matter how black and rich it is or how much you have of it!" He went to work for his Uncle Ronald, as night manager of a small tourist court on the edge of Hammond. He was a voracious reader, especially of anything about the Civil War. He could sit in the little office and read all night. He read biographies of all the major figures in the war. He read the classics, and histories. He read contemporary novels and volumes of poetry, whatever he could get his hands on. There was *quite a* large collection of dusty books scattered around in our rambling old family home, an eclectic assembly of almost everything, from the Hardy Boys to Greek drama, from *Forever Amber* to *David Copperfield,* from *Don Quixote* to *Gone With the Wind.* My father claimed to have read *Gone With the Wind* sixteen times. I never doubted it. He carried a copy of it throughout his war experiences. He kept that particular book, with its warped cover and wrinkled pages, in a locked drawer of his desk.

One of the biggest quarrels we had when I was in high school was when I came home one day and told him that I thought *Gone With the Wind* was a piece of commercial trash. I was only repeating what my English teacher had said, but my father became so angry he turned crimson. He was a big man, heavy-set, strong and powerful, and he struck me across the face and knocked me half-way across the room.

Junior high school was a traumatic experience for me, a sudden plunge into a culture I had not known even existed. My father had sent me for the first six grades to a school called Northside Progressive Academy. It was run by a shriveled little woman named Miss Julia Whitfield (a great aunt of my friend Tom, who has also escaped to Manhattan), and it was part grammar school and part military academy. The boys wore uniforms: gray wool ones modeled on those of the Old Confederacy. And we had military drill every day. The girls wore regular school dresses, except on Fridays, when they wore crinoline dresses with long hoop skirts and wide brimmed straw hats. After the boys had marched in formation the three blocks to the statue of the rebel soldier in the downtown park and had laid a wreath and sung "Dixie," we returned to the house and had a dance, with old fashioned reels and waltzes, Miss Julia banging away on an old upright piano.

And on those Fridays, as part of the ritual, after opening the day by singing "The Bonnie Blue Flag" on the sun-porch, we paid a visit to Miss Julia's mother, an ancient old woman propped up in a huge four poster bed with yellowing linen. We held hands down the long dark hallways of what Miss Julia called her "cottage," gathered around the bed, and the old woman peered silently down at us. We all had learned that she was the widow of a Confederate officer; we knew the story by heart. Captain James Taylor Whitfield, who commanded the 9th Alabama Rifles at Gettysburg, had been severely wounded in that battle, so that when he returned to Hammond after the war, he had walked with a pronounced limp, dragging his useless left foot behind him. He was an attorney, a bachelor, remaining one for many years until he married young Serena Simmons from Spring Hill when she was only sixteen. He was in his eighties when Miss Julia was born. It was hard for us to believe the old woman we saw every Friday morning had ever been sixteen.

As I sat with my mother in the hospital, during her last illness, I thought of all the years that had passed and were gone. I thought of Miss Julia's mother, the way she had looked fifty years ago. In the pictures in our well-worn photograph albums, my mother as a young woman was a flapper, happy and mischievous. Her hair was thick and dark, her eyes dusky in the old sepia prints with their checkered borders. She looked as though she loved posing, sometimes mugging at the camera, barely able to suppress a laugh. There is a picture of her as a baby, maybe a year old, when she had won a Most Beautiful Baby Contest at the Choctaw County Fair.

In the hospital she was wasted, worn down. She had always been a private person, even prissy, and she was now robbed of all her dignity. She didn't seem to care anymore how she looked. I knew that even up to the beginning of this sickness she had my father take her every week, him struggling to get the wheelchair out of the trunk of their Oldsmobile, to the hairdresser she'd been frequenting for years. Decades, I supposed. When I came home that one Christmas, as she sat in the den in her wheelchair reading or watching television, her hair was always perfectly coiffed, even though it was thinning so much on top her pink scalp glowed through.

"Do you want me to get Martha to come out here and fix your hair?" I asked her, and she shook her head no without opening her eyes. (The next time Martha would fix her hair would be in the funeral home, and though I didn't really know that then, I think my mother did.)

She had her lucid moments, but they were growing fewer and farther apart. Once she fixed me with her gaze and said, "You need to forgive him. You need to pity him."

"Can you do both?" I quipped and she frowned at me. She looked off out the window, at her view of the roof of another part of the hospital, a huge heating unit. I was later relieved it wasn't the last thing she saw in life.

"I am serious," she said. Her voice was weak, and it was an effort for her to speak.

"I'm sorry, Mother," I said.

"His life has been disappointment." Though my father had persisted, his political career was stymied. He never went beyond mayor of Hammond. He ran several times for the state legislature and twice for lieutenant governor, losing every time.

During my mother's final illness, my father didn't come to the hospital while I was there. He sat at home, in a darkened den.

"It's too much of a reminder," he said to me when I got back to the house.

I thought about that for a moment, and then I asked.

"Of what?" I thought he might possibly be referring to my sister's death, her funeral.

He looked at me, his eyes piercing. He sat with both arms resting on the arms of the recliner, a book turned face down and draped over his knee. His metal claw glowed dully in the light that spilled in from the kitchen. He would not get one of the new, more natural prostheses, just as he would not consider surgery for his fading hearing. He would not spend the money. He wore black horn-rim glasses that he had worn for thirty years, having new lenses put in when his vision changed.

"A reminder of my own mortality," he said. He said it as though I were completely stupid to ask.

He was two years younger than my mother. Eighty-six. He was still in pretty good shape, though he walked with a limp because he had broken his leg just above the ankle almost eight years before and it had never healed properly. He had slipped off a ladder when he was trying to trim some saplings in the yard.

"He thinks he can do anything with that hook," my mother said, "always has."

He offered me a drink, just as he had always done. It was a test. Always, all during my sixteen years of sobriety, he would still ask me if I wanted a drink. Part of him had never accepted the fact that I was an alcoholic, in much the same way he never accepted the fact that Celeste was retarded. It was as though he were confident that God would never do anything like that to him, that it must be some mistake, that there was no conceivable way his two offspring could be that flawed, that maimed. I offered to fix him one — a

225

bourbon and water, nothing else, ever — but he grunted and pushed himself up and shuffled into the kitchen. I heard him rummaging around in the cabinet. He returned to the room and sat back down with a sigh, holding the drink — dark, three ice cubes — in his right hand.

Sixteen years ago I had wound up in the psycho ward at Bellevue, with bars on the windows. That was where they put drunks in those days. A friend had found me in my apartment, in a near coma, badly in need of detoxing. When they transferred me to the treatment center out in White Plains, where I was to spend the next thirty-four days, my father was skeptical. "You're no more an alcoholic than I am," he said on the phone, "they're just after your money." When I asked him and Mother to come up for family week, as my significant others, and to even bring Celeste, he laughed. "That's a lot of bullshit, Gideon. Just be a man. Have some will power. Know when to put the stopper in the bottle. That's all you gotta do." He had refused to come, and he wouldn't allow Mother to come either. I don't think they ever told Celeste, who by then never came out of her room on the third floor of the big house. He had had the top floor remodeled for her, and I used to make him angry by referring to it as the attic.

"Typical southern family," I said one day, "keep your freak in the attic!"

"You shut your goddam mouth," he shouted. "Don't you ever let me hear you refer to your sister as a freak again!" When I laughed, he threw his drink in my face.

He reached up and switched on the reader lamp. He picked up the book he'd been reading and opened it. He turned the pages with his hook. His forehead wrinkled, the tip of his tongue protruded from the corner of his mouth.

"What are you reading?" I asked, and he turned the book's cover toward me.

I could have guessed. It was *The Collected Poems of Donald Davidson*. His favorite poet. I knew what was coming next. He squinted at the page, pulled it closer to his face. He read aloud: "...the God of your fathers is a just and merciful God." He was reading his favorite poem, "Lee in the Mountains." He looked up at me then for a moment. His eyes went back to the page and he read along in silence for a few moments. Then, aloud again, "Never forsaking, never denying His children and His children's children forever, Unto all generations of the faithful heart." His voice quaked. He lay his head back when he was finished. He sighed and closed his eyes.

He looked then like a very old man, antiquated and gray, the years like ashen tarnishes on his wrinkled face.

While I was subjected to Northside Progressive Academy, from which I never recovered, Celeste received no schooling at all. My father refused to let Celeste leave the house for most of her life. There was a short period, when she was twelve or thirteen, when she would ride her bicycle downtown to the picture show on Saturdays. I had already embarked on my young manhood of drunken, spinning nights, prolonged bouts of heavy drinking. I should have known then that I was alcoholic. I did know then, but it took another twenty years of hopelessness and desperation and a final splattering against a rock-hard bottom to rip the shrouds of denial from my eyes. I loved my sister very much. I had always been protective of her, taking care of her when we played out after supper during long summer dusks, carrying her home when the playing-doctor games started in someone's playhouse.

One Saturday afternoon, Celeste stood on the street in front of the theater, crying. She had been taunted by some high school boys, and when she'd come out after the double feature the front tire on her bike was flat. I happened by about then. I had been drinking beer with some friends all day. When I spotted my sister I knew immediately what had happened, and when I asked her who she told me. I went after them, followed by my two friends who were just as drunk as I was. We got into a tremendous fight right there in the theater, and we wound up in jail. I lost several teeth and have worn a misshapen nose all these years since.

My father, of course, was mayor of the town at the time. He was horrified and scandalized. He took away my car, an old Plymouth that I'd bought with money from my job sacking groceries at the A & P. He not only confiscated it, he sold it, and pocketed the money himself. I was not allowed to go out on weekends for months, and Celeste was never allowed to go to the movies again.

"I won't have my children actin' like white trash!" he said

I have no way of knowing for sure, but I suspect that Celeste never left that third floor after that. All her meals were carried up to her on a tray. I would come home from time to time from the university, or from Houston, then Denver, then finally New York, and she would let me come up and visit her. She was pale and freckled, her eyes faded. She was terribly thin and her hands shook.

"I have to tell somebody about this," I said to her. "The police. Maybe the preacher at the church he goes to. He's keeping you prisoner!"

"No!" she would say and begin to cry. "Please don't! No! I'm scared of him!"

"What does he do to you?"

"Nothin'! Nothin'! I never see him. I haven't seen him for a million years."

"Does Mother come up here?"

"Yes. Mama comes up here."

Then she would stare at the floor, refusing to answer any more of my questions. She would not look me in the eye.

"She's happy enough," my mother protested.

"Happy?!" I blurted. "How can you say she's happy?"

"She doesn't know any better."

"Are you sure he doesn't keep her chained to the bed?"

"Gideon, stop it." My mother looked off out the window. "We live with what God gave us, Gideon. We make the best of it." I knew there was no point in saying anything else.

I could have saved Celeste. But I didn't. And I live with that fact every day. I think of it first thing when I awake, and it is the last thing on my mind when I finally fall asleep. I could have tried harder to break through my mother's denial. I could have spirited Celeste away in the night and carried her north with me, put her in a special school, given her a life. But I didn't have the courage to face my father. In the early years I was too drunk to do it, and after my treatment I was too busy tending to my own sobriety to have time for her. I knew that if I drank I would die and if I went home and became too involved with my family I would drink. In a way, I'm just as guilty as my father for what happened. And my mother.

She sat by and watched it happen. She sat by and watched all our lives happen, the way mothers do.

I was rehearsing a new play at a tiny theater on Bank Street in Greenwich Village when the call came about Celeste's suicide. My mother traced me down at the theater by calling Tom Whitfield, after she kept getting my machine.

"She's dead, Gideon," my mother said, sobbing into the phone. "She killed herself."

"W...who?" I stammered. But I knew.

"Your sister! Oh, she's dead!"

"She...killed herself?" I felt as though the floor of the dusty lobby had disappeared and left me hanging there, dangling from the phone. It was like a surprise blow to the kidneys from behind, a heavy stick swung against the backs of my knees. I had never thought of Celeste dying, never even contemplated it. I couldn't quite grasp it. It seemed unreal, maybe a part of one of my plays. As though something intangible and unsaid on the stage had spilled out and surrounded me.

So I flew to Birmingham and rented a car and drove to Hammond. It was a long trip that day, a perfectly clear and warm April day. The hills and ridges south of Tuscaloosa were splashed with dogwood and redbud. Everything was springing to life.

Except for Celeste. I drove straight to the funeral home. Bobby Simms, the mortician, an old friend from high school, showed me the stitches on the insides of her wrists. She looked beautiful and serene, still. I was too stunned and shocked to cry. "She bled to death," Bobby said. Yes, I thought, she bled. All of her life she bled. There were three huge sprays of flowers beside her coffin, white and yellow roses and mums and lilies. I knew my father had put them there. Celeste wore a green dress with long sleeves, lace at the cuffs, hiding the stitches.

I get the two funerals confused in my mind now. My mother was alive at one, nowhere evident at the second, except hidden away inside the dark-stained cherry-wood coffin, identical to the first, with its blanket of the same red roses. There is the same preacher, rotund and too young. The church is the same Presbyterian one I was dragged to as a child, except that now it is a part of the ultraconservative branch, which I'm sure pleases my father. He probably led the secession. Only my father and I and my first cousin Miriam — daughter of my long dead uncle, my father's brother — sit on the folding chairs before the raw, open grave.

I'm sure there were people in Hammond who had no idea Franklin Westlake had a daughter until she died and had to be buried in the family plot in Riverside Cemetery. It would be whispered about and explained to them that she "was peculiar," she "was not right." Her stone, in the corner of the plot, still looks brand new when my mother is buried. It reads: Celeste Land Westlake, March 4, 1942 - April 17, 1990. There is a stone angel-child on the marker, sitting, her flat blank eyes focused somewhere off toward the river, toward some world not this one at all.

Before I fly back to New York, he wants me to drive him over to Lauderdale County, Mississippi, to visit the old Westlake Family Cemetery. I agree to it because I know that when I leave this time I am never coming back.

The Oldsmobile seems huge after the rental car. We take back roads. He slouches on the seat beside me, his prosthesis propped on the dash as though to stop himself if I should hit something. He has had many of the devices over the years, but always of the same type; they were different shapes and sizes as they became more refined and improved. As a child, I thought he was Captain Hook. He was the insane murderer in the stories that teenagers told, the one who left his hook on the door handle of the lovers parked near the river.

"Turn right up here, boy," he says.

"When are you gonna stop callin' me 'boy'?" I ask.

"When I'm dead."

We cross over the state line into Mississippi. It is not far now. Near the old Westlake Cemetery is a Civil War Cemetery, with hundreds of graves in perfect rows, marked by simple white wooden crosses. You come upon it suddenly, with no warning, right out in the middle of nowhere. The graves are almost evenly divided between Union and Rebel soldiers, most of whom were wounded at the battle of Shiloh in Tennessee and brought to a field hospital in nearby Daleville.

"Stop here," my father says.

He walks out among the graves. The grass is thick, neatly clipped. The white crosses stretch away toward a tree-line in the distance. The cemetery is manicured, well kept, and I note from a sign that it is cared for by United Daughters of the Confederacy, Meridian, MS Chapter. I think of Miss Julia, her mother.

My father stands with his head bowed, and I know he is praying. I can only imagine what is in his mind, what he must be saying to his own concept of God. I have never seen him mourn, never seen him cry. I know nothing of what he thinks about anything. When he is back in the car we drive the half mile to the red clay hill where our ancestors are buried. Scrawny cedars and patches of Johnson grass and crab-grass dot the hillside. There is a sagging old iron fence, rusted, the gate long gone.

My father heads straight to the crest of the hill, his limp like a stagger, his hook glittering in the sunshine. I scramble up the rutted dirt road after him. Yellow butterflies dart about on the sparse areas of grass, fat bumblebees float lazily in the hot, moist air. He stops at a row of gravestones, gray and lichen-splotched, the oldest ones. He leans against the tallest of the stones and looks out over the valley to the west.

I come up to him and stand beside him. We can see the Civil War cemetery, the row upon row of crosses that look tiny from here. Rolling Mississippi pastureland stretches away to the horizon; a creek with water oaks and willows and plum bushes lining its banks curves and bends through the pastures. From here we can see the old Westlake home place, marked by two lone magnolias, where the big house stood before it burned back in the thirties. There is a new house near it, long and low, ranch-style. Miriam's house, Mt. Zion Church, like a child's doll-church, gleaming white in the sunshine against the intense green of deep woods behind it, sits at the end of its gravel road.

I look at the stone my father leans against. Nathaniel Westlake, it reads. Born North Carolina, August, 1789, Died Mississippi, December, 1841.

"Your great, great grandfather," I say. "my great, great great grandfather." I have heard him point that out to me a thousand times. But this time his eyes seem locked on the horizon, the far distance, as though he does not hear me. I hear a crow back in the woods, the aimless chattering of a squirrel.

I look at another gravestone: Iva Ward Westlake, Beloved Wife, 1800-1851. These two, from whom both my father and I had sprung. And Celeste, too, I think, and Celeste, too.

I start walking then, along the ridge of the hill. After a while I stop and stand looking around me, at the thick woods, the hickory and oak and cottonwood trees, the kudzu that crowds the drooping fence. The green is fierce, the day now hot, the high sun like an unmuted spotlight. I can see my father still standing there against the stone, gazing serenely off across the Mississippi countryside. I think then of his hand, what was left of it decaying and returning to the earth of a distant island in the Pacific. I think of his great grandfather's leg, amputated in that field hospital in Middle Tennessee, likely without anesthetic, and buried there, left there, in a mass grave with the limbs of others, of strangers and brothers.

The lush green earth stretches away in all directions, as far as I can see. The gravestones all around me lean at odd angles, many of the graves sunken, the names and dates obscured, washed away by the generations and the seasons. I stand still, unmoving, for a long time. I watch a gray-brown hawk circling over a field. Its glide on outstretched wings is smooth and delicate. It is graceful and beautiful. Then, like a sudden shaft of new sunlight it slashes toward the ground, toward its prey, and disappears from my view.

OTHER TITLES

Short Stories available on Kindle from
www.sixfingerpublishing.com

The Stone Soldier

A Very Proper Resting Place

The Hunted

"Suffer Little Children..."

Glad My Eyes

Birmingham: Mother's Day, 1961

An Encounter with a Friend

Somewhere in all this Green

The Night of the Yellow Butterflies

Old Wars and New Sorrows

Passin' Side/Suicide

Walk the Fertile Fields

The Flowers of Her Summer Garden

Walking Strawberry

The Queen of the Silver Dollar

Brother Bobby's Eye

The Best of It

Full-length novel available from Amazon and all
good bookstores:

A Time to Reap (released December 2013)